An Englishman in Terror

Philip Tucker

Philip Tucker

Philip Tucker

TO HELEN

She came on my journeys with me and always smiled.

Philip Tucker

AUTHOR'S NOTE

An Englishman in Terror is a work of fiction, though a few of the events described were inspired by real incidents. The narrative that links events and characters is entirely fictitious. The characters are not real persons and are not inspired by them - they are composites of individuals I have encountered and observed throughout my life. Thus, though the Englishman bears some of my traits, he is not me. Likewise, none of the people I have met during my career, including my tour in Southeast Asia, are in this book. There is one slight exception to this: there really was a Bruce II. Whilst I have taken the liberty of using his first name, the character I have attached it to is fictitious. I hope you don't mind Bruce; you were always a good friend to me.

Philip Tucker

Out of reality are our tales of imagination fashioned

Hans Andersen

Philip Tucker

CHAPTER ONE

The Englishman was walking home from the East. Looking out towards the sun and the sea, he inhaled deeply, then turned his back on the cove and began.

Yesterday was the last day of the conference. The Englishman had already donned his walking coat and was trawling through his rucksack for his train ticket from Waterloo to Wool when the Detective Chief Superintendent beckoned him. Other delegates, Counter Terrorism Liaison Officers from around the world, were shrugging on heavy overcoats and wishing each other Merry Christmas.

The small heavy curtain juddered as it caught in the rail. An electric motor whined before the snag was freed and the dark ruby veil swung forward to meet its counterpart at the half way point. The curtains were closed. The delay caused by the trivial technical fault was miniscule, yet to the Superintendent it was another small reminder of the reluctance of his predecessor to let go of the job. Not that O'Raugherty had ever actually done the job, but he had been chosen for it ahead of the Superintendent. If he hadn't tumbled helmet-less from a motorbike taxi during his post familiarisation visit he would never have opened the way for the understudy. The Superintendent had liked the man, indeed they had been friends, in a kind of distant, collegiate way. Nevertheless, as the repatriated remains of James O'Raugherty QPM finally disappeared from view, the Superintendent felt more relief than grief. The grief at losing such a great man could not be stricken from the memories of his colleagues, but the closing of the curtains behind him meant that the Superintendent, at least, could start to move on.

The Lincoln Arms was a Branch pub and the Superintendent knew few people there, so he made his way directly to the bar. O'Raugherty's men were heading to the toilet or fussing over the hanging up of their coats. The Superintendent ordered the Detective Chief Superintendent's Guinness and whilst it settled, he bought himself a pint of London Pride, before getting the rather large round of drinks in. He was still ordering when the Detective Chief Superintendent, standing at his shoulder, raised his glass and his voice.

'Never to be forgotten,' he promised. 'Here's to James Donnel O'Raugherty QPM. The best investigator the Branch ever knew...'

'Hear, hear,' the pompous yet obsequious voice of one of the desk officers cut in. He had worked the international desk for the legendary Operation Airtight, and had thus seen O'Raugherty's ability at first hand, vicariously achieving glory himself without ever leaving the office. 'He was a great man Sir,' the Desk Officer added, quietly and confidentially, as if it were a classified matter, 'a gentleman and a scholar and a worthy holder of the Queen's Police Medal. Have the adverts gone out yet, Sir?'

'No, no. No need for adverts and all that equal opportunities stuff. This is me you're talking to. I have my man.' The volume of the Detective Chief Superintendent's voice had subsided, momentarily, as if he had forgotten that he had started to address the gathering. Nevertheless, the Superintendent was able to hear the conversation with the Desk Officer, and the suggestion that there had been some sort of nepotism involved in his selection irritated him. To start with, he was an outsider who knew no-one within the Counter Terrorism Unit. Just like O'Raugherty, the Superintendent had got through the selection process on merit. He had been waiting for a posting, that was all. In fact, he had been expecting Northern Europe, but O'Raugherty's untimely accident had left the Far East post vacant. The Detective Chief Superintendent had not even been on the interview panel and the Superintendent felt sullied by the insinuation that it had all been sorted out with a bottle of Scotch.

Drawing himself up to his full height and rocking forward on the balls of his feet, the Detective Chief Superintendent again turned towards the group of men who were now enjoying the heavenly, post funereal taste of free beer. He was a tall man, exceptionally well groomed, in a dark chalk stripe Savile Row suit, immaculate hand-made shirt and black silk tie. A Special Branch pastiche, the Superintendent considered.

'In fact, let's sort it out here and now, shall we?' He sucked the froth from his moustache as the Desk Officer eagerly rapped the side of a glass with his pen and the noisy hub-bub softened.

'Listen in chaps; I know James' body is still warm, God rest his soul, but work on the Counter Terrorism Unit must go on.'

The Superintendent cringed. Not now, not at the wake, for Christ's sake.

There was a murmur of assent from the crowd. Another sip of Guinness and the Chief Superintendent continued. 'As you know, James was an exceptional officer and his hard work, not least his role in Operation Airtight, was rewarded when he was given the tough job of representing the CTU in the Far East.' He paused, reverentially, before continuing in a choked half-whisper: 'The man gave his life in return.' The Detective Chief Superintendent looked respectfully and thoughtfully at the grubby carpet of the Lincoln Arms. Eyes were lowered all around. Still looking at the floor, he continued morosely, 'of course, his sad and sudden death means that he can't take the job.' He hesitated, lost for words perhaps, until he chuckled, 'though I wish his ghost were here to do it!'

There were nods and murmurs of approval all round. 'Here's to James O'Raugherty's ghost!' shouted the Desk Officer, raising his glass. He was now standing alongside the Detective Chief Superintendent, also facing the group. There was a general raising and chinking of glasses and group bonhomie at the mention of O'Raugherty's ghost. The Superintendent shivered.

'But, as I say, the work of CTU must go on, and I, and the senior management team, have been working hard, as ever, to select a replacement. He's known about it for a couple of days, but I'd asked him not to say anything until after dear old James' funeral.' He took a large swig of Guinness, and didn't suck his moustache, leaving it frothy white. 'I'd like to introduce you to the lucky winner of the plum job of all plum jobs. That's right, the man destined to spend his working days on beaches in Bali, Phuket and Langkawi. The man with the maid, driver and swimming pool. The man swanning around the Far East up to his neck in Oriental beauties, whilst we're up to our necks in bombs and terror.'

The Superintendent smiled weakly and, as the Detective Chief Superintendent beckoned him impatiently with his fingers, he quickly downed the rest of his pint and manoeuvred himself behind the Desk Officer. He felt the fatherly arm of the Detective Chief Superintendent around his shoulders. He was looking across the Desk Officer's carefully sculpted spiky hair, considering whether such vanity was appropriate for a funeral.

'Now you won't all know the Superintendent.' The Detective Chief Superintendent was enjoying himself. 'He's not a Branch man and hasn't got much CT experience, certainly nothing like James had, and, I think...' Turning towards the Superintendent, he asked, 'you've just come from uniform, haven't you?'

'Yes Sir. A quick spell to get myself back up to speed with - '

'But we won't hold that against him, will we lads?' the Detective Chief Superintendent blurted, smiling broadly. The Superintendent fidgeted but said nothing. 'So here he is – James O'Raugherty's replacement! Please wish him well and I know you'll give him a big CTU welcome!'

There were a few weak attempts at a cheer, but when the Detective Chief Superintendent himself failed to provide a big CTU welcome, and turned instead towards the bar, his disciples returned to their little huddles. The Detective Chief Superintendent raised his empty Guinness glass as if in toast, clinking it against the Superintendent's empty London Pride. The

Superintendent began to smile in anticipation of a congratulatory remark.

'Get the drinks in Superintendent,' the Detective Chief Superintendent ordered. His back to the mourners, he hunched over the bar with the Desk Officer, who carelessly slid his own empty glass for the Superintendent to fill.

CHAPTER TWO

He called himself the Englishman because the Australians did, and he liked it. He was the only Englishman, most of the others being from Australia. The head of the Australian Federal Police for the region was called Bruce, and the man he'd taken over from was called Bruce. Bruce II was a capable, experienced cop, he was a natural leader of men and as the commander of by far the biggest police contingent in the region, he also assumed the role of host, and he was good at that too. But he was not good at names. The Spanish National Police Liaison Officer was called the Spaniard, the BKA representative the German, the French Interior Ministry Liaison Officer the Frenchman and the United Kingdom Counter Terrorism Liaison Officer became simply the Englishman. Still, Bruce II gave him a warm welcome and had introduced the Englishman to the Australian Ambassador even before the Deputy Head of Mission had introduced him to the British one.

'Pete,' said Bruce II to the Ambassador, 'this is the Englishman.' The Englishman wondered whether the informality was genuine or if it was performed for his benefit, an Australian demonstration of a rejection of

British stiffness.

'Not Pom?' asked Pete the Ambassador, shaking the Englishman's hand very warmly.

'Not 'til we regain The Ashes, Pete. Until then, we should call him the Englishman.'

'OK mate.' Pete the Ambassador was still gripping the Englishman's hand and now he again shook it rigorously. 'Welcome to our back yard, Englishman. Have you grabbed yourself a cold one yet? Shit, there's plenty here, mate.'

'It's certainly a beautiful back yard,' returned the Englishman, indicating the well kept gardens of the Australian Ambassador's Residence.

'Shit mate. Not this back yard. Southeast Asia. It's our back yard. Now go get yourself a cold one, Englishman.'

Someone thrust a bottle of ice cold Crown into the Englishman's hand. It was served inside a small foam rubber holder to keep it cool. As he sipped, the Englishman surveyed the relaxed surroundings of the Australian Ambassador's back yard and concluded that the cordial informality was genuine. He felt himself to be amongst friends.

The Spaniard and the German chinked their bottles together. The German, relaxed in an open necked short sleeved batik shirt, had his arm around the shoulders of the Spaniard, who looked hot and stiff in his business suit and tie. Like the Englishman, all of the Europeans felt a long way from home. They were there to fight terrorism and they were all very proud to represent their countries and their police forces on the other side of the planet. It was good to be a part of the group with the Australians. They shared experiences and even information and talked about what it was like to live there, in that strange and exotic region.

The air-conditioning in the Englishman's study could barely cope. Its wheezing and the cricket-like tapping of his fingers on the keyboard were the only sounds to be heard in the large house. The Englishman pulled his clammy shirt away from his chest and wafted the material gently, in an effort to cool himself. He wondered whether he smelt and his mind drifted as he vaguely considered if battle hardened Southeast Asian insurgents, veterans of the Afghan campaigns now fighting closer to home, could discern the aroma of a white man. He fleetingly imagined himself on the run in the jungle, perpetually giving away his position because he smelt like a frightened Englishman.

Most of the night, indeed most of the last two weeks, had been spent carefully honing his first annual pre-conference report, a detailed summary of all his achievements during his first twelve months. Tonight, finally satisfied that he had captured the nuances of the post, the Englishman was confident that it would go down well with the senior management team. He pressed "Send," waited whilst the secure connection was established and then watched patiently as the encrypted document was slowly delivered to CTU headquarters. The Englishman stretched in his chair, sniffing ineffectively at his damp arm-pit as he did so, and then, hunched over the computer enthusiastically, immersed himself once again in quiet, solitary tapping, whilst the rest of the house slept. Outside, one of the security guards, patrolling alone through the neatly manicured gardens of the expatriate compound, beat his night stick against the iron bars of the children's swings, a metallic clang that showed that he had seen the Englishman's office light was on and was making his diligence known.

The guard made his rounds at least twice more before the humanity of the Englishman's chuckle suddenly cut through the monotonous mechanics of the keyboard and air conditioner. He had never been on holiday on his own, and he was delighted by his audacity. There was no walking in this city, no pavements, no air, no privacy. He rubbed his palms together with child-like excitement and anticipation.

A tiny knock on the door made him jump.

'Tea Mister?' The shrill question required no answer. A deft hand was already removing the empty mug and placing the steaming tea carefully on the coaster on the Englishman's desk. A small tray draped in a bright batik cloth added ceremony to the occasion.

'Endi? I thought you'd gone to bed?'

The maid was quick to answer, once invited. 'Mister need sleep. Endi pray now. Mister need shower also.'

'Pray? It's not 4 o'clock is it?'

'Ya. 4. Mister need sleep. Endi bring special tea for mister. Endi go pray now? Endi pray for mister. Mister wash.' She waddled out of the room, leaving the Englishman smiling as he sipped the spicy sweet ginger tea. He enjoyed her well intentioned rebukes; her interest in his welfare was genuine and unselfish.

He called after her, 'Mister smell, Endi?'

'Mister stink same like cheese,' she called back, disappearing through the kitchen into the staff quarters.

The Englishman was a handsome man, despite his boxer's nose. His eyes were perhaps a little too sunken and tired, inscrutable even. His thick blond hair showed few signs of grey, except at the sideburns and a few sprigs of wire in the eyebrows. He shaved every day and he smiled a lot, showing small, slightly chipped and yellowing teeth, of which he was embarrassed, but which no-one else ever seemed to notice. He was a little overweight, but not so that anyone would call him a fat man, and he played tennis at the American Club. He always wore a tie and cufflinks at work, and the only other person at the embassy who did so was the Ambassador. Sometimes the Defence Attaché did, but not usually.

Now the Englishman bounded happily into the bathroom and grinned into the mirror. He couldn't see his eyes twinkling the way he had imagined they were, so he put on his reading glasses. Small pupils peered out from two grey pools sunk into the depths of shadowy sockets and his untidy eyebrows bristled like uncooked prawns. The bespectacled, creased and pitted face was not one he readily recognised. He had forgotten what he looked like. What age and thirty three years of police service had done to his face, his gradually failing eyes had compensated for. Taking the dark rimmed glasses off, he saw his old familiar self in the mirror again, and smiled. The young copper smiled back. He had booked himself a wonderful walking holiday in England! A whole week of fresh English air and freedom. On his own.

In the shower, he pictured the jungle mujahedeen wondering why his scent had disappeared and was stupidly pleased with his stealth, rubbing the shower gel rigorously into his arm pits, groin and feet – the smelly bits, as his daughters called them. He imagined that he was washing himself invisible, whilst a camouflage clad, AK47 toting terrorist scratched his head in defeat. This happy thought was gradually interrupted by a nagging concern about leaving his family in the Far East throughout the conference and holiday in England. But it made no sense to fly back for one week after the conference. He was sure Elaine wouldn't mind. She kept telling him he should unwind and, after all, she and the girls were flying to meet him for Christmas when school finished, so they'd be together soon enough.

CHAPTER THREE

'Oh my God! There's someone in the house. Where are you?'

The Englishman had drunk too many Tigers, or Bintangs or Changs. 'Elaine. I had just fallen asleep.'

'There's someone in the house.' Even in his stupor, the Englishman heard a desperate fear in his wife's thin telephone voice.

'Are you sure?' He shot up from his bed and ran naked to the window, as if he expected to be able to see the intruder from his seventeenth floor hotel room, in an entirely different part of Southeast Asia. Instead he looked out on a sparkling skyline of towers - the hotels and office blocks of the wealthy quarter of some capital city.

'He was just in the bedroom. Oh my God, the girls. What shall I do?'

'Have you pushed the panic button?'

'It's not working. The alarm people were here. What shall I do?'

'Oh shit, Elaine. I don't know. It's probably the staff, isn't it?'

Elaine was sobbing with fear, hardly able to speak.

'No, the staff door's locked. It's a man. I saw him. Oh, no. He's coming back. Please help me. Please don't let the girls get hurt.'

She screamed and seemed to have dropped the telephone.

Be safe. Please be safe. He should ring the General, or the embassy. Somebody should turn out. Oh shit. Please be safe. He was pulling on underwear and a shirt as he planned a course of action. Keep Elaine on the mobile. Ring the General from the hotel phone. Oh shit, he didn't know how to access the contact numbers on his new phone without cutting Elaine off. Oh darlings, oh my lives, please be safe. What on earth am I doing on a business trip with my family stuck back there on their own? The phone rustled for several seconds, then came Elaine's weak voice on the phone.

'Why...?' she burst into tears, uncontrollable, inconsolable tears of anguish. The Englishman stood waiting, wondering whether his daughters were alive.

Late the next afternoon, his driver was at the airport to collect him.

'Good land Mister?' the question was asked with a smile, and an eager hand took the Englishman's luggage, but the driver was a family man and the Englishman felt that there was some reproach in his voice.

'Yes, good trip. How is Mrs. Elaine?'

'Man come for the killing.'

'Yes, I know. Please don't say that to Mrs. Elaine. Who at house now?'

'Missus. Girls. Mr. Henry.'

'Mr. Henry? Why Mr. Henry?'

'Wait for Mister.'

'No Mr. John?'

'Who Mr. John? I sorry, I not know Mr. John.' He

gave a little false laugh, as he often did when he was asked a question which he didn't know how to answer. He was an experienced and senior driver and he felt he should know things.

The traffic, as usual, was horrendous. The Englishman sat and looked glumly through blacked out windows into the torrential rain. A bus was crammed full of equally glum looking working men and women, their resigned eyes unable to see him behind his security glass, allowing him to survey their blank brown faces from close quarters. The bus boy, bare foot, hung out from the pole beside the open sliding doors with one hand, searching along the line of traffic for some hope of progress. His small hand clutched a wad of filthy bank notes. A burning tyre glowed and fizzled in a tiny road side banana plantation, squeezed between the shack–shops whose keepers crouched and looked glumly at the vehicles as filthy black flood water flowed unchecked from the raised road surface down between their haunches. Motor bikes laden with life weaved in and out, families of four and five on one single scooter, a tiny child asleep with its unprotected head drooping onto the handlebars. A bus passenger jumped into the path of a motorcyclist who, anticipating the move, swerved casually around him. The man unfastened his trousers and urinated on the side of the bus, just a few unobstructed inches below a face at the bus window. The bus boy watched him with interest.

It was some three hours later that the Englishman's car splashed up to the compound gates. Sitting in the back seat, the Englishman wound down the electric window and smiled at the two duck-like guards, in their pseudo-military white gaiters and helmets and draped in huge yellow plastic sheets. The heat of the night squeezed into the car, as if trying to get out of the tropical rain. A crack of lightning exploded so loudly that the Englishman instinctively covered his head with his hand.

'Big rain,' declared the driver, sagely.

The guards were taking longer than usual to check the car that they knew so well, their mirror on a stick hovering slowly under every inch of the bodywork, each door and the boot politely opened and peered into. It was clear that they felt embarrassed about the intruder. As his own door was opened, the Englishman quickly grabbed the soaking sleeve. The startled dark eyes of the guard shone out from under the helmet. The Englishman pressed some notes into his hand.

'For two,' he said, and pointed to the other guard.

The thin man gave a quick bow and the briefest of smiles and the money was spirited away. Despite the burglary, the Englishman felt sorry for the guards. They had already been sacked and tomorrow a new company was taking over the contract. The men, both fathers, were back to scratching out a living however they could. They may have been lazy or useless or both, they may even have been complicit, but they were also poor, under-paid, ill-trained, inexperienced and too servile to actually challenge anyone. Probably they had no idea what they were looking for with their mirror on a stick.

Endi was waiting at the garage door. As the Englishman climbed stiffly out of the car, she ran over with an umbrella and covered his head as he walked the metre or so to the porch. His driver was already taking his overnight bag into the house through the garage.

'Oh! Mister home. Endi pleased Mister home. Mad-man come for the killing, Mister.'

For a moment, the Englishman thought that she was

enjoying the situation, but one look at her terrified eyes told him he was completely wrong. He reminded himself that this was her home too.

'Please don't say that to Mrs. Elaine or the children, Endi,' he asked.

'Embassy man here for Mister.'

The Englishman glanced at his watch. 'Still? He here still? Now?'

Endi nodded and scuttled in through the garage, as the Englishman pushed open the main door and went in. Instead of finding the embassy's locally engaged security officer, he saw only Elaine, who was sitting, her feet up, a glass of wine on the low table next to her. She was reading. The main lights were off and the soft glow from the table lamps made the house feel welcoming and homely. The serenity of the scene looked false in the circumstances and the Englishman braced himself for the onslaught.

'Girls in bed?' he asked, gently.

Elaine looked up slowly, as if marking the spot on the page to which she was about to return. 'Yes. All the homework's done. No tears tonight.'

He stooped down to kiss her cheek, and was surprised by her warm, slow, open kiss on his lips. Collapsing onto the sofa next to her, the Englishman asked how she was. She settled her head into his chest and they slid almost into a lying position. The Englishman started to feel aroused - the very last thing he'd expected when he had walked through the door a few seconds earlier.

'I'm fine - you're wondering why. This is my home. We are going to make it here. Some bloody skinny little sod of a burglar is not going to stop me.'

She was very slightly drunk, the Englishman noticed.

Why the bloody hell shouldn't she be? 'And the girls?'

'They're fine. They know about it, of course, but we've all decided not to dwell on it. I thought about moving to a hotel, but I had enough of that when we arrived. We've only just gotten into the house, for heaven's sake. And anyway, when would we move back in? What would be the change that would make us come home? We would never come back. We'd end up in a hotel or an apartment for ever. This is my home. Our home. We've given up everything in England to be here. We're staying.'

The Englishman craned his neck away from her embrace and looked at her quizzically, trying to judge if she really felt the resolve of which she spoke so decidedly. There was not a hint of deceit. Instead there was a sultry, heavy eye-lidded sense of pride.

Elaine suddenly pushed him away. 'Don't look at me with your detective eyes! My body language won't tell you any different.' She was smiling and the Englishman suddenly felt the same sense of pride.

'Get off me and go and pour me a glass of wine. Stop looking at me, will you?' she ordered, as the Englishman had just started to pull himself closer to her. 'Oh, and there's a man waiting for you in the garage.'

'In the garage? What on earth is he doing in the garage?' The Englishman was up on his feet, straightening his tie and heading towards the staff quarters.

'I don't know. Some chap from the embassy who wouldn't come into the house. He's the embassy response to the burglar.' Looking down at her book, she called to him as he hurried out: 'Oh, by the way, mad-man didn't come for the killing, he came for the laptop.'

CHAPTER FOUR

The Englishman's hatless head was steaming, the damp woollen cap clasped between his sweating, gloved fingers. His padded coat hung open but he could still feel the moisture around his cuffs and beneath the waistband of his walking trousers. He paused and looked back. Lulworth Cove gleamed silver-grey as the mid-winter sun, a shimmering golden coin, rose above the Dorset cliffs. He checked his watch; he had been climbing for seven minutes. Ahead lay fifteen miles of chalk cliffs. The contour lines on the map told him what the brief written summary had conveniently missed out. The cliffs rose sharply from Lulworth Cove, only to dip again and rise again each time a capricious stream decided to make its way to the sea. It is said that a walker completing the entire South West coast path will have climbed the equivalent of Mount Everest, twice.

The Englishman's stomach rose and dipped as the sadness overwhelmed him again. The sudden anxiety made him feel vulnerable and ill. Had he taken his blood pressure tablets? He remembered laying them on the quilt of his single bed at the hotel. Yes, he had taken them. One less thing to worry about.

Henry stood up quickly as the Englishman walked into the garage. He wasn't wearing any shoes and the Englishman saw that there was an old battered black leather pair sitting neatly just outside the open garage door.

'Hello Mister. How are you? I come because of break-in.'

Henry was a local man, employed by the embassy as a deputy security officer. He worked for the Post Security Officer, who was retired from the army. Henry's knowledge of local procedure and, of course, the language, along with his affable personality, made him a useful contact and the Englishman already had a friendly relationship with the deputy. But it did not bode well that the man had felt too subservient to wait in the house, feeling much more at home in the staff quarters. John should have been there.

'Where is the Post Security Officer, Henry?'

'Mr. John not here, Mister. Henry in charge.' He smiled and bowed.

'Great. I'm glad you're in charge. OK, what have you done?'

'I come to house. Mr. John tell me to come to house.'

'OK. Have you told the police?'

Henry looked amazed. 'Police? What for police, Mister?'

'To solve the burglary?'

'Embassy not have money for police, Mister. Police not come to break-in.'

'OK. Have you worked out how the burglar got into the house?'

'No Sir. Henry waiting for Mister for permission to

check house.'

'So nothing's been done then? Twenty-four hours of sitting...'

'No, Mister. BP send security adviser from Hong Kong. Arrive today. He speak to landlord, discover ladder at compound wall, trees grown over security camera, discover Mister's laptop bag on roof of house. Order landlord to get new guards, get new alarm for house next door, extra razor wire for house next door, extra security lights for garden next door, extra guards for foot patrol, cut down trees that cover camera, get new camera for house next door. Find designed in security weakness in roof of staff quarters in house next door. Fix new steel gate on roof of staff quarters for house next door. Fix new bolts on door from staff quarters to main house next door.' Henry paused for a much needed breath, he didn't often spurt out this much English all in one go. 'Lots been done then, Mister.' He smiled, a triumphant grin of achievement.

'Why BP, Henry?'

'House next door, Mister. Mister next door work for BP.'

'But the house next door wasn't broken into, was it?'

'No Mister. But BP good company. Treat very serious, Mister. And landlord treat BP very serious Mister. BP pay good.'

'Did BP call the police?'

'No, Hong Kong guy say BP not got money for police.'

'And what about extra razor wire, security lights, bolts and steel roof gate for our house, the one that was broken into?'

Henry's smile evaporated as he struggled for something to say. 'Embassy not BP, Mister. But I act fast. Henry act fast.'

'But will the embassy act fast, Henry?' The Englishman doubted it. 'And in the meantime, I have a broken alarm, a panic button that doesn't work and a burglar who knows how to get in.'

'What if mad-man come back for the killing, Mister?' Endi suddenly cut in. The Englishman quickly turned to look at the maid. 'Tea, Mister?' she asked, holding up the little tray for him to take the mug.

Lulworth Cove was not disappearing. In fact it seemed to be getting closer as the Englishman climbed, until he could look down from above and see the outstretched curving arms in their entirety, a solitary yacht moored in the centre, the little inn crouching beside the tiny road. He was out of shape, but he knew also that his spirit was broken. He knew it, but could not repair it. His mind kept replaying the conversation with the Detective Chief Superintendent.

He sighed loudly and his shoulders drooped. He loved his job. He'd given his life to it, bled for it even. Serving his country abroad in the fight against terrorism was a rare and precious opportunity, the culmination of a long and dedicated career. He had dragged his girls to the other side of the world and watched them cringe at their first sight of the shocking, grubby chaos of their new city. He had moved them into a gated, secure compound and then not been there to protect them when an intruder prowled around their bedrooms in the dead of night. The girls had left their friends and their grandparents and their cousins and had supported him when he had asked them to, and had done it with unquestioning loyalty. Until, at last, they had settled. By the end of that tough first year, they felt at home. Their school work was back on track and they had new friends. And now this.

Early the next morning, Endi was serving the family breakfast when the driver stuck his head into the kitchen.

'Mr. Henry from embassy here, Mister. Big lorry. Mr. John is boss of Henry at embassy. Holiday in Langkawi. Not come,' he added, somehow having managed to do his homework even before the embassy opened. The driver's network was an intelligence set-up to be envied.

The Englishman picked up his tea and went to the main door. Henry was taking off his shoes outside the garage. He bowed and his face beamed with self satisfaction. Behind him, reversing onto the driveway was a large flat back lorry, loaded with what looked like steel railings, strong enough to keep a Sumatran tiger at bay.

'Good morning Mister. I here with strong steel fence.'

'My goodness, that was quick work Henry, I am impressed.' The Englishman had obviously been wrong to be sceptical about Henry and the embassy.

'Thank you Mister. I pleased you impressed.' Two shoeless, impossibly skinny young men, dressed only in ragged colourless cotton trousers that finished halfway up the shin, emerged from the lorry, and leapt onto the flat back. 'Mister sign for strong steel fence?' Henry looked up from under his bowed head and proffered a sheaf of papers.

The Englishman patted himself for a pen and Henry produced one. Struggling to find his reading glasses, he finally felt them hooked over the button of his shirt, and he skimmed through the official Foreign Office paperwork. 'This says swimming pool safety fence, Henry.'

'Yes, Mister. Strong steel fence keep children safe.' The two shoeless men were now holding the first length of railing behind Henry, as if exhibiting it. Endi was bobbing about, trying to work out what was going on. The driver appeared and started to chamois the spotless car windows.

'Henry, what has this got to do with the break in?'

'Mister?' He looked puzzled.

'Is this strong steel fence because of the break-in?' The Englishman marked his words carefully, keen to be understood.

Henry now looked even more puzzled. 'No Mister, strong steel fence for health and safety. All embassy house have strong steel fence around swimming pool.'

'Henry, my children are 16 and 14. They swim in the school team. That thing is ugly and I do not want it in my garden.'

'Embassy garden, Mister. Sorry, Mister. Mister take it out later. Everyone take it out later. Same strong steel fence go in every house. Mister sign please? Mr. John orders Henry get signature. Then Mr. John in clear if children die.'

'And what happens to Mr. John if my children are killed by a burglar?'

'Oh my God!' Endi's sudden high pitched shout caused everyone to look at her. She stood, terrified, frozen, her hand over her mouth, looking with horror at the Englishman. 'Oh my God,' she repeated, 'Mister think mad man come back for the killing.'

CHAPTER FIVE

The Englishman had been awarded the Long Service and Good Conduct Medal. He wore his uniform to ceremonial events, even though the heavy black serge tunic and flat peaked cap, with its shining silver braid, were too hot for the tropical sun. The others saw it as typically English, and he liked that. His diminutive hosts may have looked lean and fit in their figure hugging, short-sleeved khaki shirts, sparkling with tin and brass, but nothing looked quite as splendid in its plainness as the Englishman's traditional custodian uniform, adorned only with four chrome buttons down the front, one chrome button on each pocket, a crown on each epaulette and the Long Service and Good Conduct Medal ribbon above the chest pocket. Of course he also had the Queen's Golden Jubilee Medal, but he was less proud of that because he hadn't had to do anything to get it; one just had to be a serving police officer on the date of the anniversary.

This morning, the Englishman had attended the funeral of three local CTU officers killed the day before in a gun battle with insurgents in the jungle. He had worked hard to be close to the General, the head of the

CTU, during the long, hot ceremony. This had paid off and now he sat opposite him, dressed for an English winter, in the General's barely air conditioned office.

'So how is it you want me to deal with you, Sir?' The General smiled broadly. 'Please,' he said, motioning with his hand towards the hot sweet tea, 'have something to drink.' The Englishman resisted, waiting instead for the General to take the first sip, as his own staff would do.

'Well, I'd like us to work together. Sharing information on a police to police basis to fight terrorism.' The General lifted his cup and the dehydrated Englishman quickly followed suit.

'Yes it's true we have our problems with terrorists here. I think you know that we have that in hand.' Again, a broad smile. 'As today's funeral demonstrates only too clearly, we are prepared to engage with our terrorists wherever they might be hiding. But I think there is no connection between terrorism in my country and the Al-Qaeda inspired indigenous groups that you have at home. Nor with Irish related terrorism. Please, Sir, have some food.' He motioned towards a dainty cardboard box, half the size of a shoe box, that was placed tidily next to the Englishman's cup.

'You are right, of course, General. I must say I'm very impressed with the results your counter terrorism unit has been having lately. And it's a terrible tragedy about the death of your men,' he added. Peering into his box, the Englishman discovered a strange mixture of savoury and sweet snacks. His fingers finally settled on a miniature spring roll.

'We have arrested forty-seven and killed thirteen. Very good results I think. We have good intelligence. We work well with international intelligence agencies.'

Again the General smiled a broad, soft smile as his neat fingers unwrapped a little cake and he bit daintily into the tiny green chilli that came attached to it. 'English men do not like spicy food, I think. Too spicy.'

The Englishman selected a brown translucent lump the size and texture of a pencil eraser, wrapped in cellophane. 'Excellent results,' he said, discovering that the brown lump had no hint of sweetness or saltiness and may well have actually been a pencil eraser. 'And I think you're correct, General'. He gagged on the flavourless mass, and sucked back a gob of drawl just in time to stop it seeping from the side of his mouth. 'We do not see terrorists from your country on the streets of London. But your terrorists are also inspired by Al-Qaeda, aren't they?'

The General fingered the Englishman's business card that lay on the mahogany desk in front of him, beside the chilli stalk. 'Superintendent. Our terrorists are well trained. Many are veterans of Afghanistan. They have fought in Mindanao and in Ambon. They do not hesitate to open fire on the police. I was there last week, myself. In the jungle, leading my men against the terrorist training camp.' The General gave his broadest grin yet and chuckled very slightly. 'We have good intelligence.'

The Englishman swallowed hard and was relieved when the lump responded, passing with some resistance into his gullet. 'And our terrorists, young British men whose mothers and fathers originate in Pakistan, also go to Afghanistan to train. Some to Yemen and Somalia. And in these countries they may meet young violent extremists from here. In this way, they inspire each other, form friendships. A young man with no previous convictions from your country…'

'Clean skins, you call them, do you not?'

'Yes. Clean skins from here would be anonymous in the UK. And British clean skins could also enter here quite freely. For me, it's only a matter of time until we see that happening. If you were able to give me the list of your arrested terrorists...'

'Ah, so this is what you want.' He spoke urgently in his own language to the young uniformed Inspector who was sitting silently at the table, as if rebuking her. The Englishman looked towards her, studying her tight fitting khaki shirt as she jotted down his orders. She bowed, smiling clean even teeth, and left the table.

'I could check them against the names held back at CTU in England. I don't expect that we will get many, if any, hits. But we should try.'

'This can be done. My inspector is getting you the list now.'

The Englishman kept up the pace. 'But better still would be if you could give me the list of your intelligence suspects. Those from the camp who you are currently...'

The General cut in. Again looking down at the business card, which he skated about on the shiny surface with the tip of his middle finger, he said, 'Do you work with your colleagues in your embassy Superintendent?'

At last the Englishman reached the top of the golden hump. He was now walking along a short stretch of level, grassy path and his breath was slowly returning, though he still steamed uncomfortably. A fence made from wooden stakes and barbed wire separated him from the steep, curving bank of long yellow grass, dotted with sprigs of dried cow parsley, that disappeared out of view towards the sea. The vista was delightful, soothing. Rich, fertile looking meadows stretched endlessly ahead, like the rippling edge of a golden green blanket laid on top of the chalk cliffs. In places, this comfortable looking grassland stretched inland as far as the eye could see, curving up into a gentle ridge parallel with the cliff line and then dipping down inland. Periodically, it was interrupted by fences or stone walls, the eagerly marked boundaries of farmers' fields. The chalk cliffs cut steeply into the sea, varying in height according to the folds of the blanket, stretching out here and there in sharp, craggy outcrops of green and white. And then there was the English Channel, blue, cold and refreshing. Ahead, and far, far out on the horizon, a low, slender spit of land framed the view – the Isle of Portland. It was impossibly distant, faint and grey, not much more than a single stroke of a pen, underlining the difficulty of the feat the middle-aged Englishman had set himself. He had to reach Weymouth today, just prior to Portland, and, it being late December, he had only about eight hours of light in which to do it. At his feet, narrow concrete strips had been embedded into the chalky, flinty ground forming the bars of steep steps, which were already leading downwards. Ahead, the grey-white path dipped in and out of view like a picturesque roller coaster. The Englishman could see three or four more blanket folds ahead of him, each one meaning a steep walk down followed by a breathless drag up again. A few short steps forwards and downwards and Lulworth Cove disappeared from view behind him.

Notwithstanding his trepidation at the task ahead, vanquishing the first hill of the walk cheered the Englishman considerably. He liked the General. It had been good of him to warn the Englishman, albeit ever so subtly, that he was already working with SIS. The Englishman's own people had never warned him; not the Detective Chief Superintendent, certainly not the pompous Desk Officer and not the spies themselves, until they felt it tactically beneficial to do so.

The Fresh Faced Spy was finding it difficult to look up. He was a nice man and the two really should have been friends. The Englishman was older than the spy, but otherwise they were pretty similar types. The Englishman considered that they were in the same business and he was used to getting on with people.

'So how was your meeting with the General?'

'Yes, it went really well. He gave me a list of all the arrested terrorists so far. I've sent them to CTU.'

'What will you do with them?'

'Compare them against the lists of current targets and intelligence. I don't expect we'll get any hits, but it's only a matter of time before a terrorist from this country crops up in the UK, in some guise or other. We need to keep checking.'

'Ah, I see.' The Fresh Faced Spy looked relieved. He was the Head of Station and took his responsibility rather seriously. 'Well that seems pretty....ah,' he hesitated, 'harmless'.

'My ideal position would be to get a list of their current targets. Photographs, fingerprints and DNA if they have them, so we can compare against current investigations. What a travesty it would be if we were both working on the same target and didn't know. There would be a lot of name checking and photograph sifting to be done, but it would be worth it. It might prevent a terrorist attack in the UK.'

'Ah,' the Fresh Faced Spy said slowly, 'I see. But he didn't give you such a list, did he.'

'No. Well, I've not known him long. I hope to build up some trust with the arrested persons list first. I'm not surprised he didn't share his current suspects with me. Come to that, I wouldn't share ours with him just yet.'

'And how did you say you managed to get in to see him?'

'I didn't say. I sent him an email and he invited me to the funeral.'

The Fresh Faced Spy looked up, began to colour and looked quickly down again. 'You sent the General an email? You're supposed to get a note verbale signed by the Ambassador.'

'Oh.' The Englishman was taken aback. 'I didn't know. Nobody told me. He gave me a card when I introduced myself to him at the Queen's Birthday Party. I thought people gave you their card so that you can contact them. That's the way policemen think, anyway.'

'And the arrested persons list. How did you get the list out of him?'

'I asked for it. I think he agrees with me that it's good to share on a police to police basis.'

'Ah, I see. Police to police. Yes.'

'Yes. Police to police. It's what the police have been doing around the world for about a hundred years.'

'Yes. Good stuff. The thing is, I own that relationship.'

'Sorry?'

'Yes, you see, we weren't consulted before you came out here. I, ah, own that relationship.'

'Oh. Have I trampled all over some agreement? He didn't say.'

'Well that's not very likely is it? Given how much I pay him.'

CHAPTER SIX

Coming down from the second climb of the day, the Englishman encountered a delightful cove of golden yellow sand and pebbles. This ended with an enormous slab of white chalk cliff that protruded out of its skin of green meadow like a mighty truncated tusk. Inviting steps had been cut into the cliff, leading directly onto the beach. The Fresh Faced Spy was a good chap, the Englishman supposed. Just doing his job. The Englishman took a deep breath and looked up towards the next climb. Why the bloody hell couldn't the path just get to the top and then stay up there?

Had the CTU known all along that it would be near impossible to do what they'd sent him to do? Did they know that MI6 already had the General in their pocket? The Englishman wondered how many reports the Fresh Faced Spy had written about him, whether the traditional links between the Branch and the Old Firm had been the Englishman's undoing. Then again, he'd never actually seen eye to eye with the Deputy Head of Mission either.

'Come in Superintendent, come in.' The Deputy Head

of Mission looked tired and bored. Grey eyes peered wearily up from under heavy lids before collapsing back to the level of the computer screen. He sighed. 'Let me see. Here it is. Yes – Police Counter Terrorism Liaison Officer Southeast Asia. Yes. Er... Right then. Anything I can do for you?'

The Englishman started towards the empty chair, then checked himself. He waved towards it vaguely with his hand, a gesture which seemed to go unnoticed by the Deputy Head of Mission, so the Englishman remained standing. 'Well, I'm new in country and I thought I'd better make an appointment with you. I assume you want me to report to you in some way.'

'Yes, I suppose you ought really. That other policeman chap we had here doing the training. He used to write too much. Pages of it. No-one reads it.'

'Right. O.K. So…, what? Perhaps I can give you regular briefings. Shall I make an appointment to see you every week, or month?'

'Yes, that would be one way to do it.'

The Englishman was talking to the top of the Deputy Head of Mission's head, thick silver grey hair that needed cutting. 'Are you busy now? Shall I come back and see you another time?'

'Well, that would be an option.'

'So…?'

'Send me an email every now and then. Not too much. Nobody's interested, to be honest.'

'In terrorism?'

'In terrorism? Yes of course, it's one of our country priorities. Although climate change takes up most of my time. The, er…,' he lowered his voice conspiratorially and gestured to his office wall with his thumb, 'the boys at the end of the corridor have got terrorism. They own all the key relationships. Have you met them yet?'

'Yes, I have, thanks. I'll send you an email occasionally then, shall I?'

'Yes. That would be an option.' The Englishman turned to go. 'Oh, by the way superintendent,' the Deputy Head of Mission suddenly sounded enthusiastic.

'Yes?'

'You left your computer screen on yesterday evening. Don't forget our green targets.'

The Englishman felt a slight soreness at the heel of his right foot, similar to the tingle of a stinging nettle. He had bought new boots for the holiday and, although he had made efforts to wear them in, he now reflected that he had not subjected them to any serious gradient before today.

'You need to piss on them,' the Post Security Officer had advised him. 'An old army trick. Breaks them in.'

The Englishman had opted not to urinate on his new boots and, as it was clear that the soreness was just a fleeting niggle, he sniggered to himself at the ridiculousness of the Post Security Officer's advice. His soles were now bashing heavily into the hard mud as he gathered speed on a steep descent, his knees, and even his teeth, jarring with each step. Then, starting to climb, his breathing quickened and shallowed until it came only with difficulty. Once again he felt the nettle like sting on his heel as he trudged slowly upwards; his mood darkened and his mind switched to a strange telephone call that should have forewarned him of the treachery he now faced. Deep sadness overcame him. Yesterday morning he had loved his job, looked forward to the future. Now he didn't know who he was. He was alone, in the depths of winter, struggling for breath on the edge of a barren Dorset cliff.

'How's it going Superintendent?' The Detective Chief Superintendent sounded irritated, as if it were he who had been awoken by a call from the Englishman. 'What's the matter, you sound tired? Are you coping out there?'

'No, I'm fine Sir. I was in bed, that's all. It's rather late here.'

'Well, it's not really late though is it? I mean, it's actually only five o'clock in the afternoon.'

'It's rather later than that here though, Sir.'

'Yes, but, I mean it's not the same, is it? It's not like you've lost touch with the real world so soon, is it?'

'No Sir.'

'So how's it going Superintendent?' Your Desk Officer suggested I should give you a call.'

'That's very kind of him, Sir. All good my end, thanks. The family's settled in. We're now getting over the burglary. I had to get the landlord to put razor wire on the back wall and fit some extra security lights. I thought the embassy would see to that, but apparently that's my responsibility. They've fitted a four foot fence around the swimming pool though. In case my sixteen year old falls in, I suppose.'

'How's your relationship building going? SIS?'

'Yes, very well, I think. I've had a bit of a problem with the spies, but that seems to be on its way to being sorted.'

'Problem? What sort of problem? I don't want problems with the Service.'

'Well that's good, because there isn't one. Just at the beginning, they seemed to resent me going in to see the CTU General, but I think that's OK. I was out to dinner with the General last night.'

'I want that relationship to be a good one, do you understand? Mutually inclusive. That's how I want it. You sort it out.'

'I have sorted it out, Sir.'

'And I'll tell my Foreign Office contact on the Programme Board that you're having problems and we'll see if that helps.'

'Thanks, Sir, but I think it's not really...'

'And are you going to the Ambassador's weekly meeting? I'd heard that you weren't.'

'No Sir. I went to two, but they're not restricted. They were about plans to arrange next year's QBP'

'QBP?'

'Queen's Birthday Party'

'Oh heavens. You're not to get involved in that sort of thing. You're out there to fight terrorism. Do you understand your role? Your Desk Officer thinks you're not sure about it. I know you haven't got much CT experience.'

'Yes Sir. I quite understand my role. I just don't think the spies got it at first.'

'I'll get someone out to see you to sort out your problems with them. And make sure you attend the Ambassador's weekly meeting. You've got to get these relationships right, Superintendent.'

'Sir. They're fine. I was just trying to explain that they were problematic at first.'

'And the General? You see him?'

'Yes Sir, no thanks to the spies. I was at dinner with him last night.'

'Why "no thanks to the spies?"'

'Well, they seem to, shall we say, fund him? We could really do with a strategic meeting your end Sir.

Sort out the relationship between the CTU and the Service so that the spies and I have clear guidance this end. I don't think there are any personal reasons why we shouldn't get on. He's just looking after his organisation. But some clarity from your end would be most helpful.'

'I don't think you're aware of your role there, are you?'

'Sir, I do wish you wouldn't keep saying that. I'm well aware of my role. But MI6 don't seem to have been told about it.'

'Don't call them that on an insecure line. Are you mad?'

'No Sir, I just thought I'd answer your questions, that's all.'

The low winter sun created a beautiful yellow light which now bathed the ancient coastline in gold. The Englishman looked vaguely at the map and forced himself to read the names of the landscape that he had so desperately wanted to enjoy and remember. But his efforts were useless: Dungy Head, St. Oswald's Bay, Durdle Door, Swyre Head, Bat's Head – all went unnoticed as the Englishman trudged blindly past. For company he had the words of the Detective Chief Superintendent and his grovelling little side kick, the Desk Officer. He hated them.

The Englishman was on his way to see the Fresh Faced Spy when the Deputy Head of Mission called wearily from his desk.

'Is that the police chap?'

The Englishman reversed back a few steps and hovered in the office doorway.

'You've stopped going to the Ambassador's weekly meetings. You're the only one.'

'I've explained my absence to the Ambassador and he seemed very satisfied that I was concentrating on my role here. In any case, they're not restricted. I can't contribute to an unrestricted meeting. What would I talk about? The weather?'

The DHM looked momentarily interested. 'The weather? Have you noticed it lately? Have you signed up for the Earth Hour?'

'No. What's Earth Hour?'

'All embassy staff are asked to switch off all lights at their houses for an hour this Saturday evening. It's a small contribution to climate change, but it has a huge educational impact. My family are all rather looking forward to it'

'Well it's certainly an option.'

'Now, shall I tell the Ambassador you'll be there this week?'

'No, I'm afraid I'm flying out on Tuesday. I have an operational meeting about the suspects in the church bombings. I've briefed the Ambassador and I sent you an email about it.'

'Oh yes, you did, didn't you? Let me see, climate change, climate change, illegal logging…, oh – did you read this one? There's an OUI gathering this evening. Are you going?'

'OUI?'

'Orang-Utan Initiative.'

'No. I'm the Counter Terrorism Liaison Officer.'

'You probably need to speak to the guys along the corridor.'

The view from the top of Bat's Head was stunning and

the Englishman, panting after the slow upward plod, stopped for a moment or two, coat hanging open, hands on hips. The chalk cliffs swooped down and up again in a long smooth dish-like curve, the grass of the cliff top grey and bleak, the sheer white walls magnificent and terrifying. The English Channel shone in the cold morning sun, gentle waves breaking blue and white on a colourless gravel beach far below. The Englishman's feet were sore after the steady climb. He considered stopping and checking that his heels were not beginning to blister, but he felt he must make more progress first. The peak ahead of him, White Nothe, appeared to be at a higher altitude than he was now at; he resolved to reach that point before stopping for a tea break. He recalled the advice of the Marine from Mandalay, the soldier who had walked alone from Second World War Burma: rest for ten minutes every hour. The Englishman felt that this was sound but still he knew that he must make progress or risk finding himself stranded in the cold darkness of a Dorset December evening, unable to see the cliff edge. Yes, he would stop for tea after White Nothe.

The cold sea air filled his lungs and he tried to remember the smell of seaweed and shellfish. Linda and Katherine often tried to describe smells to him and now he pictured his daughters on the beach at Exmouth, giggling as one covered his eyes and the other waved a seagull-cracked mussel under his useless nose, desperately willing him to guess. 'Ice cream,' he would say, or 'coffee,' and they would snort with laughter, though of course he could see the mussel through the small fingers. The wind gusted in his face and moisture sprang up in the corners of his eyes. How could he have let them down so badly? What could he do to make it right for them? They were so happy. His chest surged and for a moment the Englishman had the ludicrous feeling that he was going to cry. He gulped in a shallow mouthful of cool air, shrugged his walking coat back over his shoulders and the odd moment passed. Carefully, he started the descent. His heel slid in his boot and a sharp needle like pain caused him to wince. The crisp air blew the dry salty lines back across his cheek bones.

CHAPTER SEVEN

The thunder grumbled and groaned discontentedly, continually shifting position, heavily and uncomfortably, as if it were trying to sleep, desperate for rest. There had been no dry season. The city was damp and rotten, its crumbling and unfinished walls stained black with mildew, the stagnant, fever ridden swamp on which it had been built rising inexorably above the pot-holed roads. The jungle sprang up from the filthy black ditches, drinking in the long wet summer until its foliage shone, huge and heavy. The naïve and unprepared shack houses around the British International School of the Orient flooded every afternoon, the raised concrete of the new school buildings sweeping the thick brown water into the hovels of the poor. At the beginning of the gravelled school drive, a bright orange Bajaj lay squashed like a dead beetle under the trunk of a mighty roadside tree that had come crashing down when the rain washed away its anchor. The thin, elderly driver stood emotionless beside his stricken machine, his soaked clothes hanging as helplessly on him as his future, the large, warm raindrops plopping relentlessly around his feet.

The Englishman's driver stopped the car outside the first gate, showed his pass and they were allowed into the "air-lock," the secure gap before the second gate. Here the underneath of the car was searched with a mirror on a stick, the doors were politely opened and the Englishman was scanned with a hand held metal detector. He noted with satisfaction that there was a police officer sitting in the little wooden booth, his automatic weapon hanging from his slim shoulder. They were cleared to drive through the second gate, but here the Englishman was required to get out and walk through the third gate, the security guard there again scanning him with a hand held device. No private vehicles were allowed beyond this third gate, and as the driver swept into the driver's compound to see how many of his friends were here today, the Englishman put up his umbrella and walked the two hundred metres to the reception. The impressive fleet of school buses, each identical and with blacked out windows, stood dormant to one side, there being another hour or so of lessons before they were pressed into action. Each one of them carried a tracking device, so that the school knew where every bus was all the time.

The headmistress was an ageless, plump and tall, grey haired English lady, wearing a white long sleeved shirt, which hung loose, undoubtedly in a useless attempt to conceal her enormous bosom. Glimpses of a pristine white lacy bra could occasionally be had through the gaping slits between the buttons. She had a compelling smile and a warmth about her that made her very popular with pupils, parents and staff alike. The Englishman wondered whether she was older or younger than he was.

'No Elaine today?' she asked. There was a green

cardboard file of papers open on her desk.

He looked up as she did. 'No, she's doing the soup run today. She's been cooking all week. Well, she and the maid have been.'

'I knew she was the type to get involved. Well, do say hello for me. I like Elaine. Positive right from the start. That's what's seen the girls through, I think.'

'Yes, Elaine's been a great support for me. It can't be easy, following your husband to the other side of the world. I can immerse myself in work, but she doesn't have that to prop her up.' The Englishman was sweating profusely, despite the air conditioning. He didn't know if it was the effect of the bosom or the short walk from the car.

'And you should be very proud of Linda and Katherine too. They've adapted so well here, though Katherine had her problems at first, didn't she?' There was another glimpse of white lace.

'Yes. She found it rather difficult to make friends, I think. It's not an easy age.'

'But wonderful GCSE results. She's had a very good six months. You need to make sure she's settled for her A-levels next. Will you be staying?' Her heavy breasts swayed gently as she spoke, mesmerizing the Englishman, whose eyes followed the movement in spite of his diversity training.

'We certainly hope so. My secondment is three to five years. I'd like to provide some stability for both girls really, which means staying another four years, which, as you say, will see Linda through her A-levels.'

'I think you've got the right idea. A little stability would be good for the girls now. Which one do you want to see me about today?'

'Oh, I'm not here as a father, actually, I'm here on

embassy business. I'm not sure if you know what I actually do at the embassy?'

'I assumed you were MI6,' she said, nonchalantly.

The Englishman laughed. It amused him to be mistaken for a spy. It made him feel so much younger. 'No, I'm not a spy,' he reassured her, 'though I guess that I would say the same thing if I were.'

'Yes. It wouldn't do for us all to know who the spies were, would it?' she smiled broadly. 'So what are you then?' she asked.

'I'm a policeman, a Detective Superintendent. I'm here in Southeast Asia to fight terrorism, or at least to help the locals to, and to monitor the situation to see if there are any links between terrorism in the region and terrorism back in the UK.'

'I see. How interesting.' She leant forward with her elbow on the desk, resting her chin on a surprisingly girlish fist, the apparent youth of which was betrayed by the matronly bosom that again swung forward and pressed against the thin shirt. 'And so what can a school headmistress do for you in this fight, superintendent?' A swathe of curved white lace came into view.

The current fight was not against terrorism. He mustered every effort he could to raise his eyes from the opening in her blouse and look into her eyes. This simply added to the intimacy of the situation, and the Englishman felt like calling for help. Dragging his professionalism up from its knees, he just about won the battle to stay focused. 'It's actually a matter of what the embassy can do for the school,' he managed to say, 'I'm impressed with what I see here...'

'In terms of...?' she asked, smiling - perhaps, the Englishman thought, coquettishly.

'In terms of security. A strong outer perimeter, well

protected, but I wondered if you thought there were any vulnerabilities…?'

'We could do with a radio,' she said, after a pause, 'we used to be on the embassy's radio network, so that we could call direct to the embassy guard house in emergencies. It proved to be very useful during the tsunami. But then it broke and the embassy took it away again, and we've never had one since.' At last she sat back again and the delicious white lace disappeared.

'What a relief,' said the Englishman, realising only as it came out of his mouth that he'd said it aloud.

'A relief? What's a relief?' she asked, leaning forward again, instantly putting him back under pressure.

The Englishman needed to focus on terrorism. 'It's a relief that there's something positive I can do for the school,' he asserted. 'It's not just my children, it's all the children who attend. This can be an unstable country. If there were to be an incident like Beslan, a radio call might make all the difference to the safety of the children. I can get you a radio. I know just the man for that.'

He had succeeded in breaking the spell but the headmistress's face had become unexpectedly drawn and pale and worry showed on her handsome face. 'Beslan?' she blurted, 'why do you say Beslan? How many innocent, beautiful children died there? What hell did they go through before they died? Who could do such a terrible thing in a school?' Her hands were on her face, and she seemed to be picturing the nightmarish scene, the slim little bodies lined up in bags, distraught parents scraping at the polythene as they were hoisted away. Her fingers dug deeply into her soft cheeks, pulling them downwards, exposing the red inner flesh beneath her moist eyes.

'Terrorists could do such a thing in a school,' he reported blandly. And then, more compassionately, he added, 'but don't worry, it's unlikely, of course. I wish I hadn't said it. But even though it was in Russia, the Beslan terrorists were Islamists and the terrorism here is Islamist. There are similarities. The justification for extreme violence is found in the distorted version of Islam that they preach. They feel justified in killing non-Muslims. The British School makes a good, high profile target. It's got the word "British" in its title, to start with.'

The headmistress stared into the space between them. She was still in Beslan.

'But don't worry. I've got great relationships with the local counter terrorism unit. That's what I'm here for. That's what the embassy's here for. I'll get you that radio.'

In the car he had reflected on a successful meeting and had pondered how he could convince Henry to get her a radio, but now, now that he had time to think, now as he trudged along the coast path, now as he dived into his memories to find evidence that he had not been good at his job, he looked upon the meeting differently. He pondered instead on how he had managed to infect such a beautiful, girlish woman, a loving and dedicated school head, with his own filthy job. She had been going about the business of educating eight hundred and fifty children, teaching them how to contribute to a nicer world. A nice lady doing the world nothing but good. And he had violated that goodness.

He lived and breathed terrorism, he worked with it, he studied it, he talked about it and in the evenings he read about it. He had breezed into her office and threatened her with Beslan. If there were degrees of terrorism, Beslan was an example of it at its most horrific. And he disgusted himself too; he was a voyeuristic pervert. Even if she had been flirting a bit, that's what happens in a nice world, isn't it? But now he saw that even the flirting was probably just a product of his filthy mind. There she was, trying to educate his daughters and he had been looking at her breasts. He sickened himself. She was nothing but good and he had stubbed her out. It was as if he had stamped on a small bird. A brutality, a trespass. A nasty, clumsy copper in the office of a gentle, nice lady. A wave of deep shame broke over him. He was sick of it. Thirty three years of dealing with the worst that society can offer had culminated in murder and terrorism. What a career path. Perhaps the Detective Chief Superintendent had been right: perhaps it was time to give up this job he had loved, that had defined him, that had broken his heart.

Step by tender step, the Englishman trudged upwards. A small acorn on a wooden post told him he was heading in the right direction. He reflected that a few such signs might have been useful over the last twelve months. Fucking bastards. How dare they send him out there without making it clear what was wanted of him? How dare they allow him to talk his family into moving to the other side of the world and then allow him to fail? Why should he now make it easy for them? There had never been an ounce of understanding from CTU HQ of what it was like fighting bureaucracy, incompetence and terrorism in the Far East. Of course he wouldn't give up his job. Fuck them. He strode out with determination.

The Englishman got up from his desk and walked into

the small kitchenette. He'd run out of PG Tips and the two local tea bags he'd left soaking in a mug of hot water had by now formed a darkish brown cloud that didn't quite fill the mug but which, if carefully mixed with just the right amount of long life milk, would probably produce a passable brew. The Deputy Head of Mission came in carrying a chamomile tea bag in one hand and an embassy radio in the other. Glancing across to the Deputy Head of Mission's office, the Englishman could see that the Post Security Officer was sitting there. He wondered why the Deputy Head of Mission was only carrying one tea bag.

'You coppers do like your tea strong, don't you, eh?' His voice was chirpy and pleasant.

'We most certainly do. And you foreign office types like your herbal stuff nice and weak, don't you, eh?'

'Well, it's the caffeine you see, it makes me buzz.'

'I can well imagine.'

'Have you been up to BISO recently Superintendent?' The kettle boiled and, tucking the radio under his arm, the Deputy Head of Mission poured some water into a saucerless cup, not looking up at the police officer.

'BISO? Is that orang-utans or logs? I don't recall.'

'It's the bloody school, for heaven's sake!' The Deputy Head of Mission's pink fingers closed around the little hot bag.

'Yes, of course, I was up there yesterday. Actually, my girls were in the gala. In fact, your daughter was in one of the races, wasn't she John?' the Englishman called across the corridor to the Post Security Officer, 'didn't I see you there? Nice day, wasn't it?'

The security officer didn't answer. Instead the Deputy Head of Mission spoke again, still looking down at his cup of water, swinging the little scented bag over the surface, as if contemplating another dip. 'And have you been there in a professional capacity at all?'

'Not for several weeks, I don't think.'

'Ah. But you have been there in such a capacity?' The bag plopped into the water, making a little splash that caused the Deputy Head of Mission to jump back.

Tiny, translucent, crystalline brown flakes had appeared on the surface of the Englishman's tepid tea.

The Deputy Head of Mission scooped out his chamomile bag with a stained and bent teaspoon and thrust his thumb aggressively into it, squeezing until his nail turned white. 'You gave the headmistress a radio didn't you?' he blurted loudly, twisting his neck and looking at the Englishman for the first time, dropping the spoon, letting the bag plop back into the cup and whipping the radio out from under his arm and waving it in the Englishman's face.

'Yes, I did.' The Englishman paused for a second and added, 'of course. That was when I was last there professionally. I gave the headmistress the embassy radio she'd asked for. Is there a problem with it?'

The Post Security Officer cleared his throat. He seemed to have slid further back into the Deputy Head of Mission's office, so that now only his twitching, crossed legs were in view. 'Is there a problem with it?' the DHM mimicked, 'the problem with it is that the school had it.'

'It was signed out properly, wasn't it? I asked Henry to make sure that it could be properly audited. Or is the headmistress not happy with it?'

'The head is delighted with it. Of course she is.'

So politically correct of him to drop the mistress from the job title. 'So what's the problem then?' the

Englishman asked. The Post Security Officer grunted.

'The problem, as I am trying to explain, is one of liability. We do not give out embassy radios willy-nilly. The embassy has no wish to become liable for the health and safety of children attending the British school.'

'But your children go there. And John's.'

'Yes. And I have no desire to accept liability for what happens to them there.'

The Englishman looked into the Deputy Head of Mission's face, waiting for the punch-line that did not come. 'So the official line of the British Embassy is that it wants nothing to do with protecting British children who attend the British school, including our own children? What planet are you on?'

The Post Security Office's legs jerked as he growled out: 'We could be sued if we assume responsibility for managing the risks at the school and someone gets hurt. BISO is a private company. It is responsible for managing its own risks. It is not for the embassy to mitigate those risks.'

The Deputy Head of Mission had crept back across the corridor and now stood just inside his office. His mug twitched a little in his hand. 'Precisely,' he added, 'it's not for the embassy to manage the risks.'

'We don't look after British children?' the Englishman asked.

'Watch my lips.' The Deputy Head of Mission seemed to have gathered confidence from the Post Security Officer's support. He spoke his next words with forced enunciation: 'The FCO does not accept liability for managing risks that private companies should themselves be managing.'

'Well it should do.' The Englishman grabbed his tea

and, without removing the two tea bags and without adding milk, he swept into his own office. Dark brown splashes on the carpet marked his route. He sat down, pushed his computer mouse a couple of times and got up again. He walked into the Deputy Head of Mission's office. 'I thought you were in the army,' the words were spat out towards the Post Security Officer, who sprang to his feet and backed away, his mouth hanging open, his hands rising. The Englishman walked out again before the ex-soldier could answer. Swooping up his tepid tea, he took a large mouthful before slamming it down again on his desk and breezing back once more into the Deputy Head of Mission's office.

The Englishman caught him smiling wanly at the Post Security Officer, as if asking for his efforts in confronting the police to be seen as a victory. The damp chamomile tea bag hung exhausted from his finger, dripping.

'Have you two prats never heard of Beslan?' the Englishman bellowed, and stormed out again. He stood for several minutes at his office window, spooning his own two tea bags. He stared out at the traffic and the rain, until his train of thought was interrupted by the little bleep to indicate an incoming email message. He shrugged his shoulders, put down the empty mug and sat down at his desk. The new email was from the Deputy Head of Mission and was headed, "Practical Limitations for the Embassy in Accepting Liability for British Institutions Overseas." The email was not addressed to him, it had been sent round to every member of staff. The Englishman deleted it without reading it.

CHAPTER EIGHT

By the time the Englishman reached the top of White Nothe, he knew his heels were blistered. It was mid morning on the first day of a six day, seventy-five mile trek and he had blisters. He cursed his own stupidity and lack of judgment. His obstinacy in pressing on had damaged his feet. He blamed the Detective Chief Superintendent for distracting him, for putting him into turmoil which had occupied his mind when he should have been taking care of his feet.

The familiar acorn sign sat atop a simple wooden post that also had the words "Coast Path" written vertically. An adjacent sign said, "White Nothe. You may walk on the undercliff at your own risk." The path at this point ran between a little row of coastguard cottages and the cliff edge. Looking over, the Englishman could see another grassy cliff top fifty feet below him and it was clear that a substantial chunk of the cliff had slid towards the sea. A precarious path picked its way up from the beach, a smugglers path no doubt. The brown dwellings looked sad and unused, their black windows staring blankly outwards, as if they were contemplating throwing themselves into the sea, far below. They had enjoyed their role as guardians of the coastline and now that smugglers no longer came ashore in the dead of night with their contraband, the cottages had lost their sense of purpose. Unable to abandon their post, they sat silently with their memories, waiting to slip into the sea.

There was a long, level section ahead of him, followed by a steady descent to sea level at Ringstead Bay. The Englishman decided that he would dress his feet and open his flask of tea on the beach there and so he limped onwards, reflecting on his own role as a guardian of his country.

The Englishman's job involved preparing for the next big terrorist event affecting British people in Southeast Asia. There hadn't been a big one since just before he had arrived in post. The separatist insurgencies in the Mindanao region of the Southern Philippines, the somewhat less frenetic but still lethal insurgency in southern Thailand and the more rampant terrorism in Indonesia aimed at establishing a Muslim state, meant that there was a constant flow of terrorist incidents, though most of these were not aimed at foreigners. In Thailand, home-made roadside bombs delivered by rather mysterious unknown terrorists regularly killed or maimed police officers, soldiers or dignitaries of the Buddhist state. In the Philippines, a fight for a Muslim enclave in the south, independent from the Catholic state, led to jungle warfare, and there were regular gun battles between the police and the insurgents, resembling conventional war. In Indonesia there had been a movement aimed at transforming the country into a Muslim state ever since post-war independence from the Dutch, so that most weeks there seemed to be small bombs exploding somewhere across the seventeen thousand islands, killing somebody or blowing somebody's limbs off. Malaysia, Singapore and Brunei seemed to be terrorism free, but there had been nasty incidents of religious intolerance in Malaysia and at least one serious plot in Singapore, so that no country was immune from the terrorism threat.

From time to time, there had been much larger attacks. The ruthless Abu Sayyaf Group sunk a 'super-ferry' in the Philippines, killing more than a hundred people. Two huge bombs in Bali killed hundreds more innocents, among them twenty two British citizens, including several teenage rugby players celebrating the end of a tour. Prestigious international hotels in the centre of Jakarta had been bombed twice and a terrorist training camp discovered in Aceh revealed that the thirst for terrorism was still as strong as ever. The often brutal nature of it was exemplified in the beheading of three catholic school girls. It was this last case that caused the Englishman to worry that the type of massacre that happened in the little school in the Northern Russian town of Beslan could happen in Southeast Asia: terrorists in Southeast Asia had already shown that they were prepared to execute school children in furtherance of their cause. Perhaps he had been right to mention Beslan to the headmistress of his children's school, after all.

The thrust of the Englishman's work was to understand the situation on the ground and report it back to CTU, all the time sifting for any links to the United Kingdom which might suggest that the Southeast Asian threat was turning towards home. The United Kingdom came second or third on most Islamist terrorists' lists of target countries, after the United States, and in this part of the world, Australia, it being their back yard.

The technical side of the Englishman's work was not in itself challenging. The Counter Terrorism Unit Desk Officers would send him enquiries, links to British terrorism investigations, that needed answers. These might simply be finding out about the use of a particular mobile telephone, taking a statement from an immigration officer about the movement of a terrorist suspect through the region or trying to trace the sources of terrorist finances. But these relatively simple tasks were inordinately difficult to achieve in countries that had no interest in their outcome and whose police chiefs had nothing to gain from the extra work that their local resources, busy enough already, were expected to carry out. Busy Southeast Asian police officers had no time to deal with British requests for information, so that even the most simple of enquiries required the investment of hours and days of diplomacy and relationship building before there could be any hope of success.

At last the Englishman crashed onto the pebbles at Ringstead Bay. He sank down onto the cold stones, which were hard against his aching buttocks. He took his flask from his rucksack, poured himself a cup of steaming grey tea and began to unlace his boots.

The Attorney General had chosen the most exclusive restaurant in Chinatown and was sitting waiting, sipping tea, when the Englishman and his two British colleagues arrived. He stood up and bowed, gesturing towards the female officer to sit next to him, waving the palm of his hand over the plush cushion of the chair. He smiled, in a puzzled sort of way, his smooth brow crinkling above the otherwise flawless skin of his soft, round face.

'Please, please sit down,' he invited, graciously, the puzzled look returning to his happy face. 'A beautiful restaurant, is it not?' he asked, using his arms, magician like, to direct the gaze of the open mouthed visitors to the confused display of Buddhist, Hindu and Chinese statues that adorned the private dining room. They were decorated with little twinkling candles, miniature baskets of offerings and burning sticks of incense. The eclectic collection would not have been able to withstand any sort of religious, geographical or historical scrutiny, the various gods probably not entirely happy with each other's company, but it certainly was a wonderful display of Eastern charm. The table was set with a pristine white cloth, batik napkins in silver rings and a large shiny green rubber tree leaf with the words 'Attorney General' in neat white English painted on it. 'Mmm, mmm,' he added, seeming to approve of his own recommendation.

He turned towards the woman detective and, scrutinizing her with a bemused smile, he spoke to the Englishman, not taking his eyes off of her. 'So, we have some guests in our country, Superintendent. Mmm, mmm.'

The Englishman introduced his guests: a CTU Detective Chief Inspector in charge of a complex investigation into terrorist financing and the Crown Prosecution Service lawyer, advising on the case.

'Mmm, mmm. Detective Chief Inspector.' The Attorney General drawled out the words as he looked her up and down. It was so blatant that one expected him to ask her to stand up so that he could take a closer look, or to lift the table-cloth and examine her legs. Seemingly fascinated by the figure and perhaps the sheer size of a slim English woman, he slowly managed to draw his eyes away from her towards the other visitor. He spoke slowly as he squinted into the eyes of the second visitor. 'A lawyer for the Crown, mmm. I too am a lawyer. I am the Attorney General, but you may call me...' He paused, puzzled. 'Mmm. Attorney General.'

The Englishman wondered if the Attorney General was over stretching his language abilities a little. He constantly looked as though he were struggling to understand, albeit he seemed very happy in this perpetual state of wonderment. The two visitors looked towards the Englishman, unsure of how to interpret this rather strange, puzzled little man, in his immaculate brown suit, khaki shirt and brown tie. But then he burst out laughing. 'Ha, ha! Good joke, eh! You can call me Attorney General! Ha, ha, ha! I like your guests, superintendent, my country is theirs also.' He stood up and presented each guest with a business card, holding it neatly between his two neat fists, his thumbs pointing forward. He offered the card with a little bow, muttering 'mmm, mmm' as he did so. The inspection was over and, without either guest having said a word, the ice had been broken by the Attorney General's odd sense of humour and the little card giving ceremony.

The first course was already arriving when the Attorney General pulled out a mobile phone from a pouch on his belt and made a call. The language was too fast for the Englishman to catch any of it and the three sat awkwardly waiting for their host to invite them to start the meal. The call over, he smiled, puzzled, at his guests. 'Please, please eat,' he said, waving his arm above the food. 'This is the oldest and finest restaurant in Chinatown.'

The Attorney General was a gracious and generous

host and course after course was laid out before them. The conversation revolved around the English Premier League, the local man demonstrating an impressive knowledge of Manchester United in particular.

'They had plans to visit,' he said, forlornly, after the long discussions about their form and future fixtures had reached a natural end, 'and I had arranged with my friend, the Chief of Police, for my family to have dinner with the team. We would have had many photographs, mmm, mmm.' He smiled gently and appeared to be quietly contemplating what might have been. 'But the Jakarta hotel bombs prevented them from coming to the Far East. This terrorism is bad for the economy. I am sometimes unsure about the benefits of democracy. There was no terrorism before it. Mmm. Mmm.'

'Attorney General?' asked the Englishman at an appropriate point between the dim sum and the fried grouper.

'Mmm. Mmm,' he answered, looking not at the Englishman, but into the Detective Chief Inspector's eyes.

'My guests would like to brief you on their case. I brought you the papers a couple of weeks ago. We were rather hoping that you'd be able to carry out the arrest and interview that we asked for.'

'Mmm. Yes. You did bring them. Very interesting case. Very good letter. I have given it to my subordinates to copy to use in our own cases.'

'And do you think it might be possible to carry out the arrest?' he asked. The guests were looking anxiously at the Attorney General. They had been working to assemble a prima facie case for two years and the interview of the Southeast Asian suspect was all important.

The fish arrived before he could answer. 'Please, please - eat,' is all he said. It was a relief to be served a spoon and fork with the battered grouper, having spent five courses chasing slippery food around with chopsticks, but the purpose of the lunch still hung awkwardly in the room. The Attorney General seemed not to want to speak of business.

Suddenly, a young photographer, a heavy professional camera slung around his neck, entered the room. The Attorney General quickly shuffled his seat close to the Detective Chief Inspector, put his arm around her shoulders and smiled. The photographer took one snap, looked at the image briefly on the camera's small screen, smiled at the Attorney General and backed out of the room. The host was already back in his position, nibbling on the final course, small lychee like fruits which he called dragons' eyes. 'Mmm, mmm,' he said, removing the large, round black stone from the sweet, perfumed white flesh, 'lychees heat the body after such a meal, but dragons' eyes have cooling properties. They aid digestion.'

A knock on the door signalled the arrival of the Attorney General's driver. He was waved away with an uncharacteristic hint of irritation, but it was clear that the Attorney General was preparing to go.

'So, do you think we might be able to meet you tomorrow to brief you on the case, Attorney General?' asked the Englishman.

'No,' the Attorney General smiled, looking puzzled, 'I am not available after today. The work of an attorney general is very demanding, Superintendent.'

'I know, Sir. But this is a very important case for the United Kingdom. We cannot proceed at home until we understand the role of the local man. Can we meet a subordinate tomorrow - ?'

The Englishman was cut short by the Attorney General's mobile phone ringing. Their host stood up, walking towards the dining room door, spending a few seconds listening. 'Mmm, mmm' he said, every two seconds or so, before stowing the phone back in his belt pouch. The Englishman was on his feet, the operational officers looking at him imploringly.

'I like you, Superintendent, mmm, mmm,' the Attorney General said slowly, 'and I like your guests too.' He was looking at the Detective Chief Inspector again. 'You should try a massage before you leave,' he said to her, 'you will enjoy it.' He reached for the door handle and then looked back into the dining room. 'No, you may not see a subordinate of mine tomorrow, because it is no longer necessary. Mmm, mmm. But you should call my good friend the Chief of Police. By a happy coincidence, his officers have this afternoon arrested your suspect, who will be ready for you to interview tomorrow morning. Mmm, mmm.' He seemed somewhat puzzled as he grinned widely at the three British officials, before bowing slightly and walking out of the room.

The Detective Chief Inspector punched the air with glee and the lawyer hugged the Englishman spontaneously. They were thus embraced when the door re-opened and the Attorney General's round face appeared.

'Is no-one hugging this beautiful woman?' he asked puzzled. The Englishman and the lawyer dropped each other. 'The Chief of Police is a good friend of mine, mmm, mmm,' he continued, 'you should call him…mmm, mmm…,' he paused, 'Chief of Police!' and, chuckling to himself, he left again. 'Good luck, my friends,' he called back as he crossed the restaurant floor.

CHAPTER NINE

The sea crashed noisily onto the beach, casting the flint pebbles like unwanted toys, before whimsically dragging them back again. The Englishman sat amidst the gushing and clattering and contemplated his pink steaming feet. He had two large, taught bubbles on his heels, each blister covering the entire heel area. He tried to compare the size with that of a coin, but there was none large enough. The blisters were bigger than a two pound coin. Then he got it. They were the size of the Churchill Crown that he had been given as a child when the great man had died – he estimated nearly four centimetres in diameter. They were impressive blisters. He looked at the special plasters that he had brought with him and that now sat curling in his hot palm. They were only half the size of the blisters. Carefully unpeeling the protective tape from the first of the translucent gelatinous pads, he applied the cushion to the top half of one blister. Next he stuck the second pad below and slightly overlapping the first. Repeating this for the other foot, he managed to cover some eighty percent of each blister. It was the best he could hope to achieve. He gradually peeled his socks up over the dressing, taking care not to lift the edges of the pads. Finally, he eased each tender foot back into its boot, sucking in his breath as the painful bulge slid over the unforgiving anklet of the boot. He fastened his laces as tightly as he could, keen to prevent the boot moving and rubbing against the raw swelling.

He downed the last mouthful of dull tea, dropped the flask back into his rucksack and struggled to his feet. Turning his back on the sea, he resumed his journey, hobbling unsteadily like a very old man. The dressings were near useless. The way up was depressingly steep and every step involved a torturous jab of intense pain into the hyper-sensitive, childlike softness of his heels. He longed to be wearing his working shoes – smart black brogues that had been heeled and re-heeled, but which were well and truly worn in, comfortable and easy to wear.

As he tripped towards Westminster Bridge, the Houses of Parliament came into view across the wide expanse of the Thames, shining silver in the low, early sun. There was a stiff breeze in his face and the Union Jacks flying from the top of Westminster Palace flapped potently. The Englishman loved his country. One of the reasons he had wanted to walk alone along its Southern rim was to remind himself of the England he was serving in the Far East. Now it seemed that the Far East had come to England as an early coach-load of Japanese tourists disembarked across his path, photographing each other standing at zany angles, their fingers inexplicably held up in a 'V'- sign, with England's most famous landmark as the back-drop. Stopping with them to admire the view, the Englishman took out his own pocket camera and snapped the scene: the golden yellow stone of parliament and of Big Ben, the pale turquoise of Westminster bridge's flattened iron arches and the bright red of the double-decker buses, warm against the flickering silver cold of the Thames. The noisy tourists might have irritated the Englishman on another day, but today, his first day in England for more than a year, he enjoyed their enjoyment of his country. Leaving the view behind him, he headed off to the conference.

It infuriated and embarrassed the Englishman to think how positive he had felt about his job just a week ago. He felt stupid and naïve. His stomach churned and he found himself groaning out loud in response to the humiliation. He paused to unfasten his jacket and let off steam. His neck and chest were clammy with sweat and his damp cuffs stuck to his wrists. His heels stung cruelly in spite of the dressings and his knee joints seemed reluctant to lever his stodgy body up each step. The cold wind blew in his face as he looked down at the Channel far below, trying to settle his respiration rate down to a less dangerous level. A week ago he had been part of the team that protected England from terrorists, now he was isolated. Looking back towards the peak of White Nothe he thought that he could just make out the black, cartoon-like silhouette of another lone walker in the distance and he wondered if he, too, was lonely.

'Get down on your knees you English bastard.' The terrorist screamed angrily, bitterly at the Englishman. 'Now you die for everything you have done to Muslims.' He was salivating, spitting with hate. The automatic pistol he gripped in both hands was inches from the Englishman's forehead. It twitched and shivered tangibly.

'No, no', the Englishman whimpered, his open palms lifting to the level of his face in submission, 'please don't kill me'. Dipping his knees without warning, the Englishman ducked below the kill zone and grabbed the barrel of the gun with both hands, twisting it violently outwards and away from him. The terrorist screamed in agony as his trigger finger broke in two places with a loud snap, crackle and pop, and the gun was safely in the Englishman's hands.

'Well done', the terrorist muttered, in reluctant respect, 'very quick indeed.'

Pleased with his performance, the Englishman blew across the end of the barrel of the yellow rubber Baretta. 'Now I'll be the terrorist,' he said, grimly.

During the break from conflict management training, the Englishman and his counterpart in Yemen, the two eldest of the group of seventeen counter terrorism liaison officers attending the conference, dunked digestives in their red hot tea and shared experiences. They were perched on the edge of a trestle table in a Territorial Army function room somewhere in central London.

'So how's the Far East treating you?'

'It's great. Tough at first, you know, settling the children down and trying to make the place home. I'm sure you've had the same problems in Yemen.'

'Not many! And my post is unaccompanied. Heaven knows what it must be like with a wife and kids! How are you getting on with the embassy?'

'Oh, great. No problem. They've made me feel right at home.'

'Ah well, at least you've got that in your favour. They've treated me like shit. The spies see me as a threat, the Foreign Office is full of weirdoes and, to be perfectly honest, this lot aren't much support, either. They either micro-manage everything I do or completely ignore me for weeks. The only ones I get any sense out of are the local cops.' The Englishman had not met his counterpart in Yemen before he had tried to kill him with the rubber Baretta. He had seemed a placid, gentle man, but now he was becoming animated and angry, his hot tea splashing onto his thigh, causing him to jump up, the trestle table and the lethally hot urn rocking precariously.

'Oh.' The Englishman hesitated a moment. 'I'm rather glad you said that. I thought I was the only one.'

'Well you're not. The problem is that most of them are doing the job to avoid real police work. Not many are old gits like us who can retire. The Boss has got a real hold over them all. They do as they're told, they don't speak out, they get their heads down. One wrong word and they're back on Borough – custody sergeant at Lewisham. Don't get me wrong, I'm not saying they're lazy; they're not. They do what they're told, that's all. Make no waves with the Boss. You won't find many who'll criticise the CTU, that's for sure. Keep your head down and don't be noticed.'

The conflict management instructor, a huge, pleasant lump in an obscenely tight tracksuit, was dragging a full-size legless rubber man into the centre of the hall.

'OK gentlemen, finish your tea,' he bawled, his round, shaven head smiling broadly, 'let's practise fighting unarmed, legless, rubber terrorists, shall we?'

The Englishman and his counterpart from Yemen arose carefully from the wobbly table and began to pull on the boxing gloves they'd been given. 'The Boss believes the job's a doddle and he likes to think he's rewarded us in some way by giving it to us. Never worked abroad himself, of course.   Branch man, through and through, I suppose. Loves the spies. He's alright, if you don't upset him, but he doesn't expect you to have an opinion other than his.' They joined the rest of the world's Counter Terrorism Liaison Officers, who were now standing in a line, chatting idly, kneading their gloved fists, waiting for the order to punch the rubber Al Qaeda operative.

The path up from the beach at Ringstead Bay had levelled. The gradient of the coastline this side of the bay was much less severe and the Englishman was gradually able to get into a steady stride. The regular thud, thud of his boots became a metronome that guided the rhythm of his thoughts, measuring and ordering them, filing them in their proper places and soothing his anxiety. It was a state of mind that the Englishman knew and cherished. It was why he walked. A moment would be reached when the body functioned automatically, the legs strode, the arms swung and the mind ticked like the movement of a fine time-piece. Even if he were with Elaine, his voice would be silenced for an hour at a time, chiming only occasionally to remark upon a bird or an unfolding landscape. The steady tempo was reassuring, regular and predictable. It generated reinforcements for the psyche, bolstering its defences against the onslaught, perhaps preparing the emotions for siege. Once so corralled, the mind was free from the intrusion of harmful distortions and was able to function efficiently, like a machine into which problems could be inserted, processed and resolved.

The Englishman considered his life as a policeman. It had been a good one and he had been a good copper. He had been a decent father and an honest, faithful husband. He had put his work first, that was true; but that was his duty. He had always put duty first. He had not changed when he had arrived in the Far East and the transition had been tougher on his family as a result. But he was preparing for a Beslan, preparing for the day when a terrorist attack happened on his watch. It would have been no good if British citizens had been targeted in Jakarta, Singapore, Bangkok or Kuala Lumpur and the Englishman didn't have any law enforcement contacts there. That was why he worked so tirelessly to build a network of local allies to whom he could turn when the big one went off. That's why he'd been able to get the Detective Chief Inspector and the Crown Prosecutor in to see the Attorney General.

Such was the Englishman's mind as he arrived on the outskirts of Weymouth, where two long curving arcades of sky blue and cream arches appeared out of nowhere on the beach, a rigid and ordered, slightly grotesque, piece of architecture that shouted out against the silence. The Englishman stopped and looked. The Riviera Hotel. In the height of a childhood summer, the teeth-like arches, once a 1950's holiday camp, may have represented a broad grin, but in the bleak cold of a December evening, they looked altogether more sinister: a sanatorium, or worse, an Orwellian creation of some sort, perhaps a series of torture chambers. Nearby, an industrial slab of blue and white beach-huts did little to relieve the stark imagery. A prison-like row of cold, bolted doors kept unwelcome visitors firmly outside. The rust seeped from their heavy padlocks and stuck to the cold blue steel like dried blood.

In welcome contrast, a cheery row of multi-coloured bed-and-breakfast hotels, tall, terraced houses with bright door canopies, pristine white window frames and dangling 'Vacancy' signs reminded the Englishman that he was home. Whilst his hotel was not in one of these traditional old houses, the Smack Inn was another typically English phenomenon: a rough seaside boozer, a pub that looked as if it had witnessed many a fracas and whose seedy, damp bedrooms seemed to retain the DNA of their secret occupants in their sheets and carpets. Worn and thirsty, the Englishman pushed noisily through the heavy swinging doors and found himself in a big saloon bar. Two late afternoon shoppers, an elderly couple, looked up from their drinks and stared, whilst an unshaven barman dragged his eyes lazily away from the half-time football results. The Englishman had downed three pints of John Smith's before he thought of unzipping his coat.

Later that evening, in the Bengal Spice restaurant, the Englishman met a young Kashmiri man from London working as a waiter, but whose dream was to be a writer. He served the lamb tikka with ambitious stories of his other life, not yet lived, and the Kingfisher beer was cool and the Englishman escaped east with him and was happy. But when it came to telling his own story, he found himself talking not of the achievements of his career, nor of his beautiful daughters and sexy wife, but of his conversation with the Detective Chief Superintendent two days ago.

'Sit down, Superintendent. There's something I need to say to you.'

'Sir?'

'You're under performing, Superintendent.'

'I beg your pardon, Sir?'

'You're under performing.'

"Under-performance": politically correct police

parlance used to describe the lazy and incompetent. 'What do you mean, Sir? Who says I'm underperforming?'

'I say. You've not overcome any of the relationship problems, you can't get on with the spies, you have no friends in the host police forces, the Foreign Office say they never see you and now I understand you're not completing the enquiries we send you.'

'What?' Never in thirty three years of service had he received a bad appraisal. 'I don't know what to say. That's simply not true.'

'What isn't?' The Detective Chief Superintendent, who had been leaning forward casually, as if talking to a friend in confidence, sat back in his chair and crossed a slim ankle over his knee, so that his chalk-stripe trouser leg formed a barrier between the two men. 'What part of it isn't true?'

'None of it is, Sir. I have good relationships with everyone and I do everything that the CTU sends me. My intelligence reports make it into the CTU daily summary almost every day. Most days I'm the only contributor.'

The Detective Chief Superintendent smiled without emotion, a practised mask. 'Look here Superintendent, this isn't about detail. You haven't got the right experience for this job. You can't go round upsetting the spies or the Foreign Office, you know. They report back on everything.'

'So someone's done that, have they?'

'I understand they're going to. Bloody mess. No bloody CT experience. You have to get on with people if you're going to work in CT.'

'But I do get on with people Sir. My relationships out there are really rather good. The General passes me everything we expect him to. Take that suicide bomb at the police mosque – the report was on your desk before start of play in London.'

'It's not the locals I'm worried about. It's our people. FCO. MI6. What the bloody hell have you been doing out there?'

'I thought I was there to work with the local CT unit.'

'Thought you were? Thought you were? There you go, you can't articulate your role properly. You're under-performing. Your post's up for evaluation after Christmas.'

'Evaluation? But what about my pre-conference annual report, Sir? I spent days preparing that. It outlines all the problems I've had, how I've overcome them and how I intend to go forward next year. I thought that was the evaluation.'

'Your so-called "pre-conference annual report,"' the Detective Chief Superintendent mocked, 'is just a load of excuses as to why you've upset everyone.'

'But I ran it past the Ambassador and the spies - the Head of Station, in fact. It seemed to go down rather well.'

'Perhaps you should have attended a few of the Ambassador's weekly meetings instead of spending your time constructing complex reasons as to why you have to act differently from every other liaison officer in the programme.' The Englishman started to speak but the senior man interrupted. 'Your heart's not in the job and your post will be evaluated early next year. It's time to start thinking about the next step of your career.'

The Englishman imagined himself having to tell Elaine and the girls. 'But what about my family, Sir? My kids have only been in the school a year.'

'You should have thought of that before you upset everyone.'

'But I didn't know I'd upset anyone. No-one has given me any hint of this whatsoever. This is the first I've heard of it.'

'Clumsy. No diplomatic skills. And your Desk Officer says you're adding no value at all to our investigations.'

'I don't know what you mean by that, Sir'

'I mean, for Christ's sake, that James O'Raugherty would have done the job better than you're bloody doing it!' The Detective Chief Superintendent coughed it up as if it had been lying on his chest.

'But James O'Raugherty's never done the job, Sir. I'm not sure it's fair to compare...'

'Look, Superintendent. Don't you say a word against James O'Raugherty. He gave his life for the CTU. He knew the job. He had what you haven't got. He got things done.'

'Could you give me an example, Sir? I don't understand why you would say that.'

'Well, that arrest and interview for the financial team, for example.'

'Yes Sir. A cracking result. I included it in my report. '

'Yes you did, didn't you, giving yourself plenty of credit, I notice. But that didn't have anything to do with you. You, whose only job was to get the investigating officers access to the prisoners, you nearly blew it. Cracking result? What are you talking about man? You didn't do a thing! The Attorney General took one look at the strumpet and the job was done!'

'And how do you think we got in to see the Attorney General in the first place? My ground work, that's how.'

'Ground work, my ass. He likes English women. That's all there was to it. '

'You've been talking to that bloody Desk Officer. He's a knob.'

'Now, now. Don't bring the desk officers into it. They keep this unit afloat. I can't imagine James ever saying a thing like that.'

'Could you get me in to see our Attorney General, Sir? Do you have any idea, Sir, how much hard work it takes so that a liaison officer can get to the point where he can even be in the same room as the Attorney General? And I've got six or seven of them across Southeast Asia to try and get to know.'

'But it's not just that. You're not getting the job done. Upsetting people.'

'But there's no evidence of any of this, Sir.'

'No evidence? Bloody cheek. Don't you threaten me.'

'Threaten you Sir? I'm not sure I understand...'

'Do you think I'm stupid? Suggesting I would bring up an officer's under-performance without something to back it up with? Are you a bloody Federation rep or something? Of course there's evidence.'

The Englishman stared at the Detective Chief Superintendent. Why on earth was he talking about the police officers' staff association? 'Well no Sir, I'd be surprised if you would bring something like this up without considering the evidence first. But I'd like to know what the evidence is. I have a right to reply, you know. And of course I'm in the Superintendent's Association like you Sir, not the Federation.'

'Oh, I see. That's your game. You're not bringing me down. I would've thought better of you, Superintendent. I thought you were an old fashioned type. I'd have thought you'd have had no truck with that equal opportunities nonsense. James O'Raugherty was one of us. He'd have thrown himself on his sword in this situation. That's the difference. I'll find the evidence alright. I'm not having my job put on the line by the likes of you.'

'So, what next Sir?'

'What do you mean, what next?'

'What happens now, Sir?'

'You go on your bloody walking holiday, I guess. You've got no bloody commitment to the job, after all. You're too old. You should've retired by now. You'd never have gone out there at your age if James hadn't died. I'll see you after Christmas.'

'But what do I tell my family Sir? They're committed to the next few years in the Far East. Linda and Katherine have taken a year to settle.'

'Linda? Katherine? Who are you talking about now? Go and have your bloody holiday and we'll talk through the evidence after Christmas.' He took out a small pocket diary and flicked roughly through the pages, ripping them every so often. 'Come and see me on the tenth of January. I have a week's holiday after New Year.'

'But I fly back on the fourth.'

'Well you'll have to delay your flight back. That's just the type of thing I'm talking about. No commitment.'

The Englishman had a headache. He was alone, vaguely aware that the Detective Chief Superintendent was now talking to another Counter Terrorism Liaison Officer. Sitting on the edge of his seat, in the front row of the conference room, dressed in his bright blue walking jacket, a rucksack at his feet, the Englishman bowed his head and looked down at the ticket between his finger and thumb. When he next looked up, he thought he saw Wool station flit by in the darkness.

CHAPTER TEN

The Englishman's night at the Smack Inn was spent with James O'Raugherty. He had dreamt him alive, living in the Englishman's house, the father of his children, Elaine's husband. O'Raugherty had been there when it mattered. As the Englishman stood impotent, naked on the end of a phone, O'Raugherty fought off the intruder before tucking the girls into bed and slipping in beside Elaine. Henry stood in the garage and watched from behind a strong steel fence with Endi and the driver as the naked Englishman took a chamois to O'Raugherty's pristine car. He repeated the Detective Chief Superintendent's words over and over again until, even in sleep, the Englishman was exhausted.

At some stage, the dark night became dark day and it was time to get up and out, to make the most of the few hours of daylight. He had to cover some fourteen miles today to reach Abbotsbury, in spite of the fact that he was too old, incompetent, and under-performing. The Englishman lifted the damp, grey quilt cover and swung his old aching legs out of the bed. If the Smack Inn boasted any en-suite rooms, the Englishman's was not one of them and, in wanting to inoculate his tired feet against the grubbiness of the landing carpet, the Englishman slipped his boots over his sockless feet, instantly crying out in pain. The fatigue, the beer and the stories of the night before had meant that he had forgotten his blisters. Now he realised that he couldn't walk.

Under performing. Bloody cheek. He fell back onto his bed and, shifting his weight without using his feet, he sat on the pillow with his back against the headboard. He was too old. His thin bare legs protruded from his boxer shorts and ended at the heavy walking boots. He loosened the laces, so that the boots were opened as fully as possible and then painstakingly removed each one. Even the slightest contact with his heel caused excruciating pain. He had no commitment. He took his reading glasses from the Formica bedside table and examined the damage. The neat round bubbles of yesterday were gone. In their place, two large open wounds. James O'Raugherty wouldn't have got blisters. The bubbles had burst, ripped open, revealing a thin layer of sore dark-pink virgin skin beneath them, almost too thin to hold back the blood, which seemed to be flowing just beneath the gossamer layer. The Englishman was reminded of a pathologist carrying out a post mortem examination on a murdered man, except that he was looking in at himself, his pink insides being exposed in a way that didn't look healthy. Clear evidence that he was under-performing.

They were the type of wounds that needed professional treatment. The torn skin 'lids' were very thick, perhaps a millimetre, showing just how many layers of skin had been damaged. These discs of blistered skin were white and moist, most of their circumference ripped painfully away from the foot, but each hanging on by a centimetre or so of thick, living, nerve carrying skin. The Detective Chief Superintendent's words were spoken again and again in the Englishman's head, even as he tried to concentrate on his feet. His pre-conference report was just a list of excuses. The gel blister plasters were still stuck firmly and uselessly to the skin flaps, albeit they were curling away at the edges, like grubby little petals, fluff and dirt clinging to their sticky surfaces. The Englishman gingerly pinched the edge of one of the plasters between his finger nails and tried to peel it off. It was at one with the skin, and instead of coming free, the disc itself began to tear at the point that it joined his foot. The Englishman winced as the blood, already close to the surface, immediately began to trickle from the wound. He was to be evaluated in the New Year. The pain caused by this tiny rip was intense, agonising. It was focused and sharp and small, but deep and pointed and jagged. The Post Security Officer had been right about one thing, at least: he should have pissed on his boots.

The Detective Chief Superintendent spoke aloud. 'Give up,' he said, you've got no commitment. You're too old. O'Raugherty wouldn't have got blisters. Give up.'

The Englishman laughed loudly, surprised to find that his nose was suddenly running. 'No,' he replied, aloud, his voice bubbling up out of his throat. 'No, I'm not giving up.'

'Give up,' insisted the Detective Chief Superintendent. 'You're finished. You've been evaluated and you're under-performing. You can't do your job and you can't finish this walk. Give up.' The words fell clumsily from the Detective Chief Superintendent's mouth as if he didn't want to enunciate them.

The Englishman looked at the moist dead skin of the blister discs and wondered at what stage they would rot and start to smell. He imagined himself skulking along the coast, the jungle mujahedeen hot on the scent of the rotten flesh of a frightened Englishman.

Elaine was crying. 'Don't give up. Don't let us down again. You're no good at your job, but you can walk. Don't give up on this.' She was sobbing loudly, her words deep and rounded in her throat as she wept. 'You weren't there when we needed you. Don't give up now. Don't give up this fight as well. We can't tell Linda and Katherine that.' Elaine's tears flowed freely. They flowed from the Englishman's eyes. Her sobs emerged from his chest, which convulsed with sorrow. Tears and snot dripped from his face onto the worn grey bed-sheet as he spoke Elaine's words and wept her tears. The Englishman looked at the treacherous wounds that revealed his incompetence and at the thin old legs onto which his face was dripping and he was reminded of another time.

It was a Saturday afternoon and the young copper's girlfriend had popped into a shop to buy a card for their friends' wedding. The odd cumin-like smell of cooked frankfurters drifted from the open doors of the Wimpy into the new indoor shopping centre, which was full. Elderly couples with brown PVC shopping bags and drooping shoulders explored without buying, using the nice new toilets before returning to the high street market to buy potatoes and a cheap screwdriver. Overweight poor families, all three generations dressed in cut-price sportswear, milled about with a slight belligerence, grunting unhappily at the lack of cut-price sportswear in the men's fashion shop next to the one in which Elaine was searching for a card. And a gang of about a dozen young men stood fashionably bored, facing each other in a circle, like young policemen listening in at an ad hoc briefing before a raid.

The young copper's face burnt as one of the gang yawned and stretched, reminding him of the treachery of his own body. On his way to a dangerous situation, like a pub fight or a violent domestic, he often found himself yawning and stretching in his terror. The same thing had happened at Orgreave, during the miners' strike.

The gang were 'casuals' and so were well dressed in pastel coloured Pringle golf sweaters, slim cut Farah slacks and Burberry bomber jackets. The young copper, just a young man like any other, was dressed the same way. He was impressed with his ability to blend in and imagined himself undercover. 'Dressed like a scrote,' his sergeant would say.

Among the gang was a big, smiling but quiet, strong looking blond youth. He was well known for breach of the peace and drunk and disorderly, but he'd dyed his hair blond and the young copper hadn't recognised him at first. He made a mental note to tell the collator about the change, and he shifted the shopping bags resting between his feet, looking back to see if Elaine had had any success choosing a wedding card. When he turned back, just a second later, the gang was gone. The young copper was puzzled; there hadn't been enough time for them to leave the shopping centre and be out of sight.

Then it became frighteningly clear. Fighting back a sudden yawn, the young copper felt the gang brush past him, from behind, from the men's clothes shop. They were like a fleet of fork-lift trucks, their arms in front of them laden with heavy dark expensive denim. *Steaming* they called it and it had become fashionable in Oxford Street. It was a terrifyingly brazen crime, relying on fear, not stealth. Gangs walked into shops and took whatever they wanted, young shop assistants standing by helplessly.

They were close enough to reach out and touch. The young copper could easily just step into their path and stop them. His mind writhed with discomfort, fear and duty. It was his duty to do something. He had sworn to the Queen that he would protect people and property and the solemnity of the oath weighed heavily on the young copper. What would happen if it was discovered that he'd witnessed the robbery and hadn't done anything? What would his peers think of him? He'd heard them talk behind the backs of probationers, judging them.

The young copper turned and took one step to the side, blocking the path of the gang. His hands rested on the powerful powder blue chest of the big blond one, who appeared to be the Ringleader.

'Stop. What do you think you're doing?' His mouth was so dry that he could barely form the words and his voice waivered with uncertainty. He was aware of a sticky white spittle forming at the corners of his mouth.

'What's it fucking well look like?' The Ringleader stuck his face in the young copper's face and the citrus scent of his aftershave wafted incongruously from his smooth chin. The muscles of his thick neck rippled with hate.

'I'm police.' The group looked at him stupidly. There were too many of them for him to arrest single handedly and they knew it. The young copper hoped that they would think he was a part of an undercover operation. What if they stabbed him? Once the young copper had seen a scrote get stabbed in the arm. A fountain of bright red blood pumped two feet clear of his arm each time his heart beat. He recalled the Joseph Wambaugh book in which the LAPD street cop gets shot in the stomach - the regret of it all, the pointlessness of it all. The period of clarity as one lies bleeding. Although suburban London was somewhat different from Watts, Wambaugh had a way of capturing the camaraderie of a group of police officers, a true to life realism that young coppers enjoyed, a way of seeing the world. Them against us. The Englishman's shift rather imagined themselves as the Choirboys. They called people scrotes.

The gang closed in around the young copper and the Ringleader was still grimacing in the young copper's face. Beyond him was a wall of violent pastel pullovers, all of them looking as if they were pumped up with steroids. Their arms were all still full of Levi 501s.

'Put them back.' The order was weak and the young copper felt that even the scrotes knew it.

The big blond Ringleader squeezed the words out from the thick neck with rage: 'You wanna learn to fight properly and stop fucking.'

The young copper didn't see anything coming. His face suddenly exploded as a sledge-hammer crashed into his nose and eyes. A single blow so hard and unforgiving, it instantly took him off his feet, snapped his nasal bone, crushed the sinuses and pulverised the cartilaginous septum into a distorted, squashed 'S' shape, blocking both nostrils forever. A perfect head-butt delivered by neck muscles that had been honed just for the purpose.

The young copper found himself alone on the floor,

surrounded by blood and jeans. There was a lot of blood and the Levis he had stood up for were irreparably damaged by it. The gang had dropped the jeans and fled. The young copper's nose had become the epicentre of his head, smashed, dripping blood and mucus onto his legs and radiating bolts of searing pain in ever increasing intensity. The aftershock came as a wave of nausea. He wretched deeply and vomited on himself. The young copper was covered in blood, mucus and vomit, kneeling on a pile of jeans in the middle of a shopping centre on a Saturday afternoon, looking like a scrote. Before he passed out, he was vaguely aware of a woman from the shop ordering him to put the jeans back, at once.

The Englishman didn't normally cry, of course. Women don't like men who cry. Neither did the Englishman. Crying was unproductive. Policemen don't cry.

Sometimes he had wanted to cry. As a Senior Investigating Officer, an SIO, he had found himself having to explain to traumatised parents the manner in which their beautiful son had been stabbed outside a night-club, or how their only daughter had been raped before being strangled. They always wanted to know the details. The SIO would explain carefully, watching the reactions in their tired faces as they tried to absorb the horror. They wanted to know, but it broke them and, as they wept, the SIO wanted to weep with them. His head would throb, his heart would die a little with theirs, his stomach would sink and churn and his cheeks would burn as he fought back his emotions. But it was important not to cry. They were relying on him for justice. He became the means by which their child's death was explained, their opportunity to tell the world about a decent, ordinary life. They wanted the senior detective to be human, to empathise with them, to hate the killers with them, to be strong and to solve the murder, but they did not want him to cry.

He had no recollection as to whether Elaine had helped him up, or whether he had dragged himself up. He remembered the first officer on the scene. Although he must have been taken, he didn't recall going to hospital. He knew that he couldn't taste his food afterwards, gradually learning that this was because he'd lost his sense of smell. Only his taste buds told him whether food was savoury, sweet, salty, sour or bitter. He could smell neither the death that he encountered in his police work nor his new born daughter. The last thing that he had smelt was the aftershave of the thug that had robbed him of his sense of smell.

There were more blister plasters in his rucksack. He had a couple of small bandages in his first aid kit and he had some Savlon. He would need to keep infection out; if these holes turned septic, he would be in big trouble. The skin discs themselves could act as both a barrier against bacteria and padding, preventing the raw new skin from chaffing against the leather of his boots. If he could position the discs against their wounds and stop them from moving, he might stand a chance of getting through the day. By evening time the new skin may have hardened slightly. The Englishman gently smeared each sore with the antiseptic cream. It made him wince again to touch the wounds, but the cold of the cream acted like ice on a burn and the pain actually eased a little whilst he was rubbing it in. With a small pair of scissors, he trimmed off the grubby and flapping pieces of yesterday's blister plasters. Then he used two new plasters on each skin flap, to try and tape them into position and to provide some cushioning around the exposed edges. Finally, he wrapped the heel in the thin cotton bandage, binding as tightly as he could in order to try to stop the ripped skin discs from moving. Over the bandage he slid his walking socks. The dressings felt thick and firm and the Englishman was much more confident as he eased his tender, bulging feet into the unforgiving boots. He gritted his teeth as he pulled the laces as tight as they would go, the sturdy leather clamping around his ankles.

Clinging to the wardrobe and the bedroom door handle, he levered himself to his feet and supported his weight as best as he could with his arms.

'OK, here we go,' the Englishman grunted aloud and he let go of his hand-holds. He half expected to fall, but his feet felt steady and firm in their tight bindings. There was surprisingly little pain - until he tried to walk. When he did, the raw circles of pink skin stung as if they were completely uncovered and unprotected. They scraped against the inside of the boot, the pain cutting into him like a cheese grater on his bare flesh.

He stumbled down to breakfast a cripple. The rank bar where he had guzzled his three pints of beer had been lazily transformed into a grimy breakfast room. Under-performance: he hated the stupid expression and the stupid man who had used it so flippantly. The stupid Detective Chief Superintendent who knew nothing of the Englishman's past but had been so quick to destroy his future.

The greasy old pub carpets made for a slightly revolting backdrop for eating, and when the sausages, bacon, black pudding, mushrooms, baked beans, tomatoes and fried eggs arrived, the Englishman wondered what sort of kitchen had produced them.

The snout looked around the interview room suspiciously before sitting down.

'I know where there's a stolen kitchen.'

The Detective Sergeant held back a snigger. 'Kitchen? How can somebody steal a kitchen?'

'It was in a van.'

'A kitchen in a van?'

The Detective Sergeant's colleague sniffed, looked at his watch and started to stand up. 'What a waste of time. Let's get rid of this idiot.'

'A fitted kitchen. Ready to be fitted. It was all loaded up in a van and it's been nicked. I know where it is.'

'Where?'

'It's been fitted already'

'Are you sure this isn't a fit up?' The two policemen laughed, but the snout just continued as if he was used to people laughing at him. He didn't even appear to be offended.

There was supposed to have been a system, but the truth was, it was difficult to get a warrant at the weekend. It was Saturday evening by the time the Detective Sergeant found himself at the duty magistrate's house, swearing out the search warrant. Another family weekend ruined. The magistrate used the same fit up joke before he signed the warrant. An hour later the Detective Sergeant and his colleague were inside a shabby terraced council house that sported a pristine, state-of-the-art fitted kitchen.

'My son brought it me,' asserted the lady of the house. She was a skinny blonde whose leathery sun-tanned skin made her look older than she probably was, though she was not unattractive. 'He's a good boy.

He's no angel, but he's a good boy.'

'And where's your son now?'

'He's asleep upstairs. You can go and wake the lazy bugger up if you want.' She nodded towards the open-plan staircase that ran up from the side of the kitchen.

'There's no need.' A deep, coarse voice boomed from the top of the stairs, 'I'm up.'

'He's up,' echoed his mother, 'there's no need.'

The flimsy wood above their heads creaked dangerously under heavy steps before a pair of expensive trainers and legs wearing grey jogging trousers came into view. A bare torso and chest appeared next, followed by a thick neck and what would have been the head, but for the fact that the man was pulling on a black tee-shirt, which momentarily obscured his face. He was a mass of huge, veined muscles, so much so that he was having problems getting his thick arms over his head and through the sleeves of the shirt.

'He might kick up,' said his mother, casually.

Both detectives took a step back, towards the door. There would be no winning in a fight against this man-mountain. As ever, they had left their truncheons in their desk drawers but, in any case, they would have been mere twigs against this hulk. They carried their hand-cuffs, but his wrists were far too thick for them, even if he were to be compliant.

'I ain't gonna kick up,' growled the deep voice through the material.

'He ain't gonna kick up,' translated the mother, 'he's a good boy.'

At last the tee-shirt was pulled down over the pumped up body, but the taut cotton stretched across the biceps and chest had the effect of making the man appear even more intimidating. As the face popped out into view, the Detective Sergeant recognised the Ringleader immediately. He began to stutter some sort of ridiculous greeting, before realising that the Ringleader had no idea that they had met before.

'I'm Detective Sergeant…' he began.

'I know who you are. You're Old Bill,' the Ringleader interrupted. 'Who grassed me up?'

'We've got a search warrant. We've come about the kitchen…'

'I know that. Me mum didn't know it was nicked. I told her I bought it for her. You don't need to nick her.'

'He's a good boy,' his mother cut in.

'We're going to have to search the house,' the Detective Sergeant's colleague said, with some relish.

'What the fuck for? The fucking kitchen's under your fucking noses.' The Ringleader became quickly angry and the mere mention of noses made the Detective Sergeant automatically reach to protect his own.

'It's what we have to do. You've more or less admitted stealing the kitchen. You know we have to check for other stolen property,' the Detective Sergeant explained.

'Alright, alright. You do what you've got to do. But there's nothing else here. You leave me mum out of it and I won't kick up.'

The Detective Sergeant's colleague shot up the stairs. 'I'll do the bedrooms,' he called out, disappearing out of view.

The Detective Sergeant asked the Ringleader and his mother to come and join him in the lounge and he started a tidy search of the sideboard drawers. The room was not unlike that of the Englishman's mother's home, the terraced council house in Shoreditch that had been his home too just a few years' earlier. There was nothing of any interest in the lounge and the Detective Sergeant moved back into the kitchen to start recording the stolen cupboards and appliances and to make arrangements for their recovery and transportation to the police station. He could already imagine the property sergeant's angry Monday morning objection at finding an entire fitted kitchen crammed into his store.

The Detective Sergeant's colleague came bounding down the stairs. 'Look what I've found, Sarge,' he said with glee. He held up some pornographic magazines and two dildos.

The Ringleader's mother's neck reddened in uneven patches. 'They're not mine...'

Her son's chest puffed out like a gorilla's and his elbows closed, his immense fists coming up to fighting height. 'You fucking bastards. I play the fucking game and you fucking...'

'Put them back now!' ordered the Detective Sergeant, and he instinctively put his hand on the Ringleader's chest. He could feel the heat and the ripples of his anger through the thinly stretched cotton.

'But Sarge, the magazines look obscene to me. They were in her bedside cabinet, we can nick her...'

The Ringleader grunted.

'Put them back where you found them,' the Detective Sergeant reiterated, slowly.

His colleague turned and began sheepishly to make his way back upstairs with his booty. The Ringleader moved closer to his mother, his chest heaving, his face red and hot. His hands came together, he flexed his biceps and he massaged his massive knuckles as he let out an immense yawn.

'I'm sorry,' the Detective Sergeant said to the Ringleader's mother, 'we didn't come here for anything but stolen goods. We didn't mean to embarrass you.'

She chewed her lip as her son yawned again, shifting the weight of his feet. 'Your mate's a bleeding knob. Get him out of my house,' she screamed, 'before he kills you both.'

CHAPTER ELEVEN

There was a clear blue sky and the Eastern face of the Queen Victoria Jubilee Clock shimmered in the cold early sun. The flat, gently curving promenade, with its cafes and amusement arcades, provided an inviting enough start to the day, even if it did all look a bit tired. The Englishman walked awkwardly, desperately trying to maintain a normal gait in spite of the pain, lifting his boots in an exaggerated fashion, belching as he went.

He had been at his peak. Detective Superintendent is a decent rank in itself; a Detective Superintendent in the Far East, fighting terrorism, is a worthy role indeed, and one of which he had been very proud. At 53, he had known that he was coming to the end of his police career, but he had not foreseen the detail. He had never considered that he would fall from the peak in such an undignified manner. Could O'Raugherty really have done a better job? He would have to tell Elaine and the kids that he had lost his job, for it was clear that the Detective Chief Superintendent intended to find whatever evidence he needed to justify replacing him.

They would have to come home and the girls would have to find new schools. He could retire. Perhaps he really was too old?

Even before he had reached the end of the promenade, the burning in his feet was excruciating and getting worse. He had hoped that he might have been able to walk the pain off, but it was now clear that his make-shift dressings were not adequate. This was ridiculous. He was supposed to have been on a holiday, having fun, relaxing in his beloved home country, "decompressing," as the Foreign Office called it, after a long spell in a tough region. But the nature of the walk had changed. Everything had changed.

Covering seventy-five miles of this relentlessly whimsical coastline in December was always going to be challenging, but now it had become something else. He had to prove that he could do it. Getting to the end meant beating the Detective Chief Superintendent. The bastard had told him he was no good at his job. Told him he was too old, that he was the wrong person, that a dead man could have done it better. The Englishman had been ripped from his life and abandoned on the south coast. He had to figure out what to do. He would have to explain to Elaine what he had done wrong. She would want an explanation. He would have to tell her that he hadn't done his job properly. She would ask him for examples and he would explain that he'd asked the Detective Chief Superintendent that same question, and that the man was clear that there was substantial evidence against him. He would return to London on the 10th January, after Christmas and New Year, and the Detective Chief Superintendent would hand him a thick file of evidence. He had stolen an embassy radio and given it to a private company. He had failed to understand the Foreign Office's subtle approach to risk management. He had called the Deputy Head of Mission a prat (and the Post Security Manager). He had failed to respect the dignity of the Headmistress of the British School in the Orient, looking at her bra through her blouse in a manner unbecoming of a police officer. And he had terrorised her with threats of Beslan coming to her school. He had claimed success when it wasn't due to him: the meeting with the Attorney General had been successful because of the man's liking for British women police officers, not because of the Englishman's relationship building. He had let his wife and family down, being absent on so-called "relationship building" meetings when they were burgled in the middle of the night. He had paid gratuities to his security guards even though they were complicit in the burglary and had circumvented embassy protocols for the installation of security measures at his home. He had upset MI6 and had talked inappropriately about them on an open line. He had undermined a key government relationship with the General by approaching him directly instead of following embassy protocols. The Englishman could see it clearly now: he was in a lot of shit. It was clear that everything had been reported back to London. Everything he did, said and wrote was watched and scrutinised and reported back. They were probably even watching him now.

The Englishman had been at the peak of his career, but he'd not been smart enough to step up to the big league. This international stuff was too big for him; the Foreign Office, MI6, the Attorney General, even international school heads, they were all above his grade. He was just a London copper, a boy too stupid to see a head-butt coming. He had been at the peak, but had been found wanting. He wasn't up to it. He hadn't even attended the Ambassador's weekly meetings.

But he had to finish the walk. Just as it became clear to him that he had failed in his work, so he knew that he must not fail in this walk. At the end of it he would need to tell Elaine and the kids that he'd not been all he said he was, that he wasn't good at his job, the way he'd always said. He would need to admit that he hadn't achieved much in the Far East, that they would have to come home in disgrace. Probably they would be allowed to return to empty their home and his office, but they would need to find new schools for the girls straight after Christmas. The poor things had held grand leaving parties from their old English schools and had departed for the Far East with some pomp. He would need to tell them that he had failed in his fight against terrorism, that they were bringing him home, that he hadn't been able to make it at the top, that the life he had promised them would last for five years had come to a sudden end. They would have to come back with their tails between their legs. They had followed him to the end of the Earth and he had let them down. Elaine had left her job, the girls had given up their friends and they had suffered for his sake. He had failed.

And he would not fail this walk. If this was his walk of shame, he would complete it. He had his cross to bear and he would carry it. He would not give up because of blisters. If they were watching him now, they would see him, limping and in pain, humiliated. But they would not see him give up. They would not break his spirit. He would finish this walk on bleeding stumps if necessary, because the Detective Chief

Superintendent expected him to fail. He would walk home because it was one thing he could do better than James Donell O'Raugherty.

Weymouth harbour came as a pleasant surprise after the rather drab promenade. It was a bitterly cold Sunday morning, but the sunshine had brought out the early sailors and the yachts that were anchored there were alive with activity. Their halyards jangled musically against the masts and the Englishman held his head high, smiling as he admired the beautiful English scene. Two impressively large catamaran ferries gleamed white, red and blue at the harbour mouth, prompting the Englishman to think of Ratty and his desires to jump aboard and travel the world.

An acorn and arrow set into a wall at the end of the harbour indicated that the coast path followed a set of fine old stone steps, which led upwards to the cliff-top gardens above Nothe Fort. The gentle beginning to the day was over. The very first step upwards caused the boot to grate and a searing pain shot through the Englishman's already sore heel. He gingerly brought his trailing foot upwards and placed it next to the other. He stood silently on the first step looking up at the thirty-nine or so more that lay ahead of him on this first 'zig' of what was clearly a 'zigzag' flight. Was this feasible? He saw himself as a limbless soldier, the victim of an Afghan insurgent's landmine, wearing a prosthesis strapped to a tender, bleeding stump. Such men had walked to the South Pole to raise money for charities. Surely he could walk to Exmouth with a couple of blisters? He hoisted his sore leading foot onto the second step. His feet hurt him. That was all there was to it. At least one of those sleek new blade-like false feet couldn't get blisters. It would be marvelous to be walking on cool sprung steel, without nerves and without tender, exposed and bleeding skin. He now stood on the fifth step, hands on hips, contemplating the rise ahead as a soldier contemplates a mine-field, choosing carefully where to place his foot next. His eye chose a level and dry piece of stone, his back tilted forward, his hip began to elevate, his knee bent drily, his weight shifted. The pain of movement in the lifted heel and from the foot now bearing his weight surged simultaneously to his brain as raw exposed flesh rubbed against unforgiving leather. He winced. He rested, one foot on the new step, the other poised for movement. His eye picked a level and dry piece of stone…

Thus the Englishman picked his way to the top of the 'zig', then looked with dismay at the 'zag,' before starting the process again. Hadn't some Chinese philosopher said that "every journey of a thousand miles starts with a single step"? Well, that's how I'll do it, he thought. One painful step at a time, I'll do it.

The problem of the short winter days came back to him. Why had he tried to do this at the end of December? The day after tomorrow would be the shortest day of the year. He couldn't be out on these cliff tops after dark. He knew that he needed to walk much faster. Elaine and the girls were arriving at Exmouth on Christmas Eve and he had to be there to greet them. But how could he possibly speed up with his feet in this state?

Stinging salt spray swept in from the sea and hit him hard in the face as he completed the final flight of stone steps. He was standing on a thick spit of land, a nose like promontory which projected into the sea. He picked his way woefully along the cliff-top path, until he found himself looking towards the rear fortifications of

Nothe Fort, an imposing Victorian slab of Portland stone. Below him to his left lay Weymouth Harbour, its flotilla of sailing boats comfortable in their haven, whilst to the right was the immense Portland Harbour, looking barren, cold and unwelcoming, its angry waters anything but a safe place in which to anchor. Beyond this, the island of Portland itself, topped with a second citadel fort, the two forming a double deterrent against the ambitious French navy of Napoleon III. This was the thin pencil line of land that the Englishman had seen in the extreme distance the day before.

The wind whistled through the exposed ramparts of the western side of the fort. The sound was almost melodic, like a lonely soul whistling a sad air. A group of middle aged men, perhaps a historical society, emerged from behind the defences, examining a gun emplacement that was being buffeted by the cold December gusts. Their coats rippled and their grey hair waved liked bunting. Below them, the barbican protruded from the walls, its narrow slits affording a clear shot at anyone attempting an assault on the landward entrance. The mournful whistling sound seemed to come from within the fort itself. One of the men, dressed in light coloured clothing, stood atop the barbican, below the main group of men, looking not out to sea, but up towards the Englishman himself. He stood casually and whistled with the wind, capable and strong. It was James O'Raugherty.

The Englishman was momentarily delighted at the opportunity to be able to talk things over with O'Raugherty. He shouted to him, 'James. It's me. I'm walking to Exmouth,' but his voice was lost in the salt wind that blew in his face.

'Exmouth? You've got a long way to go.'

The response cut in from somewhere much closer. The Englishman turned and saw that he was standing amongst the faded plastic tables of a small cliff-top café. A large, red-faced man was wiping down the damp tables with a crisp white cloth and, smiling at the Englishman.

'Can I get you anything?'

The Englishman looked at the friendly face and back towards the fort. James O'Raugherty was gone. Had he spoken aloud? Had he really called out to O'Raugherty and told him where he was going? Had he gone mad? He was bound to be depressed about his job. Were hallucinations a symptom of depression? How bad was his mental state, that he was seeing ghosts?

'The whistling reaches up here some mornings. It's a cold one today, too. Snow, I reckon. Can I get you anything? A cup of tea?'

The Englishman looked again at the café owner and then beyond him to his gaily coloured hut, from which beach balls, buckets and spades and inflatable bananas hung ridiculously, given that the man was predicting snow.

'I need to speak to people,' the Englishman said, at last.

'We all need to speak to people, mate. Can I get you anything?' He continued wiping his tables.

'I'm sorry. I've been a bit lost,' the Englishman found himself saying.

'Not on this part of the coast path, mate. You can't get lost here.'

'I meant in my thoughts. I'd love a cup of tea please.'

The café man weaved his way to his hut and disappeared inside. The Englishman sat close to the counter. It was utter relief to rest his feet. He had covered less than half a mile in nearly two hours. He could not possibly reach Abbotsbury before dark at this rate. He looked dolefully down at his boots. Bloody things.

'Just waiting for the urn, mate,' the café man said, dragging a basket full of beach-wear out to the front of the hut, 'might be my last day today, if the weather does break.' He wore a thick fleece jacket and fingerless gloves. He started to hang bright yellow and orange snorkels, masks and flip-flops from the awning of his little café.

The Englishman unfolded his map and studied it. He had to make his way South to Ferry Bridge, which linked the mainland to the isle of Portland and, from there, turn Northeast, hugging the coastline of the East Fleet and West Fleet, the strange lagoons formed between the coast and the impossibly straight sand bar of Chesil Beach. At West Fleet he had to turn inland and cut across country to get to the village of Abbotsbury, where he was to spend the night. It was about twelve miles. He had about five hours left of guaranteed daylight. Covering more than two miles an hour across this landscape would be tough for the Englishman in any circumstances, but with his feet in this condition, it was impossible.

'There's your tea, mate,' the café man plonked it down. 'You haven't got to get to Exmouth today, have you?' he asked, nodding towards the map.

'No. Though it might as well be Exmouth. My feet are ruined and I've only just started. I've got to get to Abbotsbury today.'

'Boots no good? You didn't wear them in properly, I reckon mate.'

'Bloody things.'

'It's not the boots' fault, mate.'

'I think you're probably right,' the Englishman conceded, 'but it's too late now. I can't finish my walk in these. I think I'll have to get a cab from here.'

'Flip-flops and espadrilles is all I can do you mate,' the café man suggested, 'and I can't see you getting to Abbotsbury in flip-flops. Not if it snows.'

'Espadrilles? Are they the canvas and string things?'

'Yes, mate. Two quid a pair this time of year. Same as the flip-flops. A fiver in August, but this might be my last day if it snows. I sold a snorkel and mask set yesterday for four quid, believe it or not'.

'Have you got any size nines?'

'I think so mate. Let me see'. The café man disappeared into his hut, emerging just a few seconds later with a transparent polythene bag containing about twenty pairs of flimsy looking white espadrilles, wrapped in blue elastic bands. He opened the bag on the Englishman's table. 'Let me see,' he muttered, 'sixes, sevens, eights, here we are – nines: three pairs, and tens: two pairs. Two quid a pair. Put them in your rucksack and treat them as slippers when you get back to Abbotsbury.'

'I'll have five pairs,' said the Englishman, quickly, 'all three pairs of nines and both pairs of tens.'

'I can do you discount for five pairs,' the café man said. 'Give us nine quid. A tenner with your cuppa. Christmas presents, are they?' As he spoke he put the lightweight shoes into a pale pink and blue striped plastic bag and handed them to the Englishman.

'No, I'm going to walk to Exmouth in them.'

'You'd be mad to do it in flip-flops,' the café man said with a serious air, and then added, 'if it snows.'

It was probably madness to do it in espadrilles. Sixty miles of some of the most challenging coastline in the country, in December. Nevertheless, it was a much more content Englishman who stood, finishing his tea, looking out towards Nothe Fort, than the man whose pain and inner turmoil had led him to conjure up images of James O'Raugherty as he had stumbled up the steep steps thirty minutes earlier. Hope had returned. He would finish this walk. He would talk to people. He would not get lost in morose imaginings. He was a good man. He had been good at his job and he had been treated unfairly.

He wondered what the girls would say about his appearance. He carried a huge, heavy rucksack, now bulging and heavy with his boots and the spare beach shoes. He wore a blue waterproof walking coat over several insulating layers. He wore gloves and a woollen hat, a thick scarf, two pairs of walking socks and a sparkling pair of white espadrilles. But his feet were in heaven and he was in a much better state of mind. It would be difficult, but he would do it. The café man reappeared at his side and the Englishman finished his tea, his eyes scanning the solid ramparts as he silently said goodbye again, this time forever, to James O'Raugherty.

'The old fort's haunted. I suppose you know that, do you mate?'

The café man's words stayed with the Englishman for several miles. The fort was haunted. But by James O'Raugherty? That was unlikely. Perhaps each man saw his own ghost there? Or James O'Raugherty's ghost was following him, haunting him still here in England as it had in the Far East. He wished he could talk things through with him.

CHAPTER TWELVE

The espadrilles were ludicrously comfortable; the low and soft canvas backs meant that there was very little contact with his open wounds. For the first time since the stinging had started soon after he had left Lulworth Cove, the Englishman was able to walk without pain. The path beyond Nothe Fort followed the level route of an old railway, with a smooth tarmac surface. Although the cuttings prevented any views of the sea and created a tunnel effect, the Englishman was able to walk fast, making up for some of the time he had lost in the slow climb up from the harbour. The soles of the espadrilles, made of a single layer of string, felt flimsy and thin and, of course, they had no heels. The Englishman wondered if walking in these flat shoes would damage his feet or cause referred pain somewhere else in his legs, tendonitis perhaps. But, for the time being, he was simply delighted to be pain-free.

As long as the weather held, he would be OK. The temperature was low enough that muddy paths were frozen; the problem would not be one of getting wet feet, rather of lacking the protection of a sturdy sole against rock and stone and of slipping in early morning ice. He looked up and examined the sky. It was cloudless and pale blue. No snow would fall today. He just needed to make as much ground as possible whilst he could. And he needed to shake off O'Raugherty's ghost, which he imagined had been deployed by the Detective Chief Superintendent to keep an eye on him.

The Englishman had upset the spies. Doing so had been a stupid and naïve mistake. The General had warned him that he was in the pay of the Fresh Faced Spy - a friendly gesture of caution from one senior police officer to another. It was the job of the Secret Intelligence Service to recruit agents; of course some of the Englishman's other contacts would also have been recruited, it stood to reason. The Attorney General, surely. The headmistress? Perhaps the Deputy Head of Mission himself was an undeclared MI6 officer? Henry? The guards at his house? Endi, even? Perhaps his laptop had been stolen by the spies? That would make sense. It would explain why his house was so poorly secured in the first place. And why the police didn't attend the burglary. What had been on his laptop? Had he kept any classified documents on it, things that shouldn't have been there? He didn't think so. But he had used it from time to time to write unclassified emails to his own police contacts. Perhaps the spies wanted to see what he was up to. And he had looked at pornography, too. Everyone did, didn't they? It was only harmless stuff, nothing illegal. But he'd told his vetting panel that he didn't use the internet to look at pornography. That would be enough to prompt the spies to get access to it, to prove he was lying. He looked self-consciously over his shoulder, sure now that he was being followed, knowing that he wouldn't be able to see anyone if he was. If the DCS chose to mount a surveillance operation against him, he would never know. People liked to think they could spot a police officer a mile away, but the Englishman knew this not to be true.

The huge articulated lorry reversed slowly into the small, damp yard. The Victorian entrance had never been intended for vehicles of this size. After several efforts to get it far enough in to enable the gates to be shut, it eventually stopped with the cab protruding into the small East London side road.

The Regional Crime Squad Detective Inspector's earpiece crackled into life, as the officers in the observation post broadcast what they were seeing. 'From the O.P., the driver is out, out, out and standing in front of the target vehicle.'

The Detective Inspector pushed the button on the vehicle's covert radio microphone. 'Five-three, yes, yes.'

There was an uncomfortable wait and the Detective Inspector and his driver took the opportunity to open their cold pies and take greedy, untidy bites. 'Standby, standby. The driver has been approached by two men from the yard and all three are standing in front of the target vehicle. Wait one.'

A long hiss of white noise and then a further tense delay, followed by a loud and excited burst. 'And it's a contact, contact, contact on the target. The target is one of the two men with the driver. He's talking on his mobile phone. Are you getting this five-three?'

'Five-three, yes, yes. Are you able to get photographs, O.P.?'

'O.P. yes, yes'. Then another excited burst of raised voice: 'Standby, standby, standby. The target is in, in, in to the target vehicle, the driver is in, in, in. Engine started, manoeuvring, manoeuvring and it's off, off, off, towards you five two.'

'Five-two, yes, yes. Five-two has the eyeball and the vehicle is held at the junction with Cambridge Heath Road'

'O.P. can I come in?'

'Five-two, yes, yes.

'From the O.P., the third man remains at the yard and is making a call on his mobile phone. For your information, five-three.'

The Detective Inspector squeezed his button. 'Five-three, yes, yes. Back to you, five-two.'

'Five two still has the eyeball. The target vehicle is held, offside indicator, and it's a right, right, right onto Cambridge Heath Road.'

The Detective Inspector's pager vibrated and he read the message. 'Get me to a T.K., quickly,' he snapped to his driver. Then, into the radio: 'Five-three, can I come in?'

'Five-two, yes, yes.'

'Five-three is leaving the plot to get an update.'

'Five-two, yes, yes. It's a left, left, left onto the Mile End Road and it's over to you five-seven'.

A woman's voice took over the commentary: 'Five-seven has the eyeball, on Mile End Road, speed three-zero, four vehicles for cover....'

The Detective Inspector, dressed in jeans and a baggy sweat-shirt in order to hide his covert radio and a loose bomber jacket that concealed his side-arm, leapt from the car and into the filthy red telephone box. The floor was coated in a layer of damp black muck and it looked as if it stunk of urine. Brightly coloured business cards with lurid drawings of buxom, stocking and suspender wearing women offered him various sexual services. Tapping in his phone card number, the Detective Inspector called Scotland Yard's 'Little Room,' which managed all police telephone intercepts.

'Hello?' a cautious voice answered.

'Can I speak to Ivan, please? One-three-nine.'

There was a short delay, then, 'good morning, Ivan speaking.'

'Hello Ivan. It's the D.I. from the Regional Crime Squad here. One-three-nine.'

'Hello, Boss. It sounds as if it's all happening for you, is it?' It was the friendly deep London voice of 'Ivan,' the pseudonym of the man the DI had never met, but to whom he had spoken twenty times a day from telephone kiosks around the country for the last six months.

'Yes, it looks as if it's coming off today. What have you got?'

'The target's spoken to someone to say that the driver's here. Perhaps someone inside the slaughter? Then B's just made a very interesting call.'

'That's great, he was at the slaughter with the target when the U.C. arrived with the lorry. The U.C. and the target have gone off in the lorry. B stayed at the slaughter.'

'That makes sense. Don't stand your O.P. down, because it looks as if they're coming back. B's put in a call to say that the target has met Joe and has gone with Willy to look at the paperwork. That'll be the money, I presume?'

'Yes, Willy's the undercover driver. The money's with the other U.C. But who's Joe?'

'I'm not sure. It's a new name. But it looks as if the drugs are with B and someone else, perhaps Joe, at the slaughter, so today could be the day it all comes off.'

'That's great news. I'd better get back to the plot. Cheers, Ivan. Keep me posted.'

'Good luck, Boss.'

The Detective Inspector wondered if they really would be putting in a strike today. It had been a long and complex surveillance operation that had seen him and his team working sixteen hour days for the last three months. Before that there had been months of preparatory work. There was not much they didn't know about the target: what time he got up, who his mistress was, where his children went to school, which bank he used, his favourite hotel, pub, betting shop and gym. They knew who he met and where he met them. They had even had a surveillance officer swimming lengths next to him in his local swimming pool. They had been close to success a few times before, but today looked as if it would be their best opportunity yet. The combined use of informants, telephone intercepts, undercover officers, mobile surveillance and probes had built up an intelligence picture that had led them to the brink of the largest quantity of cocaine ever seized in the United Kingdom. Arriving back at their position, the mobile surveillance convoy was still out of range and the Detective Inspector was able to call the Observation Post.

'O.P. from five-three. Are you getting anything on the probe?'

'Yes, yes. Target two has returned inside and is talking to an unknown male. They're waiting for target one and Willy to return.'

'Five-three received.'

'Five-three from O.P.?'

'Yes, yes.'

'I think the gear's there. The unknown male has

talked about three tonnes, over'.

'Say again the quantity, over.'

'Three tonnes. Three thousand kilos.'

There was a faint crackle of interference and then both the Detective Inspector and the Observation Post realised that the remainder of the surveillance team had come back into range. The Detective Inspector's mobile telephone rang – the undercover officer's controller.

'Hello Guv. I'll keep it short 'cos I know you're up to your neck in it. Willy's managed to put a quick call in. He's shown the target the money and he's well pleased. They're going back to the slaughter to hand over the gear. It's three thousand keys, Guv!'

'And the target's going to be hands on, is he?'

'It looks like it, Guv. He was with Willy.'

'That's great news. Looks like today's the day.'

'One thing though Guv. He's got the gun on him. Be careful Guv.'

The Detective Inspector's mouth was dry and his heart was beating unhealthily fast. The undercover officer, the telephone intercept and the probe all suggested that the principal target was about to sell three thousand kilograms of cocaine. There would be plenty of evidence not just to convict, but to secure a guilty plea. Surveillance operations were difficult, but the evidence they generated was difficult to challenge.

'From five-seven, it's a nearside indicator, followed by a left, left, left as the target vehicle approaches the target premises. And it's a stop, stop, stop, immediately outside the target premises'.

'Move up, for Christ's sake,' the Detective Inspector snapped at his driver. 'Get closer.'

'From the O.P. The target is out, out, out of the

target vehicle and in, in, in to the target premises.'

There was a pause as everyone waited for the Detective Inspector's instructions. He stretched and yawned, reached under his armpit and felt the uncomfortable lump that told him his Smith and Wesson revolver was where it should be. It looked like a cowboy gun. He yawned again, pushed the microphone button and, his voice wavering like a boy's, he shouted 'Strike, strike, strike,' before jumping from his car and leading his team into the yard.

The Englishman had begun to feel like a criminal. A part of him knew this to be irrational, but another part feared the police and the fear made him feel like the enemy. He had done nothing wrong, but he felt a sense of closing ranks, of efforts being made to find evidence against him by those who saw him as an outsider. The Desk Officer and the Detective Chief Superintendent hunched over the bar together at O'Raugherty's funeral, plotting even then to bring the Englishman down. Waiting for a slip-up. Watching him, all the time, and waiting. He knew from his own experience the extent of the intrusion that could be authorised if the target justified such surveillance. If the Detective Chief Superintendent considered it to be proportionate and necessary, then the Englishman could well be under surveillance right now. He had stolen the embassy radio and that was something that could justify all sorts of intrusive techniques. Even in the barren December countryside there would be ways of watching him. Aerial surveillance perhaps? Maybe a tracking device had been placed on him. Thankfully, he'd not brought his mobile phone with him, having had it sent on to Exmouth with the rest of the conference trappings. The

Englishman had wanted solitude to help him relax; now it was driving him insane. And he could watch it happening: almost as an objective observer, the Englishman was able to see the effects that the solitude and the pain and the Detective Chief Superintendent's investigation into his poor performance were having on him. He waddled along in his flapping espadrilles and worried.

His counterpart in Yemen had told him to keep his head down and not to upset the Boss. That's exactly what the Englishman had intended to do next year, but it now seemed as if it was too late. There wouldn't be a next year for the Englishman. He had upset the Deputy Head of Mission, the Post Security Officer and the Fresh Faced Spy and, as a result, he'd upset the Detective Chief Superintendent. And he doubted whether MI6 needed authority to mount surveillance. They were supposed to comply with the law, but did they? Probably there was some other secret law that enabled them to do what they wanted in the interests of national security.

The Englishman had emerged from the railway cutting into open countryside and now was able to look across The Fleet to the pebble strip of Chesil Beach. A small community of huts and boat sheds huddled together against the cold on the distant bank, looking like Captain Scott's South Pole encampment. The Englishman had once seen Scott's journal beneath a glass case in the British Library and the humanity of the handwriting had really struck him. A living man's written words found next to his frozen dead body, a piece of his life left after death. 'Things have come out against us, but we do not complain. Instead we bow to the will of Providence. For God's sake look after our people.'

What would the Englishman leave behind? He didn't keep a journal. What was the point of a journal of a walk along the South-West Coast Path, when Englishmen such as Scott had already written about extreme suffering? What could the Englishman add – the horror of blisters and dank hotel rooms? Once he would have left behind a reputation and that would have been enough, but he had ruined that when he had failed in the Far East. He had nothing to leave his wife and daughters but shame - the will of Providence.

The sun was low above the horizon by the time the Englishman reached West Fleet, where a handful of miserable swans were dotted on the bleak water. The path here was barely discernible and the map showed that it turned north, inland, and made its way across country to the village of Abbotsbury. As he turned his back on the coast, he calculated that he had covered some twelve miles since Nothe Fort - not bad for a man in a pair of string and canvas shoes, haunted by ghosts and under MI6 surveillance. What's more, if he was able to keep up this pace, he could easily cover the remaining couple of miles before the sun disappeared. He laughed aloud at his victory and, casting his eye about the deserted hilltop, he got the sense that he had managed to shake off his cover.

Emerging from the edge of a small copse, its leprous trees naked and twisted and covered with curling flakes of grey lichen, the Englishman found himself at the bottom of a damp, green meadow. The grass was long and lush and the soil saturated with water, so that it resembled one of the paddy fields of Indonesia, except that it was freezing cold. Little translucent thin crystals of ice, like gossamer, had started to form at the edges of the small muddy pools, making tiny crisp sounds under his feet. His espadrilles absorbed the moisture like a sponge and his feet were quickly sodden. The path, which the map told him led through the middle of the field, had disappeared amongst a series of deep, muddy bogs caused by the hooves of many cows. The entire herd stood in a narrow gap between a stream to the right and a barbed wire fence to the left. Heavy with milk, the huge black and white animals mooed loudly, and a little aggressively, the Englishman thought, as he approached.

His feet slid in the wet mud as he trudged nearer to them. The ground close to the stream was even more soggy, and the stream itself, perfectly still, was starting to ice over. As a result, the Englishman chose to stick to the barbed wire fence to his left as he crept ever nearer to the herd. The cold of the approaching evening pulled at his moist nostrils. He had got within a few metres when the animals nearest to him began to move away. However, finding themselves facing the cold stream, and blocked from behind by their companions, they turned back on themselves, squeezing the cows nearest to him out of the comfort of the herd and propelling them reluctantly towards him. The Englishman started to back away, but the circular movement created by the cows escaping the stream picked up speed and the cow nearest to him collided with his face. A huge white and pink snout, like some giant and grotesque kitten's, nostrils steaming slightly, butted heavily into his cheek, smearing him with warm bovine snot. The beautiful eyes, their lashes curling, stared emotionless into his, their heads at the same height. The Englishman turned and tried to run, but the smooth string soles slid banana-skin like on the soaking ground, his feet left the earth for the sky and he fell heavily on his rucksack laden back.

The herd instantly surrounded him. He kicked and squirmed like an over-turned beetle trying to right himself as the small sharp hooves stamped and slid around him. One threatened to come down on his chest and it took all of his might to force it aside with the outside of his arm. The warm dangling teat of an udder brushed revoltingly against his lips as he levered his hands into the freezing wet mud and, finding purchase against the heels of the udder's owner, he slithered to his feet. The curved, fat backs of the beasts undulated just below head height and he looked across them in the half light for an escape route. Without warning, a heavy thud in his back hurled him forward, knocking the air out of his lungs. His string soles slid uselessly on the sodden grass and mud and he was propelled against the flank of another beast, as the soft brown eyes of a third looked bewildered into his face, her warm breath on his neck. The cows continued to circle wildly, panicking, squashing the Englishman alarmingly, so that it was becoming difficult to breath. He raised his arms up to try to get some purchase and climb up on top of their backs, but it was the worst thing he could have done. Unable to use his arms to push the animals away from him, he was lifted helplessly off of the floor, his arms flailing above his head and his chest pinioned. His ribs were unable to expand and the air was being squeezed from his lungs. He was carried by the ceaseless movement of the herd, which still circled in a chaotic panic to avoid him, their efforts at escape as ineffective as the Englishman's attempts to draw breath. The strange thing was the absence of noise. Just as punches in a pub fight lack the

Hollywood style slap and biff sound effects of those in a cowboy saloon and real knives are drawn silently, without the accompanying metallic zing that directors feel so obliged to add, so the Englishman was being killed amidst the backdrop of quiet Friesian pants and the squishing of hooves. Similarly, the Englishman made no noise as he wheezed, feeling like a balloon deflating in slow motion. Unable to call out, he was being constricted to death, quietly. The base of his metal flask was pressed painfully into his kidney and, his arms still uselessly waving in the air, he was dying. So this is what Providence had willed for him. 'For God's sakes take care of our people.' He started to feel peace. He guessed he hadn't breathed for nearly a minute and he knew that he was finished. He was a policeman, he'd investigated many murders and suspicious deaths; he knew how people died. Even as his life slipped away, he knew he was dying and could see the post mortem examination of his own body, opened without dignity on the slab. The pathologist sniggered as he declared the espadrilles to have been the cause of his death, and the Englishman slipped silently into unconsciousness.

He was instantly back alive, freezing, wet, submerged. Dark water swirled across his open eyes and he instinctively sucked it into his vacuous lungs as he tried to take a breath. He burst up into air, water pouring from his open mouth like a village pump. Noise returned as the cow that had been compressing his chest was struggling to drag herself out of the stream, mooing frantically, her front legs pawing at the soft and crispy soil, her massive hind quarters finally managing to propel herself clear and to safety. The herd was also mooing loudly. The Englishman bobbed up to his chest in the icy water for a second, getting his breath, then realised in a panic that he had to get out. The water that had saved him was now killing him as surely as the cold had killed Scott. He heaved himself out and ran up the meadow, water streaming from his rucksack, his socked feet sucking noisily in the soft mud, his toes curling for grip, his sodden, filthy espadrilles floating in the stream behind him. He reached the narrow lane at the top of the rise. From here, in the half-light, he could just make out the wooden finger-post that marked the way of the next section of the route to Abbotsbury. Ignoring this, the Englishman turned left and jogged down the road in his socks, his rucksack bouncing on his back.

CHAPTER THIRTEEN

It was dark by the time a dripping, shivering and steaming Englishman, covered in thick black mud from head to ankle, but wearing a brand new pair of white beach shoes, pushed open the door of the Ilchester Arms and ordered a pint of bitter and his room key.

'What happened to you there, boy?'

The Englishman stopped mid swig and looked towards the voice. A badly shaven face, clumps of silver bristle showing here and there on the chin and cheek and tiny brown eyes beneath a tweed cap. The skin of his face was engrained with dirt, so that his lips where they touched looked clean and young in comparison. He stood with his fingers wrapped around an empty beer glass, elbow on the bar, his foot resting on the brass foot-rail. It was the same position the Desk Officer had been in as he had conspired with the Detective Chief Superintendent. 'You fall in a stream, boy?' he asked, his brown skin wrinkling as he smiled.

'I'll tell you after a hot shower,' the Englishman replied, feeling the delicious headiness of the beer take its effect as he finished it in one slow and even pour.

The Ilchester Arms was cosy and welcoming, its

Christmas decorations a riot of clashing colours that reminded him of real Christmas, childhood Christmas, not beige and mauve shopping mall coordinated spend-all-you-can Christmas. English Christmas. His comfortable and well heated room was in a terrace of rustic looking bungalows behind the inn itself. Most luxuriously, it had a bath. The Englishman stripped off as it filled, the steam swirling boisterously around the slightly dated but efficient and large bathroom, which besides the bath, sink and toilet, also had a large piping hot radiator on which he hung his soaking clothes. Before getting into the wonderful hot water, the Englishman checked the contents of his rucksack. He assiduously kept everything inside its own plastic bag and he was quietly pleased with himself on discovering that, although the bags themselves were wet, the contents were more or less dry. Carefully placing the bags so that they would dry, he dotted the contents, spare clothes, flask, first aid kit, compass, map case, espadrilles and boots about the large bathroom, turned the rucksack inside out and hung it above the radiator, and sunk into the bath.

He felt strangely elated, and laughed when he thought of his near-death experience. Cows! What an idiot. For an hour or more he had not thought about his job and his future and the disappointment of failure. He sighed loudly and felt a wave of embarrassment as he remembered his failings in the Far East. It was the same feeling as when his parents had died. You would gradually forget as time healed and then, suddenly, just when happiness was returning, you'd remember that they were dead and you'd feel loss and sadness and guilt. It really was the same feeling. The cows had nearly killed him, but they'd also enabled him to forget. After the elation of surviving, the returning depression and guilt seemed worse than ever.

He checked his blisters. A day without rubbing had been good for them. Certainly they were no worse. He might even be able to get his boots back on tomorrow.

Nearly two hours later the Englishman stepped, warm and dry, out of his bungalow and into the Christmassy bar. The old man who had tried to strike up a conversation before was in exactly the same position and still clutched an empty glass. It was like déjà-vu when he said, in the same tone of voice, as if the evidence was still plain to see, 'you fall in a stream, boy?'

The Englishman faltered as he decided whether to engage in conversation with the man and whether to tell him the truth. Somehow he felt that he'd be buying all the drinks. But, for the sake of his sanity, he'd decided he needed to speak to people and he could stand the ridicule. 'You guessed right there, my friend. Yes I did. There was a herd of cows.'

'Down by the bottle-neck?' the old man asked.

'The bottle-neck? Maybe. It was a narrow gap between the stream and a fence. I tried to squeeze past them, but when they moved towards me, I slipped.' As he had expected, the old chap was quick to accept the Englishman's offer of a beer. The barman removed the empty warm glass and slid a full one into the curled fingers that were still propped up by the elbow on the bar.

'You're wearing the wrong shoes, boy,' the man said, and he nodded slightly towards the Englishman's feet.

'Oh, I wasn't wearing these,' the Englishman said, quickly, thinking of his first pair of espadrilles which he'd left floating in the icy water.

'I'd hope not boy. You'd be bound to slip in those.

It ain't safe to slip amongst a herd of cows, boy.'

The Englishman downed his pint quickly. He was very thirsty and knew that he should be replacing his fluids with something other than beer, but there was nothing quite like a pint of good English bitter when you'd been deprived of it for a year in the Far East, especially when you'd walked fifteen miles and had been through a bovine near-death experience. The old man had not touched his drink and the Englishman berated himself for thinking it was going to be an expensive evening. He had used to be able to read people; perhaps he was losing his touch? As he placed the Englishman's foamy pint in front of him, the barman nodded, without speaking, to his companion's glass. The curled fingers were in the same position, the elbow propped on the bar, but the glass was empty! How had that happened? He must have guzzled it down in one draft as the Englishman had ordered. The Englishman nodded wordlessly back to the barman, who prised the empty glass from the fingers and inserted a full one.

The old semi-plucked face showed no acknowledgement. 'You frightened of cows, boy?' is all he said.

The Englishman was taken aback. He'd never considered the question before. 'Am I frightened of cows? Maybe. I'm a towny.'

'I thought as much, boy. They can smell it,' he said, sounding vaguely Glaswegian. The local man spoke with a strange blend of regional accents, sometimes one coming to the fore, as the Scottish one just had.

'Smell what?'

'The fear,' he drooled, 'they can smell the fear.'

The glass was suddenly empty again and the Englishman found himself half a pint behind. He gulped the remainder of his own drink and the barman obliged with two more pints.

'That's just folklore, isn't it? Does fear have a smell?'

'Cows can smell it alright. They don't like it. Cows like certainty and routine. Out to pasture in the mornings, in for milking in the evenings. They like to know what's around the corner. They don't, though.'

'They don't what?' the Englishman asked.

'Know what's around the corner. Same old routine every day, then one day they're slaughtered.'

'But where does the fear come in?'

'Lions'

'What?'

'Lions. It's a big animal, the cow'

'I know that alright, they're as tall as me.'

'When a lion stalks a buffalo, the hunter might get hurt or even killed in the chase,' he explained, with a slight South African lilt, 'so the Lion's frightened. And he gives off a smell.'

The barman nodded in silent assent. 'So doesn't that fill the cow with confidence?' the Englishman asked.

'No, not at all, boy. The buffalo don't know it's fear it can smell. To the buffalo, it's just the smell of a hunting lion.' He paused, before adding, dramatically, in the brogue of a Cornish pirate, 'the smell of death, boy.'

The Englishman was sure that he had been looking directly at the man as he spoke, but somehow the glass was empty again. The barman shifted his head almost imperceptibly and the Englishman nodded back - two more beers.

'It's like coppers.'

'Coppers? What do you mean now?'

'Coppers creeping round the back of buildings in the dead of night looking for burglars. How do you think they feel? They're frightened, boy. And the burglar can smell the copper's fear. But he don't know it's fear. He just smell's a copper. And the smell of a copper's fear scares the burglar shitless.'

The Englishman knew the fear of patrolling alone on foot in the pitch black, dressed in black from the tip of his helmet to the toe of his black boots, creeping silently for fear of disturbing any burglars and at the same time terrified of finding one. He had never stopped to consider that the burglars were more frightened than he was and that they could smell his fear. The Englishman liked this wise old curiosity of a man. He was enjoying the conversation and bought more drinks.

They spoke over the sounds of the jingling bells and scraping guitars of 1970's Christmas pop songs that were playing back to back in the bar. The music was on a loop and the same songs played one after another until the Englishman could predict what song would come next. It was the music of his teenage Christmases and, just as he had been then, the Englishman was happy and warm and safe. The barman nodded from time to time and the beer flowed freely.

The Englishman pondered whether he had been frightened of the cows and if they had been able to sense this. 'But what if the lion's not hungry?' he said at last, 'what if the copper's not good at his job and he's not looking for a burglar, so he's not frightened?'

'All coppers are bastards,' the old man asserted, as if with experience, 'to a burglar. He'll smell 'em anyway.'

There seemed to be something wrong with the logic of the old man's argument, and the Englishman started to think that he could no longer keep up with his companion. The weariness of a day's walking and worrying combined with the experience with the cows came together to make him feel suddenly very tired and he became aware that he was looking at the old man with one eye closed. He also needed to go to the toilet and he decided it was best to turn in. He shook hands heartily with the barman, with whom he had formed a lifelong friendship, nodded respectfully to the claw like drinking hand of the wise one and left the pub. Finding himself on a main road, on a precariously narrow pavement, he dodged backwards as a monstrous gritter lorry hurtled past. It was perilously close, its amber rotating light illuminating the clear night sky as it sprayed salt and sand up his trouser legs. He turned and went back into the pub, bowed ostentatiously to the old man's hand, reached over the bar, shook the barman's hand again and left the pub by the back door. This time he found himself in the familiar little yard between the pub and his bungalow. The night air was cold and refreshing and reminded the Englishman of the early winter walking holidays that he and Elaine had taken in Devon all those years ago - the holidays that had led them to move to the Devon seaside to bring up their children. He remembered the smell of cold salty sea air fragranced with the smell of coal fires. He could see a plume of smoke rising straight up from the pub's chimney and wondered if it smelt the same. The smoke merged with a billowy and heavy looking, starless English sky.

'Merry Christmas, England,' he shouted to the heavens, 'Merry Christmas!'

So what if he'd had too much to drink? Fuck it! I was nearly killed today! By Cows! Ha, ha, ha!

'Merry Christmas cows!' he shouted, cupping his hand around his mouth and turning himself in the general direction of where he imagined the bottle-neck between the wire and the stream to be. No more shouting, he thought. That's enough shouting for a Detective Superintendent. His bungalow key had a piece of wood the size of a small novel attached to it, and this caught on the edge of his pocket as he took it out, clattering to the floor. As he bent to retrieve it, he noticed his sparkling espadrilles.

'Merry Christmas, espadrilles,' he whispered, stumbling over the awkward word, 'you nearly killed me, but you got me here.'

He was now desperate to go the toilet and was finding it difficult to concentrate on the task of unlocking the unfamiliar door. Finally it swung open with a bash and, slamming it shut behind him, he pushed into the bathroom and ripped his flies open, urinating almost before he'd got the zip down. His rucksack, hanging inside-out from a hook above the radiator brushed his face and, turning to look at it, he was pleased to see that it had dried. As he did so, he nearly missed the toilet pan and in the process of adjusting his aim, he splashed his feet. He corrected himself, noisily hitting the water in the bottom of the toilet pan without touching the porcelain sides.

'Sorry, espadrilles,' he whispered, 'you don't deserve that.'

And then he saw his boots. 'But you do, you bastards,' he tittered and gave them a quick spray. The spattering sound of his urine on the brown leather of one of the boots was very satisfying and he returned for a quick spray of the other one.

'Ha, ha, ha! Merry Christmas you bastards!' He squealed with delight at the realisation that he'd actually managed to urinate *inside* the second boot and this encouraged him to move in for the kill.

'Ha, ha! Piss on my boots. Ha, ha, ha!' He was now in full flow. 'Fuck you. I don't need you, you useless bastards,' as he lent back and produced an immense arc, sweeping left and right, strafing the enemy relentlessly.

'Ha, ha, ha! Take that! Merry Christmas, you bastards. I should have pissed on you a long time ago! Well now you're getting it! Glad of what you did, now, are you? Pleased you ripped me to fucking shreds, are you? Fuck off! Ha, ha, ha! Merry Christmas!'

The Englishman stripped off and fell naked onto his bed. He giggled to himself, mightily pleased with his revenge; and then, for the second time in a day, he was unconscious.

CHAPTER FOURTEEN

It was pitch black and the Englishman was in a hotel somewhere in Southeast Asia. The telephone was ringing, but he didn't want to pick it up, because it meant that he'd let down Elaine, Linda and Katherine. He didn't want to hear that there had been a prowler in his daughters' bedrooms whilst he'd been drinking with a counter terrorism commander in a seedy little bar, hookers draped all over him. If he didn't pick it up, he wouldn't know. But as the telephone persisted and he gradually came to, the Englishman found he was in the darkened bungalow in Abbotsbury. An automated voice told him that this was his requested alarm call.

He groaned and his head fell back onto the pillows. He was hungover and he'd been dreaming of Beslan again. The nightmare was part of the price he had to pay for being a Counter Terrorism Liaison Officer. He had had the dream about once a week for the last eighteen months, ever since he had first seen the security arrangements at the British School of the Orient. That was when it had hit home that there were risks in this job for the whole family. He had faced many risks in the past, but his family had always been insulated from them. At least that had always been his intention. But this was different, he was knowingly leading them into risk.

Elaine's legs had buckled underneath her after she and the Englishman had waved goodbye to the blacked out school bus with Linda and Katherine somewhere inside, and watched it leave the secure compound on which they lived. She spent the day in shock and did not recover until the two girls emerged smiling from the bus at the end of the day. They had received a great welcome at the school, they loved the headmistress and their teachers and were full of happy stories of the cosmopolitan blend of friends that they had already made.

Elaine and he had decided not to tell their daughters that a hand-grenade had been thrown over the wall of the Australian school just one week before they had arrived. He knew that they would find out, but he didn't want to be the one to tell them. He didn't know how he could reassure them if he confirmed that it was true. It would be better to dismiss it as silly gossip, to play it down. The Englishman hoped that neither his wife nor his children would ever find out that three Catholic school girls had been beheaded by terrorists simply because of their faith.

He dreamt that Elaine, Linda and Katherine were hostages of the Islamist terrorists who had taken over Beslan Middle School on the first day of term, whilst parents and children alike were attending the traditional annual celebration of the school's opening. His family was held with more than one thousand hostages in the school gym, which was wired for death. Bombs were placed around the walls and in the basket ball hoops, set to detonate automatically if the military intervened.

Katherine and Linda were thirsty but the terrorists would not let them drink. They would not let any of the children drink or go to the toilet. Some silent terrorists, presumably women, dressed from head to toe in black, their faces covered, wore suicide vest bombs. In the nightmare the Englishman was the negotiator. He saw his children suffering, crying dry tears. They were so thirsty. He wanted to give them water. The bearded terrorists ordered Elaine and Linda to leave, but Katherine was forced to remain. Elaine, Linda and the Englishman walked to safety and Katherine stayed behind, in terror, puzzled, bewildered, thirsty. It was how Beslan had been. Mothers were forced to make that choice. Mothers with babies were told that they had to leave with their babies but that their other children were to remain behind. Eleven mothers walked away cradling their babies, eleven mothers abandoning their thirsty children, forced to make that terrible choice. They walked out on their children, never to see them alive again. The children were suffering when the end came. They had still not been allowed to drink. More than one hundred and fifty children died. It had been the first day of a new term and they were just children in their school. In his dream, Katherine was with them, she was one of the slim, frail bodies when the carnage was over.

He lay on the edge of sleep for another few minutes, waiting for the dread of the nightmare to pass. It would subside, but only gradually, leaving him with a sense of death that would last the rest of the day. He would have the same dream in a week's time.

He reminded himself that there was no snooze facility on the automated alarm call system and that he had to get up and be ready to get out as the sun came up. At last he swung his legs out of the bed and walked to the bathroom. His clothes lay on the floor in the bedroom doorway like a crime scene. His underpants, trousers and socks were in a single, tubular heap and his tee-shirt, shirt and sweat-shirt were layered just as they'd been in life. He stepped over them into the bathroom and put his foot down in a pool of cold water.

He looked above his head but could see no signs of a drip or leak. He stooped and felt the radiator feed-pipe and found it dry. He would have to report it to the hotel. Then he saw his boots and remembered. Being good quality waterproof boots, they were full to the brim. He tried to pick one up between his forefinger and thumb, but it was too heavy and it tipped, spilling some of its contents onto the already wet floor. He crouched on his painful ankles and stiff knees beside the toilet pan and carefully scooped up first one boot and then the other. He emptied them into the toilet pan. The fear of the dream was alive in his mind; now a wave of dismay spread up from his stomach to his face, as he confronted his embarrassment. He had pissed on his boots. Ha, ha! He laughed weakly as he recalled his exultations of the night before.

Now empty, he picked them up again and held them to his nose, but of course he didn't know if they smelt. He remembered the ammonia pong of gents' public toilets and grimaced at the thought that he might smell like that. Never mind the smell of bloody fear, I'll smell of urine, like a tramp. That'll certainly fool the burglars. He ran his fingers through his hair and sighed. Where would he stop? Not satisfied with turning the Deputy Head of Mission, the spies and the Detective Chief Superintendent against him, and acting like a dirty old man with the headmistress, he had now urinated all over the hotel's bathroom floor and he stunk like a toilet. He dried the floor with the bath towel he'd used yesterday evening, threw it in disgust into the bath and turned on the shower in an attempt to rinse it. Better that the staff had to deal with a wet towel than a filthy one. He could dry himself with the hand towel.

But could he manage without his boots another day? He had to cover twelve and a half miles to get to Seatown. It was a long way, but at two and a half miles an hour, it should take just one hour longer than yesterday's walk. The highest peak of the holiday, Golden Cap, wasn't until tomorrow. It was obvious that he couldn't wear the boots in this soaking state, so the espadrilles would just have to do – they had been blissfully comfortable yesterday in any case. Admittedly, he had slipped in front of the cows because of them, but he would never have got as far as the bottle neck without them. He could dry his boots out this evening, so that they were ready for Golden Cap tomorrow. Today he would again walk in espadrilles.

It was when he opened the bungalow door to walk across to the pub for breakfast that the Englishman discovered the flaw in this decision - it was snowing. Large, light flakes were fluttering and swirling in the air and the yard was covered with a thin white coating, bare patches of tarmac still visible here and there. The sky was heavy and low, and a cruel wind whipped around the yard, blowing the dry snow into the corners and recesses. He would have to walk twelve and a half miles in espadrilles in the snow.

The Englishman had not eaten the night before and now found himself both famished and with a stomach that was somewhat unsettled, thanks to the effects of the beer. He sat down in the breakfast room and was served by the barman of the night before, who didn't seem as friendly as the Englishman had remembered him. Nevertheless, it wasn't long before he was tucking into a decent full English breakfast with toast.

Ten minutes later, the barman returned and placed an envelope on the table. 'There's your bill, Sir,' he said. He was dressed in black trousers and a white shirt, the international uniform of hotel staff and waiters.

'Why do I have a bill? I've paid already. I paid for all my drinks, didn't I? I was a bit drunk, I think, when I went to bed. Sorry.'

'You weren't any problem, Sir. It's Christmas, after all. You paid for all your drinks, don't worry about that.'

'Well what's the bill for then?'

'Your friend, Sir. His dinner.'

'Friend? Dinner? It is me you want, is it?'

'Yes, Sir. The friend you were drinking with last night. He had a T-bone steak and a cheese board'

'Friend? He's not my friend. I just met him at the bar. I stood him all his drinks all night as it was. He can pay for it next time he comes in, can't he?'

'But he might not come back in, Sir.'

'What do you mean? He's a local, isn't he?'

'I've never seen him in my life, Sir. I don't know where he's from. He's certainly never been in here before.'

'But I thought you knew him. The little nod and everything, when he needed a drink.'

'No, I was just trying to ask you if you were buying his drinks too. I thought he was up to something.'

'Thought he was up to something? Why didn't you say so?'

'I thought he was with you.'

'Well when did he eat? I was with him all night, wasn't I?'

'Early, Sir. While you were in your room. Just after you had that first drink with him. He said he was with you and that you'd be putting it all on your bill.'

'Well, I never. How much is it?'

'Twenty three pounds all together, Sir.'

The Englishman's first reaction was to refuse to pay. After all, the trick had been played on the barman, not the Englishman. Then he remembered the urine soaked bathroom floor and reconsidered.

'Well, I guess I'd better pay then. Someone's got to.' He dug out his wallet, still slightly soggy from its immersion in the freezing stream, and paid up. 'Then what about the cows?' he asked.

'The cows, sir?'

'Smelling fear. What about the cows being able to smell fear?'

'Sounded like a load of old rubbish to me. He'd have talked about anything as long as you were buying the drinks, I reckon.'

The Englishman stood between the two smooth white pillars of the door canopy and looked out at the falling snow, then down at his feet. He'd managed to squeeze on three pairs of socks and the size ten espadrilles. His feet would start comfortably enough, but there would be no keeping out the wet. However, when he thought of the pain of the blisters and the state of his boots, he knew that he had to stick with the espadrilles as long as possible. The weather hadn't deteriorated over breakfast, at least. The road was still passable and, in fact, vehicles were travelling quite fast. Perhaps the surface had been gritted. He put on his reading glasses and looked at the map, trying to work out which direction to take in order to get to St. Catherine's Chapel, which sat on a hilltop somewhere between Abbotsbury and the sea and was his first point of reference. As he studied the map and tried to get a bearing with his compass, he noted with some relief that cars and lorries were indeed driving fast and the thought of them doing so on ordinary tyres gave him hope for his own string-tread shoes.

He slid the compass back into the map case, and looked up just as a large black car cruised slowly past as if its driver were looking for somewhere. He took off his reading glasses and saw that it was a Rover 75. These were unusual cars and the Englishman knew of only one other person who had a black executive car like this one: the Detective Chief Superintendent. It was his official car, purchased by the CTU at a time when it was considered politically astute to buy British. In fact, it had been one of the very last to have been produced at Longbridge. The Englishman was only aware of it because he had mistaken it for a hearse at O'Raugherty's funeral. Amazed, the Englishman looked into the car as it passed. He didn't recognise the driver, who was a young man, casually dressed in an open necked shirt. He was about to walk away, when the angle of the car gave him a view of the front passenger: a big moustached man – the Detective Chief Superintendent! Yes, it was him. He was looking about from one side of the road to the other as the car cruised by. Perhaps because the Englishman was obscured by the pillars, he didn't appear to have been recognised. The car gradually picked up speed and then slowly disappeared out of sight.

CHAPTER FIFTEEN

The Englishman scanned carefully from left to right and then opposite to see if there was somebody watching him. Nobody was out walking in this weather and, in any case, the light, blustery snow made it difficult to pick out details. If surveillance had been mounted on him, where would the O.P. be? He looked up at the bedroom windows of the yellow stone cottages overlooking the hotel. A curtain twitched and he fixed his eyes upon it for a long time trying to confirm his suspicions, but nothing stirred. Probably the apparent movement of the curtain was a trick of the snow. He started to walk. But he was sure now that he was under surveillance. He asked himself how they would go about doing it in this weather and rural setting. There would definitely be an O.P. Perhaps the curtain had moved, after all. Was there a probe in his hotel room? Were there agents in the hotel? And why would they follow him? What would it achieve?

In order to remove him from his post he had to have done something wrong: under-performance. But that had to be proved. The Detective Chief Superintendent had said that he would come up with the evidence.

Perhaps he was having difficulty finding it. Of course he was, the Englishman was fairly sure that there wasn't any. So now the Detective Chief Superintendent was looking to find current evidence. Perhaps they were breaking into his home in Exmouth or even in Southeast Asia, or searching his office in the embassy? If they were they would need to control him. They would need to know that he was indeed on a walking holiday on the South West Coast Path; they couldn't afford for him to just turn up as they were in the middle of their covert search. He didn't have his mobile phone with him, so they couldn't track his movements with that. They would have to use conventional surveillance. Who would the team be? Spies? This would be unlikely - unless they saw the Englishman as a threat to national security. More likely it would be a police Professional Standards team - CIB3, the ones who investigated coppers like him, with their surveillance teams and integrity tests. Did they still exist? He wasn't sure, but somewhere there'd be a department that did what they used to do.

The Englishman felt as he had done in the Lincoln Arms – an outsider. The Detective Chief Superintendent and the Desk Officer stood with their backs to him and he couldn't know what they knew. Whereas the thought of being under surveillance was merely uncomfortable, the idea of a closing of ranks against the Englishman was oppressive and isolating. The closing of ranks was such a powerful barrier to the truth.

'Gulf Charlie Nine, Gulf Charlie Nine…?'

The young copper was alone, dressed like a scrote. 'Yes, go ahead. Gulf Charlie Nine over.'

'Report of a burglary in progress. Little Park Gardens, suspects disturbed, made off through gardens towards the town, over.'

'Yes, Gulf Charlie Nine, I'm at Little Park Gardens now, over.'

It was gone 2.00 am and the lampposts had been switched off. The large detached Victorian houses squatted grimly in the darkness. A light drizzle spattered on the windscreen of Gulf Charlie Nine, a nondescript beige Mk II Ford Escort. The young copper pulled over, switched off the headlights and the ignition, wound down his window and listened to the silence of the suburbs.

Suddenly they emerged from an alleyway beside his car, two men carrying large square plastic bags. 'Gulf Charlie Nine. Urgent permission.'

'Go ahead Gulf Charlie Nine.'

'I've got two suspects. On foot in Little Park Gardens. I'm single crewed – can you send back-up, over?'

'Yes, yes Gulf Charlie Nine. Gulf Victor Seven, Gulf Victor Seven…?'

The young copper stepped from the car straight into the path of the men. 'Hello lads. Police. Nothing to worry about.' They were engrossed in enthusiastic conversation and stopped abruptly. Two skinny young men, wearing pale coloured linen suits with the sleeves pushed up to their elbows. One of them wore Ray-Bans, even though it was the middle of the night.

'Do you mind telling me where you've been lads?'

'No we don't mind. Round his girlfriend's house. Listening to records.'

'And where are you going?'

'We're going home. We live in the same street.' It

was Ray-Bans who had spoken this time.

'What records have you been listening to?'

'These.' Both boys held out their carrier bags to show the young copper their contents: He recognised ABC's *Lexicon of Love* and Heaven 17's *The Luxury Gap*.

'Do you mind if I take a look at your shoes? What's your name by the way?'

'David Tripp,' Ray-Bans answered. His hair was neatly swept back into a large, blond quiff.

'David. Could you show me your shoes please?'

David Tripp leant on the arm of his friend, turned his back and obediently lifted first one foot and then the other for examination. He was wearing white lightweight canvas shoes with a string sole, the type you would wear on a beach.

'Do you mind telling us what's wrong, please?' the other boy asked.

'Of course I don't mind. There's been a burglary and you two have come from the place where the burglars were last seen. Could you show me your shoes too?'

The boy without the sunglasses did the same as his friend had. He too was wearing canvas and string soled shoes, though these were black.

'They're spotless. You two haven't been running across any gardens have you?'

'No. My girlfriend's house is just down there. You can go and ask if you like. Anyway, we wouldn't get far running in espadrilles,' David Tripp said.

'In what?'

'Espadrilles – these shoes.'

'Gulf Charlie Nine, Gulf Charlie Nine…?'

'Yes. Go ahead. Gulf Charlie Nine over.'

'I'm just on with the informant. It might not have been a burglary. I'm waiting for further details, over.'

'Gulf Charlie Nine received. Can I have two name checks?'

'Yes, yes. Go ahead with details, over.'

'And can you cancel my back-up, over?'

'Yes, yes. Gulf Victor Seven, Gulf Victor Seven…?'

'So, what I'm going to do is just take your names and then…'

A white Police Transit van, a personnel carrier, came screeching round the corner into the road. It's blue light swept across the windows of the houses. It juddered to a halt beside the young copper and the two lads. Suddenly, a uniformed sergeant, a big, strong man, working on overtime from late turn shift, was standing with them. He wore shirt sleeves and epaulettes, no hat. His shirt cuffs were turned back two folds and the cuffs of his black leather gloves were also folded back, giving them the appearance of being too small for the large hands.

'Is this the fucking burglar?' he snarled. He grabbed a handful of David Tripp's flimsy suit epaulettes and dragged him towards the back of the van. The doors opened. Six or seven white shirts and epaulettes could be seen in the darkness. David Tripp disappeared into the back of the van and the sergeant was gone. There was a pair of Ray-Ban sunglasses lying in the kerb and David Tripp's friend picked them up. David Tripp could be heard squealing in the van. His friend looked at the young copper and the young copper looked at the ground. He got into his nondescript car and drove away.

'What did you do then?' The Detective Chief Inspector from Complaints and Discipline smiled. He was an older man, a fatherly type.

'I drove away.'

'And you didn't see what happened in the back of the van?'

'No. I could hear it...'

'But you didn't see anything happen. I have six officers' statements which say that nothing happened in the back of the van.'

'I want to tell the truth.'

'Good. That's what I'm after. So you didn't see anything happen to David Tripp?'

'No.'

'Could David Tripp already have had facial injuries before he got into the van?'

'I don't think so.'

'But it was very dark? And David Tripp was wearing sunglasses wasn't he? Probably very difficult to see whether he had facial injuries or not.'

'Yes, but I don't...'

'You don't know. That's OK. I have six statements from police officers to say that you weren't in the van, so you can't have known what happened.'

'OK.'

'So, if you'll just read this over and sign at the top of page one, that's it, under the declaration. And then at the bottom of both pages.'

'So what happens now?'

'You've got nothing to worry about, no-one's made any allegations against you, son.'

'But, the truth...'

'Sometimes, son, the truth is that we don't know. You didn't see what happened. You don't know what happened. That's the truth.'

The Englishman looked down at his espadrilles. Not

much good against police boots. David Tripp didn't
stand a chance and the investigation into what happened
to him didn't stand a chance. The Englishman couldn't
identify the Detective Chief Superintendent's cronies –
the Desk Officer, the spies, the Deputy Head of Mission
– he couldn't pick them out in the darkness of the
carrier. All his adult life a police officer and now he was
intimidated by the police. For the first time he felt that
he really understood the power that he had wielded for
the last thirty three years.

Of course he would retire from his post. He would
tell Elaine and their daughters about his failure and then
he would retire before they had a chance to remove him.
Yet retirement from the police was supposed to be a
celebration, a new life, fresh opportunity, a chance to
give something back. Now it seemed like a humiliating
punishment. As he glided along the shiny lane out of
Abbotsbury, he felt like an innocent young man shying
away from contact with a police force which terrified
him, because he had once been beaten up by it.

St. Catherine's Chapel was perched high above the
roadside and approaching it was the first physical
challenge of the day. The snow still blustered about in
light flakes, settling dryly in the sheltered corners in
which it found refuge from the biting cold wind, which
came in uncomfortable squalls that penetrated the
Englishman's cuffs and collar. But these conditions at
least kept the snow from settling and the Englishman
found no difficulty in getting purchase on the road
surface. Now he had to give up his grip on the road and
step up to a huge mound of rabbit cropped grass, the
hill upon which the chapel stood. The grass looked icy
and frozen and the snowflakes stuck more easily to the
short blades of grass than they did to tarmac, so that the

hill glistened with menace for a man wearing string soled beach shoes. For a moment he contemplated trying the boots, but he knew they were sodden. If he could just get through today, his blisters would have more recovery time and, with a bit of luck, he could dry his boots this evening.

Still he found it difficult to understand what the benefits were for the Detective Chief Superintendent and the spies in following him. Perhaps it was to monitor his conduct, in which case he'd played right into their hands last night. If there was a camera in his room, they'd have seen him deliberately urinating on the floor and damaging a hotel towel. They would have seen, and heard, him shouting at the top of his voice. The Detective Chief Superintendent had said that he would find evidence. The Englishman was now under surveillance to establish a pattern of misconduct.

Though his tread-less soles slid on the hillside, the Englishman was able to make progress traversing the steep slope and was encouraged when he came across a sign that showed that the coast path did not actually go up to the chapel, but skirted around the hill before descending to the sea. He reached a stone marker post and, scraping the snow from the carved letters with his gloved fingers, he saw that he was just a downwards sloping mile to Chesil Beach. Frowning into the snow, he thought he could just make out the Fleet in the distance.

There could be no other explanation for the Detective Chief Superintendent being in Abbotsbury. He had to have been coordinating the surveillance exercise himself. And as for the strange old chap in the bar, he was clearly a member of the surveillance team or an MI6 agent, planted there just to get the Englishman drunk and see how loose lipped he was. Why else would he bring up the police stuff if he wasn't an agent?

The Englishman tried to think objectively, but he could feel paranoia closing in. Every slip as he trudged upwards was inextricably linked to set-backs he had suffered in his work, whilst the steepness of the climb represented difficulties he had tried to overcome in the Far East. Now, as the track led down to a bleak sea level path along Chesil Beach, upon which there was no shelter from the bitter wind, he pulled his hood up around his face, but the icy flakes stung his cheeks and the wind whipped the mucus from his nose, so that his face was constantly wet and uncomfortable. He had to walk as fast as his soft shoes and aching ankles would carry him to try to generate enough body heat to stay warm. And the faster he walked, the angrier he became, until every stride was accompanied by a curse.

How his thoughts became so entwined with his walking, the Englishman did not understand, but as he tried to look in at himself with impartiality, he understood that his grip on reality was not what it should be. He saw that he was no longer on a walking holiday, he was escaping across the marshes. A distant speck was occasionally visible behind him through the snow, but he was unable to discern if it really was somebody behind him or whether it was just a part of the desolate winter landscape, distorted by the weather. Now it was the jungle mujahedeen in pursuit and he was an heroic counter terrorism officer, evading them, knowing they could smell his fear and were frightened by it; next he was a wanted man, a maverick, skulking along smugglers' paths evading his pursuers with guile and cunning. Other times he was a lonely man, in search of his home, his family and a warm Christmas fireside, pursued not by people, but by intangible ideas from another part of the world: fear, shame, embarrassment and failure. His family represented sanctuary, they didn't question his love, his sense of duty and his competence, they weren't evaluating him, they didn't want him to be a dead man's ghost, they wanted him for what he was, a nice man.

The snow blowing into his face started to have a refreshing edge to it and the constant crashing of the sea was a steadying companion. The Englishman was warm and had covered a great deal of ground along the level beachside path. The steady marching rhythm he had developed over the last mile or so had again set his mind upon its mechanistic analysis, and he was able to tell himself that it was alright to be confused. He recalled Little Nell as she escaped her pursuers and he vividly remembered a passage where thoughts of her past became tangled with her present, until the two became distorted into one haunting episode from which she found no solace until she reached her new home. This was what was happening to him.

The long level path came abruptly to an end and the Englishman was looking up through the thickening snow at a steep bank of long wiry grass. Still, when he looked at the map he discovered that he was nearly half way in terms of distance and it was only mid morning. Ever mindful of the Marine from Mandalay's advice, he decided to stop for ten minutes and have a mouthful of flask tea before heading upwards. The snow had not stopped all the while he had been walking and it continued now, occasional flakes falling into his cup and disappearing. The beach here was whiter than he had noticed it before, the snow settling on the sand, and he knew that he must push on.

He looked back on his progress and again he thought he saw a dark speck moving through the flurry. Crouching down beside the track, he squinted through the white haze. With his back to the wind, his view through the snow was a little clearer. He peered again. Yes, there was a walker. If he was one of the surveillance team, he was coming quite fast. Probably they had lost technical coverage in the bad weather and the foot man was being moved up. Of course a heat seeking aircraft couldn't go up in these conditions. Ha! Now was his chance to see what his pursuers were made of. Quickly he took off his bright blue coat and stuffed it into his green rucksack - he would be much less visible in his dark sweatshirt. Putting the rucksack back on, he scrambled through the long grass up the bank to the side of the track, until he found a spot from which he could look back down on the walker as he came past. He lay down in the cold and waited.

It was less than a minute before a panting figure came ambling untidily and noisily into sight. From his vantage point the Englishman watched the man emerge from the snow and stop exactly where the Englishman had stopped, looking ahead at the steep bank of long grass over which the coastal path ran. He wore a cap of some sort and carried a huge rucksack, twice as big as the Englishman's. Both obscured his face. He stood with his hands on his hips as if puzzled by something. The Englishman wondered for the first time if he had been leaving faint footsteps in the dusty snow. Even if he had, they would be difficult to track through the long grass up the hill. The man looked out towards the sea, then back the way he had come, before finally looking up to the right of the track, where the Englishman hid. He recognised the man instantly: the old thief from the

Ilchester Arms, still wearing the same cap and still sporting bristly outcrops of unkempt facial hair.

The Englishman silently relived the victory he had had over his boots. 'Ha! Got you, you bastard. Pissed all over you.' His instincts had been right - he was an agent, the Englishman wasn't losing it at all. 'Can you smell me? Eh? Can you smell my fear as I stalk you, you fool? Of course not. You bastard.'

The Agent pressed on up the steep bank and was quickly out of view over the first hump. The Englishman's body temperature had dropped quickly and, as much as he would have liked to have lain longer in his lair, he knew he had to get his coat back on and get walking. He poured himself another cup of tea and then set off up the bank, happy at the thought of the Agent hurtling along trying to catch him up, not knowing that the Englishman had given him the slip and was behind him. His feet slid on the increasingly snowy slope but, buoyed on by his success, he battled his way up the cliff.

The track, unused by many since the autumn, narrowed to the point of disappearance and the long grass, buffeted in the gusty wind, blew across his legs and feet. His trouser legs and socks became soggy around the ankles and, worse, his feet had become very wet. He hadn't walked much further before his toes began to hurt with cold. The going was steep, and when he finally reached the top he was rewarded with the soul destroying view of a barbed wire fence leading steeply downwards to a wide valley in which hundreds of freezing white caravans sat hunched against the weather, like penguins too stupid to share their body heat in order to survive. This walk was bloody endless.

Beyond the windswept Siberian desert of a beach lay

another hump of cliff and then another. By the time he reached the top of the second he was utterly exhausted and knew that he needed to stop to rest, to eat and to try to defrost his toes a little. He was relieved, therefore, to find himself looking down through the tumult at the ordered little harbour town of West Bay.

It was the most delicious looking pork pie in the world and he sat on the harbour wall and ate it greedily between sips of hot tea. For dessert he took some ibuprofen tablets that he'd seen behind the counter in the little shop that had sold him the pie. He had a hangover as well as aching knees, hips and ankles. The soles of his feet had taken a battering during the fast route march along Chesil Beach and were now tender and sensitive to every lump in the ground. Furthermore, his own reaction at seeing the Agent behind him, assuming he was following him and then hiding above the track like some Eskimo hunter worried the Englishman. It was not rational. He felt that his sense of reality was being distorted, that this intermingling of his anxieties about the past with his present was not a good thing. He worried that he might be feverish and he thought that the tablets might help. Perhaps it was all just the haze of a hangover. He had considered finding somewhere inside to eat, but a break in the snow had convinced him that he could survive outside and, anyway, he would make a more difficult surveillance target out in the open.

The little harbour, once the port that gave the nearby town of Bridport its name, was deserted but pretty. Two red and black traditional fishing boats sat resting together, looking snug and at home in contrast to the modern apartments that overlooked the scene. They were probably wonderful summer homes, but in this weather they looked like glass fronted bunkers, discordant with the wooden boats.

The Englishman imagined himself back at Boat Quay in Singapore where he and Elaine had enjoyed beautiful Indian food and Tiger beer in the simmering heat, watching the tourist boats plying their trade up and down the river. The spices of the East had been good for the Englishman - although he could not actually taste the food, at least his taste buds picked up some of the spirit of the cooking. What he couldn't taste, Elaine tasted for him. Over the years since he had lost his sense of smell, he and Elaine had developed an intimate eating ritual in which she would try to describe the flavours of the various dishes as best as she could. Her words would add richness to the unadorned combination of salt, heat and sourness that the Englishman could detect. She gave her interpretation and description of the subtlety of the meal, the rounded and smooth aromas that he could not detect, without boredom or irritation at his disability. She was to him like the lover of a blind man, who holds out her face with patience and trust, allowing him to feel the face of the woman he loves, seeing her through his finger tips. With Elaine's help, the Englishman had learnt to imagine the taste, to savour her words as substitutes for flavour.

They both loved the wonderful architectural blend of the remnants of empire and modernism that Singapore had so successfully put together, and that was so evident from the gaily lit water side restaurants at Boat Quay. The colonnades of the Fullerton hotel, once the General Post Office, sat majestically and comfortably opposite a huge glittering shopping mall, just minutes from the statue which celebrated Sir Stamford Raffles' landing point. After dinner, they had squeezed themselves into a tricycle rickshaw and giggled as an ancient and sinewy Singaporean stood up in his saddle and pumped them as far along Orchard Road as he could manage, before finally admitting defeat. They enjoyed a night cap at one of the many ultra-modern neon lit bars before wandering back to their hotel, sweating and happy.

It had not been easy to acclimatise themselves to the Far East, and the burglary certainly had not helped, but when he considered the rewards, that weekend in Singapore, their wonderful maid Endi, and the many embassy, police and expatriate friends they had made, there was no doubt that it had been a positive experience. Whatever happened next, they would always have that.

The Englishman pulled off his damp socks, examined the drying blisters and put on two pairs of dry ones. They were grubby. Endi would never have allowed that. He wondered if they too smelt "same like cheese." She not only fastidiously cleaned his socks, she even ironed them, folding them neatly in his drawer as if they were part of a shop display. Poor Endi; she would have to find herself another job. He breathed in deeply, letting the air escape slowly and noisily through his useless nose as he slipped on new espadrilles. The snow was beginning to fall again. Whilst the highest peak of the walk, Golden Cap, was not until tomorrow, the Englishman now had to climb from the beach to one hundred and fifty seven metres above sea level to reach the top of today's highest point, Thorncombe Beacon. He calculated the climb to be about one thousand six-inch upward steps.

But the wind had dropped, or at least it didn't seem quite as biting, and the grass was short, so that his feet stayed dryer for longer and his toes had a chance to warm through. The snow had not really got itself going after lunch and so it was not long before the Englishman was able to look back from the top of the climb and feel impressed with himself for the amount of ground he had covered. He had walked as far as the eye could see and beyond. Looking forward, the Englishman was puzzled by what seemed to be an optical illusion. The ground appeared to dip out of view before rising to an even higher peak ahead. Checking the map, he saw his mistake. He was not standing on top of the Beacon at all, he was at the highest point of West Cliff, a mere seventy-two metres above sea level, only half the height of the Beacon. To add to his frustration, the path dipped right down to the beach again before heading up. He had walked about five hundred steps up only to have to walk five hundred steps down again, all for the privilege of taking another thousand steps up and another thousand steps down before he reached Seatown. This wasn't a holiday, it was bloody torture. On the run from God knows who, in a pair of fucking beach shoes. Just to prove what, exactly? None of it made any sense, none of it. He didn't know why he was being sacked, why he was being followed, why he was walking, or why he was so determined to finish.

Seventy-two metres. How high did a cliff have to be to guarantee death if he threw himself off? Who would miss him, anyway? Not the police. He might have just slipped in the snow. No-one would ever know differently. They'd find his body on the beach wearing espadrilles in the snow and they'd assume the stupid bastard had slipped. There wouldn't be an investigation. Only the Detective Chief Superintendent and the

Englishman knew that he was being removed from post and that would be quickly reversed once his death became known. He'd be just like O'Raugherty after all. Fucking dead. Perhaps he could haunt his successor?

Was he considering suicide? No, he didn't think so. He wasn't that bad. Everyone thought it through sometimes. He didn't want to die, he loved his family too much. He couldn't do it to them. He'd seen the effects of suicide on families. They never came to terms with it. Sometimes, especially the young ones, they'd imagine everyone fawning over their body saying, 'Oh, I didn't think we'd upset him that much' and the suicide would say, 'Well, you did and I showed you well and truly. You won't do that again will you?' And they would enjoy the thought of the revenge they would inflict on their families –'You miss me now, don't you, eh?' But suicide wasn't like that. You didn't get to see the impact your death had on those who loved you. You weren't here anymore. You were dead. Oblivion.

He looked over the edge and imagined himself falling. If you could only die in the air, before you hit the beach. Sometimes they lived, forever in a wheel chair. Anyway, he wasn't considering suicide.

CHAPTER SIXTEEN

As he rounded the bend in the muddy rutted track, the new Senior Investigating Officer saw that the scene had already been secured. Blue and white tape hung limply across his path and he found himself looking at the objects to which it had been tied – a tiny twig like branch of a hawthorn and an abandoned car's door handle.

A young uniformed policeman was crouching down beside his car window, tapping gently with his knuckle. He suddenly became aware that his orange Mini was a ladies' car, something that had never occurred to him before now. The SIO wound the window down a few inches.

'Sorry mate. You can't come any further.'

'Why not?'

'There's been a shooting. We're waiting for the SIO now.' He used the acronym with a flippancy that suggested he didn't quite know what it stood for, and the SIO had to fight off an almost overwhelming urge to ask the young officer what it meant. Instead, the SIO fished through the pile of things on the front passenger seat. Amongst the mobile telephone, SIO's Policy

Books, SIO's Note Books, broken hands free ear-piece and sandwich wrapper, he found his wallet and picked out his warrant card.

Getting out of the Mini, he said, 'I am the Senior Investigating Officer. Could you let me in to my scene please?'

'Oh, er, Good morning Sir.' Saluting no longer politically correct, the police youth didn't know quite how to respond. Coming half to attention, he lifted the blue and white tape above his head, unsnagging it from the hawthorn twig, so that it was now easier to step over than under. 'Come through, Boss.'

As if they had been invisible to him before he had crossed the tape, the SIO paused to examine his surroundings. He found himself in a kind of residential caravan park, a mixture of rather grandly put together "temporary" homes with wooden railings, decking and little fenced borders alongside industrial units where oily people tinkered with cars and motor-bikes. Piles of old building materials and little wooden sheds were dotted about and abandoned cars and boats slunk suspiciously in the long grass that might have been termed a communal garden in a more salubrious area. Here and there, pieces of corrugated iron were strewn amongst the virulent May undergrowth like massive curling petals. A group of residents in vests were leaning on their flimsy looking balustrades drinking mugs of tea. They peered down at the SIO in a not unfriendly manner, whilst, below them, spanners stopped clattering, filthy faces squinted into the sunlight and a group of children stood at the boundary of the tape, gazing at him in what might have been reverential silence.

In a manner that suggested that the play had started,

an older looking officer in shirt sleeves and a pristine oversize cap suddenly appeared, striding cheerily through the long grass from stage right. The SIO was pleased to see that the officers on the scene were wearing their hats – it was a standard that had been drummed into him as a young officer and upon which he now insisted.

'Morning Sir. I'm the duty sergeant. I've taken charge of the scene, Sir. I've not been into the caravan myself, Sir, but you can see the legs through the window. We got the call at 0817 this morning. No-one heard a shot, but apparently he's been shot.'

'Is he alive? Have we carried out first aid? Have the paramedics been called?'

'No Sir. I didn't really think of that. He's been shot in the head. The man who found him says he's definitely dead. I didn't want to disturb the scene.'

The SIO looked at the crestfallen face of the enthusiastic sergeant and instantly regretted pulling him up. It probably was bloody obvious that the man was dead. 'Thanks Sarge. You've done a good job. To get it even better next time, you should go in and check for yourself. Preservation of life comes before scene preservation, OK?'

'Yes Sir'. The sergeant was happy again. 'The Crime Scene Investigator is waiting for you at the caravan.' He gestured towards a further unkempt field where a small, grey 1950's touring caravan with a rounded roof sat like a mushroom. Nearby, a longer, lower, dilapidated pale blue caravan with some of its panels missing, its windows smashed and boarded up, had several gun-shot holes peppering its doors. A thick black beard in a hooded white paper suit, blue plastic foot bags and blue surgical gloves stood between the two dwellings, looking towards the SIO. Beyond him, a plain white Crime Scene Investigation van sparkled in the sunshine. Two or three further paper clad officers were milling around the open back doors of the van, pulling on their own shoe covers or fiddling with cameras.

The SIO first turned to the sergeant. 'Thanks Sarge. Can you start a crime scene log please? Show me as arriving now.'

'A log Sir? Is it suspicious then?'

'I don't know. I haven't looked at the scene yet, but we'll start a log anyway please.'

The sergeant strode happily back towards the young officer, and the SIO imagined him practising his instructions as he went.

The SIO joined the black beard, which belonged to the Crime Scene Manager, who now had both arms held high, a white package in each hand. 'Large or extra large, Boss?'

'Extra large I think, don't you?'

'Well yes, Boss, but it didn't seem polite to say.'

'What have we got then?'

'I don't know, I haven't been inside. It's your scene, Boss. I've been waiting for you. I've had a look around outside, though. That van has a series of shot holes in it.'

They walked towards the derelict blue caravan and looked at the bullet holes. Some of them penetrated the thin steel skin, whilst others were, on closer inspection, not holes, but small round dents, where it seemed a bullet had not carried enough force to go right the way through. The flimsy door hung open on one hinge. The inside was filled with junk and rubbish, rank old carpets, black plastic bags of domestic waste spilling out Kentucky Fried Chicken boxes, car tyres, ancient faded cushions and an upturned settee. No-one had lived here for a long time.

'Let's go and have a look inside the other van then,' the SIO ventured and the Crime Scene Manager beckoned to a photographer to join them.

The doorway of the grey caravan faced the bullet holes in the blue one, just a couple of metres away. The door also hung open on one hinge, in perfect symmetry with its companion. Inside, the body of a young man was slumped on the floor, half lying, half sitting, his shoulders propped up against the wall, his chin on his chest – almost as if he'd fallen asleep reading a book. The small caravan was untidy, old and grubby, but not chaotic. Remains of a cooked meal could be seen on a plate and in a couple of pans on the two-ring gas hob. The photographer was already clicking and flashing, now crouching low, now seeking to gain the advantage of height to produce the best possible images of the dead. A black rifle lay on the floor beside the young man's legs.

He had a mop of dark curly hair and little else could be seen of his face from a standing position. He wore a grey-white shirt and a pair of navy blue trousers, like a school uniform. His young brown feet were bare. There was no sign of blood or indeed of a wound. Carefully crouching beside the body, without touching it, the SIO looked up into the boy's face. Thick, congealed blood, ruby and black, had oozed from a wound in the smooth forehead. The SIO pointed this out to the Crime Scene Manager and the photographer contorted himself impressively to photograph the face.

'Suicide, Boss?' asked the Crime Scene Manager.

The SIO looked at him blankly.

'Murder, you think, Boss?'

There was no exit wound. The body and gun were classically arranged to suggest a suicide and the entry wound was in the right place too. But where were his brains? They should be splattered up the caravan wall. Cause of death was far from clear. There were no witnesses. Nobody had heard a shot. There was no way of interpreting the scene. It was possible that the young man had shot himself, perhaps using his toes to pull the trigger. The rifle was a long one and it was difficult to guess whether he could have reached the trigger with his fingers and still have held the gun against his head. It was equally feasible that someone had shot him with the rifle and left it at the scene. It was impossible to judge, yet the difference between the responses needed for the two options was huge: the first scenario wasn't suspicious and the second was a murder, with all its implications; not least of all a costly, resource intensive and time consuming investigation.

Suicide was preferable. The tape would be lifted, the body carted away by the undertakers and everyone would go home. He wouldn't even have to do any paperwork; the Coroner's Officer would take over and the SIO would be freed up to deal with the next clear-cut murder that came in. But what if it did turn out to be a murder? Starting an investigation after the body had been moved would not be easy and many of the occupants of this site, potential witnesses, or suspects even, were likely to be itinerant. They would be difficult to track down later. But wouldn't he be criticised by the hierarchy if he spent a lot of money investigating what was clearly a non-suspicious death? He would be known as the SIO who blew the budget on a job that he should have been able to make an easy decision about. Suicide was definitely an attractive option.

'Is it suspicious, Boss?' The Crime Scene manager interrupted his train of thought.

'What?' He didn't know how to decide.

'Are you contemplating suicide, Boss?'

And then it became obvious. The only safe way to approach the investigation was to treat it as a murder. It would ensure a proper investigation that would be likely to ascertain the truth, one way or the other. If he assumed suicide, there would be no investigation. Expensive or not, it was the only way to serve the public, to do his duty. He could explain the budget to his boss, but he could never explain the decision not to investigate to the parents of a murdered boy.

The Crime Scene Manager's beard was close to the SIO and he was watching the detective's face intently, waiting for an answer to his question. He seemed to sense that the SIO was about to decide upon a murder investigation.

'It's a Saturday afternoon, Boss. It's going to be expensive if this rolls into tomorrow. We both know it looks like a suicide.'

The SIO looked into the Crime Scene Manager's eyes, half obscured and pulled out of shape by the elastic rim of his white paper hood. The distortion made his eyes difficult to read.

'It's suspicious,' the SIO said deliberately. 'We'll treat it as a murder until we can prove otherwise.'

'It's suspicious!' the Crime Scene Manager shouted happily to the photographer, who was just a few feet away.

The photographer leaned out of the caravan window and called to the rest of the Crime Scene Investigators: 'He's called it. It's suspicious.'

'Good call, Boss,' the Crime Scene Manager said, and

then began to talk in urgent tones about the details of the forensic strategy for the investigation. Outside the SIO heard one of the Crime Scene Investigators call to the Sergeant.

'He's called it. It's suspicious!'

'Murder?' he heard the sergeant question with delight, before shouting to the police youth guarding the scene. 'It's a murder…'

He could not hear, but he imagined the young police officer telling the audience that this was now a murder scene, before he made a note in the log to that effect.

When the SIO emerged from the caravan, radios were crackling and the Crime Scene Investigators were enthusiastically checking the instruments of their trade – more cameras, fingerprint dusting kits, tweezers and exhibit bags. By the time he had stumbled out of his paper suit, three more marked cars and two CID cars had arrived. He had set a circus in motion.

A fat, hard-working and experienced Detective Sergeant wandered over to the SIO. He was a peer, a career detective whose opinion the SIO valued. 'What makes you think it's a murder, Guv?' he asked.

'Actually, I don't. I imagine it's going to turn out to be a suicide. But there are too many unanswered questions for me to be sure.'

'What like, Guv?'

'Well, those unexplained bullet holes in the adjoining caravan and the absence of an exit wound are telling us something. I just don't know what it is yet. The only safe way of establishing that this is a suicide, is to resource the investigation as if it were a murder.'

'Good call, Guv' the Detective Sergeant said, approvingly, pulling up his trousers.

'Thanks. Why do you say that?'

The Detective Sergeant looked incredulously at his boss. 'Double-time tomorrow, Guv,' he grinned.

CHAPTER SEVENTEEN

He had limped sideways, trying to limit the damage to his painful knees, down to the beach at Eype Mouth, where he had crossed a little stream, and he was now well and truly up again, close to half way to the top of Thorncombe Beacon. The snow had re-started and was heavy in his face. His string shoes slipped on every piece of snowy grass and if he stood on rock, although he would get better purchase, even the smallest lump or protrusion would send intense shooting pains through his sole up to his knee. The snow and wind were different now. The flakes were wet and settled on his thighs so that he had to wear waterproof trousers and when they hit the ground they no longer blew about, but stayed where they had landed, the landscape turning whiter minute by minute. The wind had died and no longer gusted, but came steadily into his face. His face stung, his nose dripped mucus and his wiry eyebrows dripped melted snow. It wasn't easy to walk, but at least the wind was even and predictable; it was better than being buffeted all over the place. More worrying was the light. It was only two o'clock in the afternoon, yet it looked as if there was only one hour of light left. The sky had an orange tinge to it and reminded him of being a boy in London, coming home to the terraced house in Shoreditch, with the television shops all showing the football results, hoping his parents would let him watch Dr. Who. He had a vague memory of going with his older brother with a sledge to buy a gallon of paraffin at the garage, for the heater that stood in the hallway. It smelt nice, but he'd burnt his hands badly on it once and his mother had put yellow stuff on the blisters. When he considered how far he'd gone in the police, he felt that he'd done alright for a boy from a London council house. At least, that's what he had once thought about himself.

He stopped every ten steps or so, every five feet, to breathe. If he had two hundred and fifty feet to go, he'd have to stop another forty nine times. If every stop were a minute long he'd be forty nine minutes later at the top. Then it would be dark and he'd have to get down again and he'd have trouble finding his bed and breakfast place without light. He would have to put his head torch on when he reached the top. The temperature dropped perceptibly as he climbed, the ground beneath his feet growing whiter and shinier so that his leading foot skated away from him and his toes bashed painfully against the risers.

Then suddenly, he was there. It was like the top of a roller coaster – he was teetering on the edge waiting to career down again. The barbed wire fence that separated him from the edge of the cliff described a long swooping curve that accentuated the change. He wished that he could hold onto it, but he winced at the thought of slipping and instinctively grabbing a rusty barb. Just ahead was a gentle dip, followed by a much more significant downward slope that was pure white. The brightness of it seemed to illuminate the sky. This, at least, was a saving grace – the reflection of the snow might make it light enough to see, even until quite late.

The Englishman took one cautious step on the mirror-like surface of the slope and slid dangerously, twisting his knee. He recovered his balance and tried again, but this time both feet slid forward and he fell heavily onto his backside. It was going to take a long time to get down, if indeed he could get down at all. If necessary he could go back or, if it came to it, he could find some shelter and spend the night in his survival bag.

A few years earlier, an eleven year old Katherine had spent a weekend in Snowdonia with her school. Elaine and he had worried about it for weeks beforehand and even more so during the weekend itself. It was one of the downsides of being a police officer, or being married to one for any length of time, that risks and risk management were always in the forefront of the mind. Many people seemed to go through life not seeing the dangers and being very happy as a result. But the Englishman had spent years dealing with the aftermath of things having gone wrong and it shaped his view. Katherine and Linda were not allowed to cross the road on their own until much later than other children. Katherine would not be allowed to drive until she was at least twenty-one (thirty would have been a lower and more acceptable risk). She would never be allowed to ride a motor-bike. And she had not been allowed to go to Snowdonia without a survival bag, even though this was not on the list provided by the school. When she returned home and dumped her holdall of filthy things on the kitchen floor, Elaine discovered to her horror that the bag was ripped and torn, as if a polar bear had tried to maul her daughter during the night. When the Englishman asked Katherine about it, she told her father that she'd used it as a toboggan. 'We slid down the mountain in it, Dad.'

It obviously couldn't be done anywhere near the edge. Lying flat, he would just shoot straight under the barbed wire fence if he lost control. What sort of fool would they take him for if they found him dead on the beach wearing espadrilles and in a survival bag? That probably would be treated as suspicious. Or, worse still, as some sort of sexually motivated event. The Englishman dragged the bag several metres inland, choosing a level spot which led to a dip with a camber that sloped away from the cliff edge rather than towards it. Better to be at the bottom miles away from Seatown than to risk sliding over the edge. He could always find his way with his compass and map once he was down.

The Englishman noticed shallow footprints leading downwards through the compacted snow, roughly where he was aiming to make his descent. Someone had decided that, even with a good pair of boots, this more gentle and inward sloping gradient would be a safer choice. Laying the thick orange plastic bag out on an area of grass that was covered with just a thin layer of snow, he shoved his rucksack into the bottom, positioned his woollen hat so that it shouldn't come off and pulled his hood up for protection. Should he put his arms inside or outside? He knew from the cow situation that the choice was a crucial one. He opted for outside: he could use his hands to steer. Then it occurred to him that the bag might pick up a bit of speed and that his hands would be useless as brakes. What if he headed towards a rock or a tree? Delving back into his rucksack he pulled out his cold, urine soaked boots and put a hand inside each one, placing them, sole down, onto the snow. He was in a reclined sitting position, feet first, chest arched, his booted hands beside his hips as rudders. Shuffling his backside he edged the bag towards the slope.

Whooah! He was away. Much, much faster than he had imagined. Speeding down the hillside at break-neck speed, his buttocks bouncing first a few inches, then a foot, then two feet into the air. It was all he could do to keep his head from bashing heavily into the hillside. A tree came running up out of the snow and rushed upwards past him. He dug the soles of the boots into the snow as hard as he could and succeeded in getting some control. A bush, slightly to his right, but heading towards him. He dug his left boot in and the bag turned, almost too much. He brushed the bush with his head. Then another tree, thick, black and stunted, to his left, but too close. He was going to hit it at full speed. He drove his right boot into the hillside but the bag turned too far, all the way around, so that he was hurtling into the tree blindly, backwards, headfirst. He slung his arms up over his head and braced himself for the collision. A shout. No impact. Not a tree. A man with a cap and heavy rucksack. The Agent. Sprawling in the snow above him. He shot into the abyss, waving a boot at his enemy. Whooah! Whooah!

Backwards he plunged, down and down, faster and faster, expecting to have his brains dashed out at any moment. He bellowed uncontrollably each time he leapt into the air. He crossed a ditch, the small of his back taking a nasty wallop, and then he was slowing, enough to recompose his arms and to dig a boot in. He turned, feet first again, and slid expertly to a halt.

He was lying beside a stile on the edge of a tiny

hamlet, just a little huddle of buildings, and he must have sledged for half a mile, maybe more. His chest heaved and his head span with exhilaration, his breath coming in short, deep pants; the thrill of his ride had quickened his pulse. He snickered at having upended the Agent in the snow, trying to imagine what he must have thought to see the Englishman shooting past at such speed. But he was now some distance inland and had to make his way back to the coast to find his lodgings. There was no time to stand around enjoying himself. Studying his map by the light of his head lamp, he discovered to his immense satisfaction that, although he'd spent the entire day heading for Seatown, his overnight stop was actually in a village called Chideock, itself a mile inland, and just a stone's throw from where he calculated his current position to be. Fifteen minutes later he was being shown around the delightfully comfortable Blake Cottage.

The owner was a gentle man, wearing a green knitted v-neck sweater and woollen tie. His grey hair was neatly trimmed and parted to the side and he was clean shaven. He spoke slowly and deliberately as he showed the Englishman around the meticulous cottage, of which the Englishman was to occupy a converted section consisting of a downstairs lounge with a dining table and an upstairs bedroom and shower room. Evidence of out-dated and charming female interior decoration was everywhere – throws on the settee, embroidered table cloth, cotton cushion covers and gingham curtains.

'Are you a police officer?' the owner asked, gently.

The Englishman was taken aback by the meek, domesticated man's question. 'Yes, I am. But that's an odd question. Why do you ask? Do I look like one?'

'Only if one knew. You're a little unkempt for a

police officer.'

'I'm sorry to have disappointed you my friend. I've been backpacking along the coast path for three nights.'

'Oh well, one's quite entitled to look unkempt in those circumstances. Will you go up to the pub tonight or will you order a take-away? There's a very good Chinese restaurant that will deliver. I expect you like Chinese food.'

The thought of a hot Chinese curry and sour Kung Po noodles sounded perfect to the famished Englishman. 'But why would you think I'd like Chinese food?'

'I guessed you'd like Chinese food.'

Was it just a lucky guess? Most people liked Chinese food. But something about the way the owner said it suggested that it was not a guess at all. The Englishman thought of the Agent. He couldn't possibly have beaten him here. Momentarily he wondered if he'd been trapped and looked towards the door. But he was also tired, hungry and thirsty. He began to stutter out a reply but was interrupted by the owner.

'I didn't know whether to tell you. He said not to. But you seem a decent chap to me. I thought I'd decide for myself when I met you. I was a police officer myself you see. Scotland Yard. Retired. Sometimes we have to stick together, don't we? Have you done something wrong?' The owner stood erect, his hand on the door handle. He looked unwaveringly into the Englishman's eyes.

'Have I done something wrong? What a question!' The Englishman sank down onto the feminine sofa. 'Who knows, my friend, who knows? I'm sure I don't.'

'Not me, certainly. I just wondered, that's all. You don't seem the type to do much wrong. Just a little unkempt.'

'Who said not to tell me what?' The weary Englishman could not help feeling a little irritated by the puzzle.

'It's just that he said not to tell you he'd been. Special Branch, I'd say, if I had to guess, though I didn't know him.'

The Englishman sank further into the soft sofa. His eyes closed as he drew in a long, slow breath. So the Detective Chief Superintendent had been here in the little hamlet of Chideock, too. 'What did he say? Please tell me.'

'Very little actually. He arrived in a Black Rover. I've got the index number, though he might have changed the plates by now. His driver waited outside. He asked whether you'd arrived yet and he seemed a little frustrated when I told him you hadn't. Perhaps he was pushed for time.'

'Did he leave a message?'

'No. I asked him, of course. He said that I shouldn't tell you he'd called.'

'How did he know I was due here?'

'Oh, I don't know. The Special Branch has many friends, doesn't it?'

The Englishman rubbed his unkempt cheeks. 'What made you decide to tell me?'

'Oh, just a feeling. A hunch, as the Americans might say.'

The Englishman sat and stared up at the well manicured man. What a strange day. The owner stared back for an uncomfortable moment and then said, 'Do you have a mobile telephone with you?'

He thought of the surveillance team that was even now scrambling into position around the cottage. 'What on earth would you ask me that for?'

'To order your Chinese. If not, I'd be glad to call on your behalf.'

The Englishman decided to give the pub and alcohol a miss, after the shenanigans of the night before. Following his shower and Chinese takeaway, he sorted out his rucksack. His survival bag was, like his daughter's before him, ripped and torn, probably to the extent that it was now not even an effective sledge. Still he hung it in the shower to dry, just in case. He had made use of his equipment in extraordinary ways today. Who knew what tomorrow would bring? His boots had proved themselves worthy rudders and brakes and were in pride of place, drying cosily on a chair beside the small radiator.

He sat in bed, drinking tea. The room was crowded with furniture, but homely. A long bookshelf housed a collection of old 1940s and 1950's annuals: *Victor*, *Boy's Own*, *Dandy* and *Beano*. This had been a boy's bedroom. At one end were a few old novels: Orwell's *Burmese Days*, Greene's *The Quiet American* and Somerset Maugham's *Far Eastern Tales*. The owner's son obviously had an interest in the Far East. In the bedside cabinet he found *Kim* and *The Jungle Books* and James Leasor's *The Marine from Mandalay*, the incredible man who had walked from the Far East and found his way back to his barracks at Plymouth, having completed his duty.

Being in the boy's room led the Englishman to think of his family. His rucksack rested beside the bed; he took his compact Nikon from its waterproof pouch and started perusing through the photographs on the tiny screen. Ignoring the boring shots of the coast path, he went instead to the earliest ones and flicked forward. There weren't many on there, he was no photographer, but there was a lovely one of his three girls, Elaine, Katherine and Linda, each one with a delicate ivory and lemon coloured frangipani blossom tucked behind their ear, their hot faces squashed together, smiling in front of a Balinese temple. He grinned back at them; he couldn't wait to see them again. There was one of the Englishman, the General, the Spaniard and Bruce II on a golf course, raising their bottles of beer to the camera. A bemused and beautiful young caddy stood in the background. There were a couple of shots of the parcel bomb that had been sent to the embassy and intercepted by Henry. He'd been brave; one week previously a locally engaged security officer had lost his arm at the Australian embassy. Henry had spotted the one intended for the British Ambassador and called the Englishman immediately. The Englishman had photographed it in situ before the bomb squad had taken it away for a controlled explosion. It contained 200g of hydrogen peroxide based HME – home made explosive.

Next came one of him and Elaine on the tricycle rickshaw, Boat Quay in the background, taken by the sinewy rider before he knew what he was letting himself in for. Elaine was beautiful, happy.

The Englishman started when he discovered the photograph of the Houses of Parliament, Big Ben and Westminster Bridge on the first day of the conference. The palace of Westminster looked drab and beige, the bridge was grey, no hint of blue could be seen; the River Thames was colourless, brown at best, and it did not sparkle.

The Englishman slept deeply, though he awoke from another disturbing dream: his bed was hurtling over a cliff and he couldn't stop it. The dream featured none of the euphoria he had felt racing down the hillside in the survival bag. It carried the same sense of doom as the Beslan dream. It was full of risk and foreboding, connected with mistrust and with pursuit, though he didn't dream the detail, only the intense discomfort of needing to escape. The feeling stayed with him as he showered and dressed.

His body ached all over: his knees, ankles, toes and the soles of his feet, as ever; but today also his arms, shoulders and neck were stiff and painful. He could just make out the edges of a large bluish black bruise that spread from his lower spine towards his right kidney. This was very sore; he assumed it was as a result of the thump against the edge of the ditch as he had careered down from the Beacon.

He looked at his boots. They seemed like sturdy old friends that had been through the wars with him, now that he had established his superiority over them and they had been so helpful in his toboggan run. They had dried out overnight; he fondled the leather between his finger and thumb. Were they softer now? Had the urine really worked? Had the Post Security Officer been right all along? The thought of another day of slipping in espadrilles, with wet socks and numb toes and terrible pains in the soles of his feet filled him with trepidation. He examined his wounds. They were now dry, red and scabious. Cracks ran across the surface, raw crimson ravines of unprotected pain. He had more blister plasters in his rucksack. He sat on the bed and began to dress the sores.

He was surprised to find when he entered the little lounge, that the table had been laid: a pot of tea, wholegrain bread, a slab of butter and home-made jam sat comfortingly on a large lace doily. He hadn't heard any of this activity going on below him. The Englishman had once loved home-made jam – apricot and plum in particular. But for almost as long as he could remember jam was simply sweet. Shortly, the owner, quaintly immaculate in another v-neck knitted pullover and tie, brought in a simple cooked breakfast. The Englishman reached into his rucksack and took out the box of ibuprofen and his guide book and started to read whilst he ate.

'Good luck with the walk. You have an extremely long way to go today, don't you?' the owner said later, as the Englishman prepared to leave. 'Sidmouth, isn't it?'

'No,' replied the Englishman, 'Sidmouth's tomorrow. I only go as far as Seaton today. That's far enough!'

'Well, make sure that you rest for ten minutes in every hour. You'll make more progress that way.'

'The Marine from Mandalay?' the Englishman asked.

'You've read it? A good book about a fine man's dedication to duty.'

'I couldn't agree with you more. I've thought about the book several times during my walk.'

'Your boss said you were walking to Sidmouth today,' the owner continued, 'I had a feeling he was wrong. That means he'll be waiting for you in the wrong place this evening.'

'How did you know he's my boss?' the Englishman asked, 'did he say?'

'No. He didn't say. One guesses these things'.

'Do you mind if I guess something?'

'No, do go on. Please.'

'Were you a Special Branch officer?'

'Yes, I was.' The owner seemed pleased. 'Commander.' He paused, 'though that was a few years ago, of course.'

'You must thank your wife for me, Sir. It's been a lovely comfortable stay.'

'Oh, I'm not married,' the owner replied. 'This,' he gestured around the room, 'is my mother's work. This has been my home all my life.'

They shook hands warmly and the Englishman stepped out into the snow.

'Oh! You nearly forgot your guide,' the owner said, scooping the pocket sized book from the table and handing it to the Englishman, whose head drooped.

'Are you well?'

'Yes, thanks, Sir – just tired. Do I look too unkempt?'

The owner smiled. 'No, you look fine'. He straightened, and threw up a smart salute. 'Carry on officer.'

The Englishman also straightened and saluted. 'Sir.'

His heels twinged as he crunched his way up the drive, but he made no outward sign of discomfort. As he turned to walk from the driveway, the owner called out to him:

'Don't let the bastard grind you down.'

The Englishman looked back. The owner stood with his hand raised in salute, a huge grin spread across his neat face.

CHAPTER EIGHTEEN

It was a beautiful morning and The Englishman was walking down a narrow road towards the beach at Seatown. The road surface was virtually clear and easy to walk upon yet the hedgerows glistened with snow and icicles, bending under the weight. The winter solstice: it was the shortest day of the year, but today's walk was the second longest leg and, furthermore, it took in the highest peak – Golden Cap. The sun dazzled out from a crisp blue sky and the Dorset countryside, dusted in snow, looked fabulous. To his right a great bulge of hillside shone golden and white, curving away to the blue sky, the cap itself out of view. The Englishman was glad not to see the peak, for he feared Golden Cap.

The survival bag sled ride had electrified him and he'd been on a high when he had arrived at Blake Cottage. It did not surprise the Englishman that he had to come down from this adrenaline rush, but he had not anticipated the dark sense of doom that spilled over from his dream and troubled him still. At first it must have lurked unseen somewhere at the back of his mind, covertly undermining his optimism, for he felt morose from the moment his eyes opened. But within an hour it had made its way forward, arriving in the front of his mind. The notion of hurtling off of the edge of a cliff in his sleep heckled him, reminding him that they mistrusted him and were tracking him.

There was now absolutely no doubt of that. The intelligence from the owner corroborated his own observations of the day before. The Detective Chief Superintendent had monitored the Englishman's progress from the Ilchester Arms to Blake's Cottage and he'd made it clear that he didn't want the Englishman to know. He had deployed an agent who had engaged him in conversation in the pub and then followed him along the coast path.

But this was only half of the story – the more comfortable half. Being mistrusted and pursued was something he'd lived with for days now. These didn't quite account for the feeling of ruin that the dream had imbued him with. It was the consequence that frightened the Englishman. He had to confront this: it was the suicide thing. The bed hurtling over the cliff top was a representation of his impending suicide. There, he'd said it. He had dreamt the dream because he had considered suicide yesterday.

But he hadn't really been contemplating suicide, he was just thinking through his options. Most plans had an option that can't be chosen. When confronted with an armed man threatening to kill a child, one option is to do nothing. In your decision log you show that you've considered the option to do nothing but dismissed it, just to ensure that your decision making is accountable. Then you can get on with confronting the armed man. This was just the same. Suicide was the option considered so that it could be dismissed. How high did a cliff have to be to guarantee death if you threw yourself off? It didn't matter, it wasn't an option.

Yet everything seemed to have fallen into place over breakfast. The Englishman had read the section of his guide book covering today's walk from Seatown to Seaton. The book had carelessly pointed out that Golden Cap was the highest sea cliff on the Southern English coast, thirty metres higher than Beachy Head. Beachy Head, for Christ's sake! Everyone knows what makes Beachy Head infamous – suicide. There's even a patrolling pastor to counsel jumpers. How high does a cliff have to be to guarantee death if you throw yourself off? As high as Beachy Head. The Englishman felt his future plummet as soon as he read it. He knew. It wasn't something he wanted to do, it was just something that he would be watching himself do. It was something over which he would have no control.

The Englishman knew of this concept of looking in at one's own suicide. He had dealt with suicides many times. "Dealt with" – that was the police expression. I've "dealt with" a suicide. I've "dealt with" a murder. The Englishman had "dealt with" a few murders, and a few suicides, that he'd never dealt with inside. There were death scenes that no-one should ever see. But in dealing with suicides he had come across those who had survived their own suicide attempts. Of those, he had never come across someone who, being in a clear state of mind, had objectively considered all the options and chosen suicide as the preferred option. He knew that suicide terrorists made such a decision, but that was a different set of circumstances. They weren't suicidal at all, they were choosing to die as the best tactical option to kill.

But those who had spoken to the Englishman candidly revealed that, in their despondency, they felt helpless to stop their own suicide, that they were looking in on events as a bystander. The help they needed was in getting back inside their own minds, taking back control of their own decision making processes. Enabling them to consider all the options and decide that suicide wasn't one of them. The Englishman needed such help, right now. Providence had become Death and she was hunting the Englishman. And he could not smell her. He wouldn't know she was stalking him. He would just watch himself, a helpless bystander, slip into the abyss. For God's sake look after our people.

The Englishman would slip from the edge of Golden Cap in the snow and wind. There would be no investigation. There would be no shame after death. The Detective Chief Superintendent would come to his funeral and would comfort Elaine and the kids. It was a way out for them. No-one would ever say that the Englishman had not been good at his job. There would be no disgraceful and humiliating repatriation from Southeast Asia at the peak of his career. His family would not be slurred with the suicide thing. He would have died as a successful senior detective and proud Englishman, serving his country in the fight against terrorism. A terrible accident on a snowy English hillside during a break from a hard year in the Far East. He would be on a par with O'Raugherty at last.

He had promised himself that he would do the right thing for Elaine. Now he could see how that would come about. It wasn't by completing the walk at all, it was by slipping from the top. They wouldn't find him at the bottom in espadrilles, he'd put on his boots so that they would find a normal walker who had fallen. He wondered if he had been saying his goodbyes last night in bed, silently, to the photographs of his beloved girls. He had even said goodbye to England. Suicide wasn't an option, but falling was. He couldn't help it if he fell.

The bloody boots were killing him. They were affording him purchase on the slippery ground, but they were brutally rubbing his blisters, which he thought were bleeding in spite of the dressing. The clear morning had brought a drop in temperature and the surface of yesterday's snow shone and crunched under foot. Here and there it was glossy and lethal. His were the first footprints of the day. If the Agent was still out here somewhere, then he was behind the Englishman. Then again, in this glorious weather, the Detective Chief Superintendent could deploy aerial surveillance. He stood with his hands on his hips, his woollen hat in his hand, his head steaming and his jacket open, just as he had on the first sunny day out of Lulworth Cove. He surveyed the sky. Nothing. The craft could be miles away and still do its job.

The peak loomed menacingly above him. He felt in control, he felt that he could walk over the top without dying, but he knew that, nevertheless, he would slip and fall to his death. He wondered at what point he would start looking in at it, helplessly. He wanted to get on with it. He was knackered. Mentally spent. His old body ached. His head thumped and his heart pounded with exhaustion. He panted like a dog. Couldn't he just have a heart attack? He was tired with the whole thing. Inwardly, he was completely drained. What was the point of being alive if all you thought about was suicide, anyway? Nothing was the same as it was. He sighed and continued towards the peak. He'd had enough.

The forensic pathologist, the ballistics expert and the SIO, all dressed in blue aprons, face masks and rubber wellington boots, leaned intently over the young man's brain. The bearded crime scene manager hovered nearby with a small evidence bag in his hand, waiting for the next sample. The photographer stood atop a set of step ladders that he had brought especially for the occasion, getting himself some good aerial shots of the post mortem examination.

'Here it is,' the pathologist said triumphantly. The SIO could not see it at first amidst the damaged tissue and blood. 'It's travelled round and round, causing extensive damage to the brain, but not having enough velocity to exit through the cranium.' He finally held up the bloody bullet between a pair of tweezers. 'That's why there was no exit wound.' The Crime Scene Manager held out the little bag and the pathologist dropped it in.

'The powder marks around the entry wound suggest that the rifle was held to the deceased's forehead,' the pathologist observed. 'This is classically seen in suicides.'

The ballistics expert was examining the bullet in the bag. 'That's the sort of bullet I was expecting. You see, this was not an ordinary rifle. This was a ball bearing gun that has been adapted with a more powerful spring and a rifled barrel. It's almost certainly a Section 1 firearm now, though I'd have to do some tests on it to ascertain the muzzle velocity. My guess is that the marks on the other caravan were test shots to see how powerful the adapted rifle was.'

'Could he have reached the trigger?' the SIO asked.

'Yes, I believe so,' replied the ballistics expert, 'This is not an exceptionally long rifle and I have seen many suicides committed with this size of gun.'

After the post mortem, the SIO returned to the scene. Back in the caravan alone, he looked for further clues as to what had happened, physical clues that the forensic team, in their hunt for scientific evidence, might have overlooked.

The caravan was untidy. A full black plastic bag of mostly food rubbish, a custard cream packet resting lightly on top, leaned over towards where the body had been. A screwed up ball of paper was caught in one of the folds of the bag, like a rock about to tumble down the face of a volcano. Further pieces of litter, a chocolate wrapper and more balls of paper, were scattered about the floor of the caravan.

The SIO unscrewed one The appalling writing and spelling of somebody who had never been taught to write was scrawled in heavy yet uncertain block capitals.

'AR CARNT EKSPLAN'

The dead young man was starting to come alive. The SIO could almost see him in life. He wrote as he spoke, his accent apparent in the way 'I' became 'AR' and 'CAN'T' became 'CARNT'. He unrolled another ball of paper.

'AR LUV YOU. BUT AR DON NO HOW TO'

The words were cut short like the boy's life. The SIO could see the illiterate young man desperately trying to express himself, to explain his actions, his past and his future intentions, but becoming more and more frustrated, screwing up and throwing his efforts about the caravan. Another said,

'LET ME TRY TO SAY WOT AR FIL. AR WONT TO RITE IT'

There were six or seven of them scattered about the poor man's little home. Looking closer to where the body had been slumped, the SIO found one more paper ball stuffed into the gap where the wall met the floor. In the same crevice lay the pen. Unrolling this last piece of paper and reading the contents, the SIO made up his mind that this was suicide. In his thick, desperate scrawl, the young man had written:

'ARV AD ENUFF'

The Englishman winced and cringed with every step. Ahead lay the peak, where his punishment would end. He was not far from the top, perhaps two hundred more steps. This would all soon be over. He'd be asleep in bed, hurtling to oblivion. Behind him, his pursuers, his failures. He would not turn back, he would go on. But the boots were hurting badly. It was like self harm – every step was as if he were taking a knife to his tender, exposed heels. Every step was torment. Pissing on the bloody things had done them no good whatsoever.

'Ha!' The Englishman blurted, aloud, 'I can't even make it to my own bloody suicide.' He laughed loudly. 'Come on then Providence. Get me up there, for fuck's sake. I've had enough,' he hollered to the blank sky. 'I've fucking well had enough.'

He collapsed down onto his backside and started unlacing his boot. 'I can't make it to the top of the hill to throw myself off of it. Ha, ha!'

His gloved fingers slipped on the laces and he ripped the boot off without loosening it.

'Aagh!' He screamed with pain as the skin ripped open. Blood showed instantly through his sock.

'You bastard!' he shouted venomously, at the top of his voice, and threw the boot over the edge of the cliff.

He tugged his gloves off with his teeth, spitting blue

wool onto the snow. Then he pulled at the laces of the other boot, finally getting it undone and open and yanking it off.

'You're going in the sea, you bastard,' he snarled at it.

He shrugged off his rucksack, stood up and blustered over to the cliff edge in his socks, ratcheting his arm with the boot in it behind him as he went, like some kind of crazy bowler.

'Fuck off,' he bawled at the top of his voice and slung his arm forward as hard as he could, releasing the dark brown boot into a satisfying high arc that saw it destined to clear the cliff face and splash into the English Channel, a hundred metres or more below. The Englishman, desperate to see it splash, failed to correct his forward momentum until it was too late. He teetered for a split second, his arms wind milling desperately, fingers clawing at thin air, his sock-clad toes scrabbling, desperately, uselessly for something to grip. And then he too plunged over the edge of the cliff.

There was no sensation of flying. The ground rushed up and smashed into his face and he was dead.

CHAPTER NINETEEN

For a second time the pulse slowed.

Slower.

Slower.

It stopped. The machine bleeped the terrible uninterrupted tone of television drama.

Then it stuttered. And bleeped again.

Bleep, bleep, bleep.

'Please live, please live. Oh, my darling, I'm trying, please live.' Elaine's thin and weak voice.

Two nurses fiddled uselessly as the pulse slowed a third time.

Slower, slower…

A massive bearded man, wearing a green and gold Springboks rugby shirt, suddenly appeared in the doorway. 'Get that baby out of there now!' he bellowed. His accent matched his shirt. He was pulling on surgical gloves as he shouted. The nurses jumped back.

Bleep. Slower still. Too long. Once again the continuous bleep of death.

'Oh no, please, do something. Please.'

The South African was between Elaine's legs. Someone produced a huge pair of forceps, at least two foot long with a huge spoon on the end of each pincer. Still no pulse.

'OK, Elaine. One last push and I'm going to pull. Here she comes…'

Silence. Elaine's weary sobs.

Death.

A slap cut through the blankness. Then another. Then, at last, a new life was crying.

Linda.

The Englishman was prostrate, on the ground, face down, his nose pouring blood. It ran warm and sticky across his eyes and forehead and then dripped from his hair. He lay in thick undergrowth, odd woody shrubbery of the type that he'd become used to seeing at the top of the cliff. Through his sticky eyelids came light, but there was no other indication of how long he'd been lying there. His dream had been a short one.

His body was probably smashed. He opened his eyes. Dark, leafless bush all around; splatters of blood across the coarse grey stems and small thick leaves. Beneath that, the rough, greyish stone which he'd slammed into. He strained to lift his head and found that he could. He wasn't completely paralysed. Not above the neck, anyway.

Neither was he looking in. This was happening to him. His body shifted slightly, forward, of its own accord. As if some unseen force had dragged him an inch. His head swam with dizziness. The blood oozing from his nose ran into his eye. From his nose to his eye – upwards. Gravity - he wasn't lying flat at all. The earth twisted like a gyroscope; nausea and dizziness swept through his head. Like the first boot, he hadn't gotten as far as the beach. He was vertical, hanging, bat like, an upside down crucifix, on the thick bracken that clung to the sheer cliff face. He was high. He looked forwards, down. Below him the undergrowth petered out and then it was unmitigated perpendicular rock straight down to the beach, way, way below him, under his head. A tiny brown boot was moving around in the wash. Big dollops of blood and snot were dripping down the cliff face. Too much blood. He had to get back to the top and stem the flow somehow. Linda had survived. They would always be so grateful to that big South African doctor.

'What happened to you there, boy? Were it cows again?'

The Agent's pantomime pirate voice was so close. Was this another dream? Then the Englishman felt a tugging at his trouser leg. The Agent had obviously managed to scramble down to him.

'You need a hand, boy?'

'Yes. Please. I'm bleeding.'

He felt a strong, claw like grip around his ankle – the beer hand. 'Oh, God, if I ever get out of this, I'll fill that hand with beer forever,' he thought.

'Grab this rope, boy!' the Agent shouted.

A frayed old blue nylon rope came into view, dangling out of focus close to the left side of his face. But the Englishman was frightened of letting go of the bracken stems that he suddenly found he was gripping with all his might, keeping him there, alive. The claw tightened around his ankle.

'I've got you boy.'

He checked the grip in his right hand and tucked his socked feet as far as they would go into the woody roots. He could feel them, reassuringly solid for now, hard against the bridges of his feet, stopping his legs from swinging out over his back and somersaulting him to his death. As sure as he could be of his hold, he quickly grabbed the rope with his left fist and twisted his wrist into it.

'OK boy. Now you've just got to start turning yourself around. You'll be alright, boy.'

'How?'

'Look up here boy.'

Clinging on to the thick stems, the Englishman managed to lift his head and twist it back up towards the top of the cliff. The Agent's badly shaven face was only two feet away. He was on his belly, leaning over the top of the cliff. The taut nylon rope cut into the loose soil at the rim.

'I'm just here boy. You ain't fallen far. Just cling to them roots and work your way upright and you'll live. Now, I'm going to let go of your ankle. As long as you hang onto the rope, you'll be fine.'

The vice like beer grip was released and the Englishman felt a simultaneous tautening of the rope as the Agent braced himself. A blackish dollop of thick blood bubbled out of his nose and shot towards the beach. The Englishman swung his free arm from his right to below his head and grasped the bracken there. He didn't plummet to his death, he was still hanging on the vertical cliff face. In his mind he practised his next move: he bent his right leg at the knee and then out to the side of his body. This would have to be done quickly, because his feet were his hooks. In a flash he'd done it. He thought he felt the pressure increase on his left foot as the weight changed, but again, he had beaten gravity and his right foot found purchase. Next he moved his left arm upwards, then brought his left leg down to meet his right. The first set of manoeuvres was over - he had managed to turn himself a few minutes anti-clockwise. Again, he threw out his right arm and grasped at the bracken. But there was nothing there to hold, his hand scraped at the crumbly rock. His body slipped downwards and the rope around his left wrist tightened and cut into his flesh. He must have nearly pulled the Agent over with him.

'Just a bit lower with that hand boy.'

The Englishman scrabbled around with his right arm and found a strong root. It held. Again he dropped his right leg, then his left leg and finally moved his left arm upwards. His head was in a five o'clock position. Slowly and cautiously, the Agent supporting him with the rope and his words, the Englishman grappled with the thick bracken, right arm, right leg, left leg, left arm, slowly rotating on the cliff face like the hand of a clock, turning back time, feeling the shift of weight from his feet to his arms. Four o'clock, three o'clock, sideways on the cliff face, two o'clock, his head at last higher than his feet and seeing the sky for the first time. Finally he was hanging from the dense shrubbery the right way up, staring into the ugly, ill kept, friendly face of the Agent. They were only a few inches apart.

'Oh, boy - your face,' the Agent blurted, and he looked repulsed.

The Englishman chortled and blood erupted from his nose. The Agent took hold of him under an arm and heaved. The Englishman's feet flailed but then found purchase on the woody stems and he was back kneeling on the surface, next to his saviour, squeezing his nostrils to stem the blood. For how long had he bled? Could he now die of shock? After surviving that?

'Use some snow, boy,' the Agent suggested.

Lying down on his stomach the Englishman pushed

his face into the thin snow. He stumbled over to where his rucksack lay and, finding a deeper spot, once again thrust his face into the ground. Pain began to radiate; a familiar pain, bringing back memories of a young copper. His nose was the epicentre of his body. Throbbing and pulsating. His right nostril was bleeding fast and freely, bringing with it a thick mucus. There was little or no blood coming from his left nostril, although the pain was more intense to the left side of his face, spreading out across his cheek, under his eye and across his forehead above the eye. Bomb victims died of loss of blood from severed limbs. Gone was the old emphasis on clearing the airway. It was no good to get a person breathing again if blood was spurting from a massive trauma. Torniquets had come back into fashion and had saved the lives of many British soldiers who had stood on improvised landmines in Iraq and Afghanistan.

The Agent was beside him scooping fresh snow around the bloody melted mess that quickly built up under the Englishman's face. The wounded man edged forward to a fresh spot and they repeated the process. Then again and again, creeping like a slug across the snow leaving a heavy dark red mess in his wake. The red stain in the snow gradually got smaller and smaller. At last the bleeding reduced to a trickle. One hand pinching his nose, he heaved himself back up into a kneeling position and scrabbled through his rucksack. He was clambering into his torn survival bag when the Agent suddenly hollered:

'Jesus Christ! What's the matter with you?'

The Englishman patted his legs and belly for injury then, shivering, turned towards the Agent.

'You're not wearing any shoes, boy!'

His trembling shoulders showed the hint of a shrug and then the Englishman pulled the bag up around his neck and huddled close to the Agent.

'I guess you'd better radio in for some help,' he stammered.

'Or I could take you straight to the helicopter,' the Agent said.

'Better still. Is it far?'

'It's all in your tiny mind, boy.'

'What do you mean? You're SIS, aren't you?'

'I can be SIS if you want, boy. Will you buy me dinner, if I am?'

'But you are an agent for SIS?'

'OK, boy. What are you? A robot?'

'You're not working for MI6? You're not following me?'

'MI6, MI5, whatever type of secret agent you want, boy.'

'But what are you doing here?'

'What are you doing here? I'm walking the South West Coast Path. I'm nought but a walker, boy. But I'll help you boy. You'll need it without shoes and a busted nose.'

'Oh, I have shoes,' the Englishman said and then checked himself. 'But they're beach shoes.'

'Like the ones you was wearing for the cows? You know what, boy? I thought I was a little bit potty, but you take the biscuit, you do.'

'How did you know I was over the edge, by the way?'

'When I seen you trying to kill me in that orange bag last night. I said to meself, "that boy's over the edge."'

'Oh. Yes. I'm sorry about that. I didn't have the right shoes to get down safely. No, I meant, how did you know I was over the edge of the cliff just now?'

'I seen your rucksack. I knew it were you. The first thing I thought was, "I bet he's slipped in them shoes again."'

'How did you know it was me?'

'Your rucksack boy. Same one you were wearing when you were lying in the grass, top of that track, yesterday.'

'Pass it over will you? I need some tea. You saw me? Why didn't you say anything?'

'Well, I didn't like to boy. You might've taken offence at buying me that steak, for all I knew.'

'And a cheese board.'

'Right. I thought perhaps it's best just to carry on like I hadn't seen you, boy.'

The Englishman pulled his flask out of the rucksack. 'Would you like a cup of tea? I've got a flask full.'

'Ah well, now. About that.'

'What?'

'I had a cup of tea out of your flask earlier. Or were it two? Before I looked over the edge, you know.'

It was just after eleven in the morning. The Englishman had obviously only been unconscious for seconds or minutes. Long enough to dream about Linda.

'I need to push on boy. I have to get as far as Lyme Regis. I'd be pleased to help you boy, but I can't go back.'

The Agent passed the tea cup back and the Englishman drank. The Agent looked east, the back of his head towards the Englishman. Matted dark grey hair sprouted out untidily from beneath the cap. His neck was caked with old dirt, cut through by a rivulet of sweat, which was washing its way gently downwards, the erosion leaving a narrow pink line of exposed skin.

'I'd be delighted to accept your offer of help,' the Englishman said. 'Perhaps I can find a hospital or doctor's at Lyme Regis and get my face looked at.'

Climbing awkwardly from the bag, the Englishman pulled on some espadrilles, hoisted his rucksack onto his back and, arm in arm with the Agent, his right hand clamped to his nose, he slid on and upwards towards Golden Cap.

'Let's count the steps,' he said.

CHAPTER TWENTY

The Agent stayed closest to the cliff edge and the Englishman clung to his arm. He wondered if he'd tried to commit suicide, or at least if he had failed to prevent the fall. Or had he just slipped? He had been going up to Golden Cap in order to slip, not jump. In the end, he had slipped. Was it something over which he had had no control? Had he been looking in at himself?

He hadn't known this before, but he now knew that he thought he would see his tormentors in his dying moments. He thought that the Deputy Head of Mission would somehow be there, explaining why he didn't need to protect the children of BISO or, better still, explicating how he'd seen the error of his way and would now supply the school with a radio. The Post Security Officer would be there saying, 'You should have pissed on your boots.' The Fresh Faced Spy would look in and say, 'We could have got on so much better' or perhaps even 'thank God you're gone.' The Headmistress would say that she had been flirting, it was all OK or she'd be pleased that the dirty minded sod had died. The Detective Chief Superintendent; most of all him. He wasn't there, the selfish bastard. The man who had put the Englishman under such terrible pressure when he'd told him that he was no good at his job, the boss who was stalking him with such sinister malice. He simply wasn't there. The Englishman was dying because of him and he wasn't there. Likewise O'Raugherty, the spectre haunting him, from the mouths of those conspiring against him to the ramparts of Nothe Fort – the Ghost of Christmas Past. Where was he when you needed him? There had been no Scrooge-like moment. No-one argued over his things, his failures, his enquiries, his career. In that dying moment, couldn't just one of the people who represented the career to which he'd dedicated his life come and see him off? Not one personality from the job that had taken him from boy to man, that defined him, had been there to witness his passing. Bastards.

Patently it was he who had failed to conjure them up - they hadn't abandoned him; he had abandoned them. Was he, like Linda, ready to struggle into a new life?

The climb was becoming less arduous, the gradient reducing.

'Come on, boy. We're there.'

'Where?'

'You're at the peak, boy. Golden Cap.' The Agent smiled into the Englishman's face, his strange plucked cheeks red and scrawny.

'Have you farted?' he said to the Agent.

'No, I always smell like this,' he said, obviously a little hurt.

In the struggle to slide up to the peak, and count his steps and reflect on the meaning of life, the Englishman had let go of his nose. But what was that smell? Cheese. The Agent smelt like cheese.

'I can smell you!' he shouted, letting go of the Agent's arm and standing back to look him in the face.

'Alright boy. No need to go on about it. I'm camping, ain't I?'

'You smell like cheese, you dirty old bastard!' The Englishman was struggling to keep upright in the string soled shoes.

'Fuck off. I saved your life. You didn't worry about the smell then, did you boy?'

'But I haven't smelt anything for years! I've got no sense of smell!'

'No sense of smell? How can you tell the coppers are after you?'

'It turns out I couldn't.' And as he said it, the sense was gone again. Was that it? One brief opportunity to smell for the first time in thirty years and he smelt a dirty old tramp? No. No! That just wasn't fair.

'Oh, come on!' he shouted to the sky, as the Agent looked on bemused. Why couldn't it have been Elaine's perfume or roast lamb or the clean soapy smell of Linda after a bath? A filthy old, thieving old tramp?

He took out his handkerchief, held his vulnerable right nostril closed, and carefully, very gently blew through the left nostril. Nothing. The trapped air dug painfully into his right ear and his mouth popped open with an internal hiss. He tried again, a little harder. Again the popping in his ear, but this time he felt as if there might have been movement in the nostril. Once again, slightly harder still, he blew through the left nostril. Something was moving. A sharp ache radiated across his left cheek towards his ear and then a little lump seemed to move, sending a delicious shiver through his chest. Something was moving. One more blow. Suddenly, orgasmically, a hard round black and green plug of dried blood and mucus, the size of a large pea, shot out into his handkerchief. A deluge of blood followed. It flowed through his left nostril but its source was somewhere else in his head. This wasn't nose blood, this was head blood. His cheeks and forehead seemed to be emptying through his nostril as if someone had stuffed him full of string and was now pulling it out, all at once. Even the insides of his eyebrows were emptying. Fingers of movement rippled just below the surface of the entire front half of his head. A torrent of snot and blood, fed by unseen facial tributaries, was spouting out through his nostril like a geyser escaping from the earth. At last it stopped. The Agent was standing, head bent, fascinated by the flow.

'Oh my God, what have I done?' the Englishman cried, looking with dread at the huge quantity of bloody gunge on the snow. 'Are those bits of my brain?'

But as the outward flow of vital fluid came to a stop, so there was an inward rush of vapour through his nostril. He smelt the seaweed in the sea, the woody stems of the bracken, the crystal snow, the very essence of the grass. He smelt the mussels that the seagulls had dashed on the rocks two hundred metres below them, the salty spray of the crashing waves. Nature flooded his nose. Fragrances travelled miles to reach him and his brain understood them all, received them with glee. He stood in the centre of a circle of massive circumference and smells came in like radio messages from everywhere. The earth itself, the subtle creamy smell of mud, the aromatic herby smell of the leaves that still lived and the delicious warm smell of decaying leaf matter beneath the hedgerow. He looked out over the sea and the fields as they rolled away left and right and up at the sky and he could see it all so much more clearly. Then the near smells got their chance, the metallic blood in his mouth, the smell of his sweat, the plastic chemical tinge of his coat, the dankness of his gloves, the rubbery smell of the survival bag in the warm tentiness of his canvas rucksack, the revolting deep shiny grubbiness of the Agent's hat, the wax of his old Barbour jacket and the rotten, cheesy smell of his unwashed body. Everything came to him and he stood and received and translated and enjoyed.

Thank you God! He was blind and now he can see! The Englishman slung out his arms, and turned, taking in the view from three hundred and sixty degrees. He threw back his head, looked up at the sky and breathed in the view that he had missed all these years. A waft of onions cooking from some unseen cottage, the thin, clean smell of a pine tree, bitumen on a fence post. He was a child seeing the world for the first time.

'I can smell!' he shouted to the sky, 'Merry Christmas, nose!'

And then abruptly it stopped. He was blind again. Just as surely as if his nostril had been corked, the smells stopped coming in. He bent towards the Agent and sniffed. Nothing.

'You don't smell,' he said.

'You're used to it, that's all. Smells go away when you're used to them. Don't you remember?'

Yes, that was it, of course. Smells do go away when you're accustomed to them. Otherwise the Agent would repulse himself every second of every day. He ran towards a gnarly black and leafless hawthorn tree and sniffed at one of the twigs. Nothing, nothing at all. Just now he felt as if he could have smelt a bug crawling on the twig. He broke off the end, exposing the raw green interior, and held it to his left nostril. There should be a sappy, thin, acetone fragrance – he'd smelt it just now. Nothing. A large brown stone block marked the peak. It was bathed in a golden sunlight and, moments before, he had detected the baked savour of the rock as it heated almost imperceptibly in the weak December sun, like a mild jacket potato. He knelt before it and sniffed at it. Nothing. It was gone. As quickly as it had come gushing back, his sense of smell had gone again.

'Oh, no! No. Come back, please,' he begged, still kneeling before the stone.

'That's Lord Antrim. Says he's been dead since 1977. He ain't coming back, boy.'

The Englishman had expected to die on Golden Cap. Then, as he stood on the peak, came a miracle, his sense of smell had returned to him and he had smelt the whole world. It was out there waiting for him. Now, his body had shut it out again.

'We'd better get going boy. He ain't coming back.' The Agent stooped and, sliding his strong beer claw under the Englishman's arm, pulled him to his feet.

The ground on the far side of the peak was whiter and the snow more compact. Thankfully, long grooved concrete steps marked the way. The Agent clasped the Englishman's arm and they took the first step down, leaving the demons and the angels of Golden Cap behind them.

They walked in silence, save for the winces and groans of the Englishman, who made a big deal of the descent. It wasn't fair to offer him a glimpse of the world and then take it away again. It set his expectations too high. Better never to have smelt again than to have had one brief revelation.

The Regional Crime Squad Detective Inspector punched in the number. 'Hello? One-three-nine. Ivan'. He looked round at the guilty faces peering back at him from around his desk. 'Close the bloody door, Willy, for Christ's sake.' The undercover officer leaned across without getting up and pulled the office door closed. The animated chattering of the surveillance team was reduced to a muffle.

'Good morning, Boss!' Ivan's unflustered, deep voice came to the phone. 'Congratulations!'

'Congratulations? What are you talking about Ivan? There were supposed to have been three tonnes!'

'Crikey, Boss. A thousand kilos of cocaine is pretty good going. And you've got the target. And you didn't lose the flash money. No shots fired. That's pretty good.'

'Save it, Ivan. There were supposed to be three tonnes – the biggest seizure of cocaine ever.'

'Yes, Sir.'

'Now, have you heard anything?'

'No, Sir.'

'Tell me more.'

'Yes, Sir. From the moment the strike went in, the phones have gone silent. Nothing. If they're communicating, it's not on any handsets that we know.'

'And Joe?'

'Still unidentified. He's never made a call before. First mention of him was this morning.'

'Shit.'

'Have you arrested him, Boss?'

'No, we haven't fucking arrested him, Ivan. We don't know who the fuck he is or where the other two tonnes of cocaine are.'

'No, Sir. I'll keep monitoring, Sir, but….'

'Who said it would be three thousand kilos?' The Detective Inspector had dropped the phone and was talking to the room.

'The target said….' It was Willy who had tried to speak.

'What did he say? How can there only be one tonne?' The Detective Inspector stood up and shook off his jacket. He pulled at his underarm holster and it unfastened with an elasticated snap. 'Fuck,' he said, shaking his fingers, before dropping the heavy holster and revolver onto his desk.

There was a fumbled knock at the door and a young Detective Constable, wearing jeans and a t-shirt, his covert radio swinging under one arm, his holster and revolver strapped under the other, walked in carrying a brown plastic tray filled with white ceramic mugs of tea. He was beaming. 'Tea, Boss?'

The Detective Inspector took a mug, slopping some of the thin tea onto his desk.

'Great result, eh, Boss?' the Constable grinned. 'Six months following that scrote with a gun under my arm. Never thought I'd get to stick it in his face and nick him with a tonne of coke. Didn't see that one coming this morning. Well done, Boss. The blokes are dead chuffed. Coming in for the debrief?'

'Why do you walk?' the Englishman asked the Agent.

'Cos I keep pinching things,' he replied, 'I can't stay where I've just ripped somebody off for a steak, can I?'

'Can't you stop pinching things?'

'I reckon I can't boy.'

'But you'll end up in prison.'

'I started off in prison, boy. No, they won't put me

inside for twenty quid's worth of dinner.'

'Twenty three quid.'

'Is that what it was? I knew I shouldn't have had that cheese. You gonna dob me in?'

'No. How could I do that? I owe you now.'

'Alright boy. I'll have another T-bone.'

'Don't you want to change your life?'

'I have changed me life, boy. Once, I'd have just nicked your rucksack.'

'Well, thanks for looking over the edge.'

'Do you want to change your life then, boy?'

'I didn't. But I do now.'

'What, coming back from the brink of death, and all?'

'Maybe. Maybe. But it might be to do with smelling the world just now.'

'It stinks, does it?'

'No. It smelt glorious to me.'

'But it must've stunk before if you want a new life. What do you do, boy?

'I'm a copper.'

'Like I'm an agent from MI6, boy?'

'No. Really. I am a copper.'

'A copper? Fuck me. I think I've lost my sense of smell. You don't have to dob me in, you can nick me yourself.'

'I won't be doing that.'

'Why not?'

'Because I'm clinging onto your arm sliding down a mountain in the snow wearing beach shoes and sporting a smashed in face. That's why not.'

'Fuck me. A copper.'

'But why did you start walking?'

'To clear me head, boy, to think. A man can think when he's walking. You can sort things out. It's the same speed as your brain. You get walking and your brain sorts it all out.'

'And what happens if you sort it all out? Will you stop?'

'I don't know boy. Why do you walk?'

'Same reason, I guess. To sort my head out.'

'A bit of walking ain't gonna sort that head out boy.'

'It's not that bad.'

'Not that bad? Why don't you wear boots?'

'I do wear boots. But I threw them over the cliff.'

'That's normal is it boy? You got a family?'

'Yes. I'm married. And with two girls, Linda and Katherine. They're…'

The Agent cut in, 'did you jump?'

'What do you mean, did I jump?'

'Did you want to kill yourself?'

The Englishman stopped walking and the Agent, holding onto his arm, also halted. The Agent was looking out to sea and the Englishman was again looking at the back of his grubby neck. The stream of sweat had dried and the pinkness of the skin was already fading as new deposits of grime were laid down. 'I did. But I couldn't make it,' the Englishman said.

The Agent turned his face towards the Englishman, who started to walk once more, looking ahead at the snowy coast. 'So what was you doing over the edge?'

'I slipped when I threw my boots over.'

'But you wanted to die boy? With a wife and two little girls waiting at home?'

'I don't know. I thought it was going to happen anyway,' the Englishman replied. 'Can't we change the subject?' he added, abruptly.

'Alright then, why was you spying on me yesterday?'

The Englishman, his head forward, glimpsed

sideways at the sprouting chin and the creased eyes under the greasy shade of the cap. 'I thought you were an MI6 agent following me.'

'Why?'

'Now that I don't know. That's the bit that needs sorting out.'

They walked side by side, the Englishman sliding here and there and clinging to the Agent's arm. Every so often they stopped to allow the Englishman to blow some more blood and mucus from his left nostril. Then he would sniff at the air and at the Agent's coat or bend to some plant, twig or clump of grass.

Presently they were back at sea level, crossing the River Char at the small town of Charmouth by way of a small arched wooden footbridge, slippery with its dusting of snow. Once over this, they stepped onto a bleak and empty car-park, with the tidy bungalows of the town displayed before them. The Agent stopped, looking out to sea. He pulled his arm away from the Englishman, who stood looking at his own gloved hands.

'Well, this is me boy,' the Agent said.

'What do you mean? I thought you were going on to Lyme Regis?'

'Did I say that? No, boy. This is me. You go on now.'

'But...'

'You don't need me boy. The coast path goes inland here and follows the road. It's boring as hell, but it's good walking for beach shoes.'

'I was going to buy you dinner,' the Englishman offered, hopefully.

'That's kind boy, but there's campsites here and places for me to be fed.'

'But…'

'I walk alone boy. That's me. That's how I deal with my head. Now you go and deal with yours. And bleeding good luck to you boy.'

The Agent turned and the Englishman threw himself on the old tramp and hugged him, a bloody, swollen cheek against a grubby and poorly shaved one. He was crying. The Agent stood with his hands by his sides and the Englishman came away and wiped his sore eyes. He held out a gloved hand, then removed his glove and offered his hand again. The Agent took the Englishman's hand in his beer claw, gave a brief shake, then turned and walked back the way he had come, crossing the little footbridge without looking back, his legs moving at the same speed as his brain.

CHAPTER TWENTY-ONE

The Agent had been right; the path between Charmouth and Lyme Regis did indeed follow the road inland. The Englishman trawled uphill, walking in the brown slushy gutter of an urban bypass. Though cold, the snow had turned to dirty surface water on the well used and gritted road. Lorries thundered past, much too close for comfort, and he was splattered by their spray. His espadrilles soaked up the black grimy water and his feet were sopping and bitterly cold. The low and weak sun disappeared behind a mass of snow-laden cloud. Though it was early afternoon, the sky was dark.

The Englishman felt very alone. Even as a pursuer the Agent had been company. The boots had even been company in their own way. His hatred of them had given him focus. Now they were probably far out to sea. His face and chest, which had obviously taken the brunt of the fall, hurt him. The rest of his body hurt less, but no part of him was pain-free. The coast path turned at last from the main road and ran haphazardly and very steeply through a little wood before emerging onto a golf course. Two pairs of golfers pottered around, perhaps looking for a lost ball. They looked freezing. The path cut straight across a bleak fairway and then emerged back onto the main road into Lyme Regis.

By the time he spilled out onto the promenade, any trace of blue sky had gone and the wind blew heavily into his face. The sea was brown and angry, pebbles crashing and rattling. He pulled up his hood, dipped his head against the wind and plodded west, watching the filthy espadrilles take their steps. Every so often he looked up, hoping for seaside fish and chips or pie and mash but, although there were a few people about, nowhere was open. Shutters were pulled up against the season and there wasn't a Christmas decoration in sight, save for an orange traffic cone that someone had shoved on top of a street sign.

At the very end of the promenade, a little café was open. It was a dismal box, almost as cold inside as it was out. Why would you open a café and not heat it? A smile-less girl, no older than Katherine, stood behind the counter in fingerless gloves and a coat. Her nose was pierced and the lobes of her ears had been disfigured by the insertion of two huge plastic hoops within the flesh itself. Her dyed black hair hung in ten or so grimy plaits and a dark mauve tattoo was edging out of her black roll neck jumper. Black eye liner and mascara turned her puffy eyes into lazy looking slits. She looked like a savage. There were no signs of any cooking, so the Englishman ordered two toasted teacakes with butter and a pot of tea. He was the only customer.

The girl disappeared and he sat down in the furthest corner from the door. He had taken his coat off, but now he put it on again, pulled up the collar and looked blankly out at the drab esplanade. A little grey puddle formed around his sodden feet.

'Yeah. Yeah. I got a customer, yeah. His face is all bleeding. No, I know. I thought she was going out with Daniel,' the girl's voice emanating from some unseen kitchen. 'Yeah. This customer, right...No, Daniel. He wants a toasted teacake. Yeah. No, two toasted teacakes. Yeah. No, I know where the toaster is. But I'm like, what's a teacake? Yeah, I know, but what is it? We don't do cakes, do we? What? Where do you put the butter?'

The Englishman got up and walked out. This is what he was coming back to. It started to snow as he climbed steeply up a bank with his back to the English Channel, before the path turned and ran once again with the sea to his left through some pleasant and level woodland.

He wondered where the Agent was and how he would spend the rest of the day and the night. Why had he turned back? He'd said he didn't go back. Just to give the Englishman a chance to get clear of him? Perhaps he was behind the Englishman even now. If he was, at least the Englishman had established that the Agent wasn't an agent and hadn't been following him. But why, then, was the Detective Chief Superintendent stalking him?

Had he intended to slip? The Englishman didn't like the idea of being a person who had tried to commit suicide. It was unbalanced. It was also like letting Elaine, Katherine and Linda think that they weren't enough or that they'd done something wrong. That wasn't fair, because it wasn't true. They were the perfect family and they'd done everything to support him. It was the Detective Chief Superintendent, not them. Had the revelation that the Englishman was not as good at his job as he thought he was really driven him to the brink of suicide? Further even, to actually attempt suicide? If it had, then he didn't like himself. There was no pride in letting someone do that to you. Thank God he hadn't gone through with it. The boots had saved his life. They had been warning him not to go any higher. And to think he'd pissed on them.

But could the Detective Chief Superintendent's words really have had that effect? Had the Englishman ever caused that reaction in someone who worked for him? He had had to tell people that they needed to improve their performance. Had he ever done it in such a way as to drive someone to take their own life? None of his officers ever had taken their own life. That was a relief, anyway. What a dreadful responsibility. But if he had ever made someone feel as ill, as low, as worthless and guilty as the Detective Chief Superintendent had made him feel, how terrible.

The way had become boggy and wet and his foot got stuck in thick mud. As he tried to pull it out, his espadrille was sucked off. The mud was black and oily, the type that used to have a strong pungent aroma, especially when the tide was out at Southend, when he was a boy. He grabbed a branch for balance and, standing with one foot on top of the other, he pulled the espadrille from the mud and held it to his nose. He touched the thick mud to each nostril and tried to suck in the smell.

The Englishman decided that he didn't want to die and that he had never wanted to die and that he hadn't attempted to commit suicide. He had been in a bad way, but when it came to it, he had not deliberately done anything to put his own life at risk. But why did his predicament go round and round and round in his head? Why did it never stop? And why was it somehow connected to his sense of smell?

Asking this question was enough. He understood. The rhythm of the walking through the level, sheltered forest had worked. His legs must have been going at the same speed as his brain. It was because he had no future.

He had been at the peak of his career. Not the beginning, not halfway up, he was at the peak. There was nowhere to go but down and he hadn't seen it. The moment was always going to come. The moment when he took the first step down. If the Detective Chief Superintendent had told him he wasn't any good ten years ago, he would have shrugged it off. Not lightly, but he would have done it. He would have had time. There were other senior officers who liked the Englishman. The Detective Chief Superintendent would have moved on and somebody new would have come in and the Englishman would have been off again. Or he'd have changed departments or forces, or looked for another job abroad. The options were endless. But the Detective Chief Superintendent had been callous. He had pushed the Englishman as he stood at the peak, nudged him so that he slipped and fell.

The Detective Chief Superintendent had been too impatient. The peak is only a little patch of scrubland and you don't spend much time up there. You have a look around, hopefully enjoying the view. Some people's peaks are probably so high that they're shrouded in mist and it's difficult to see your way down. But whoever you are, you're not there long. Some people might choose to go back down the way they've come, revisiting the sites they've enjoyed on the way up. That would be OK. But others, the Englishman imagined most people, would want to go on. They would come down another way, enjoying new experiences, new points of view, even new peaks. But if you don't give a man a chance to choose, if you push a man while he's at the peak, he slips and falls, or jumps. And if the peak is high enough, say as high as Beachy Head, it might be enough to kill him.

In the Far East, the Englishman had known that he was at the peak, but he hadn't yet entirely processed this thought. It was still in his unconscious mind. He hadn't yet said to himself, 'this is the highest I'll get in the police. What shall I do next?' He was enjoying himself up there. And he was damned good at it too. But he wouldn't have been there long. He knew others were waiting. He would have chosen his route. He had been a policeman for thirty three years and he'd loved his job. He'd really enjoyed the walk up. But he knew that the time for walking down was approaching. And that careless bastard had just shoved him off.

That's why the Englishman had feared Golden Cap. He didn't want to confront the peak question. He didn't know how he was going to deal with coming down. He had no future planned. It wasn't until he smelt the world that he knew that there was a future. He suddenly sensed the whole world below him in a fresh new way - an exciting, aroma filled kaleidoscope of options. And suicide definitely wasn't one of them. It didn't matter now if he never regained his sense of smell. For one brief moment, at the peak of his career, he'd smelt the entire world and anything that smelt that good had to have a future in it for the Englishman.

The Englishman brushed out from the woodland onto an exposed concrete road bridge on the edge of Seaton. The snow was so heavy that he could only just make out a row of terraced fisherman's cottages on the far side. He strode with his face into the wind, the cooling flakes soothing his hot wounds. The broad Esplanade was deserted but a string of coloured Christmas lights swinging in the wind hinted of a town that was enjoying the cold afternoon indoors, in front of a log fire, perhaps with a glass of wine and…and a hot buttered toasted teacake. He could almost smell it.

The woman on the reception at the Eyre Court Hotel looked at the Englishman without speaking. Her mouth opened to speak but it failed her.

'Ooh, your face,' she said at last.

'I slipped in these espadrilles,' he said, like a prisoner with unexplained facial injuries.

Nevertheless, as soon as he was in his room he headed for the bathroom mirror. He looked like a television image of an elderly victim of a serious assault, a photograph published to generate maximum sympathy in order to encourage witnesses to come forward. An oxygen tube wouldn't have looked out of place taped across his mouth or nose. The shape and colour of his face had changed; it was swollen and distorted, mauve, yellow and red. He saw his father's face, old and worn, and beaten - an ageing version of the boy who had been head butted by the Ringleader. He imagined the face he saw in the mirror being broadcast as part of a police appeal. Who would come forward on his behalf to finger the Detective Chief Superintendent as the assailant?

The reflection depressed him and he turned away. He'd had enough depression. Things had changed now. He wanted to look forward. He wanted the walk to end so that he could see Elaine and tell her about the future, how he had sensed that there was something out there for them. Two more nights and he'd be at home in

Exmouth, one further night and their flight from Singapore would arrive – Christmas Eve. Perhaps he should drive to Heathrow and meet them? No, it would be better to prepare the house for Christmas. He'd buy the tree and put up decorations. There would be practical things, too. The boiler might not light.

In the shower, the Englishman washed his damaged face and it felt good. He massaged his spongy aching cheeks, the sides of his nose and the tired temples with the tips of his fingers. He discovered little scratches and nicks and he washed the grime out of them. He lifted his face to the spray and enjoyed the sensation of the water pattering against the pain. He imagined the smell of jasmine oil and he and Elaine were sharing a massage room. Piped Eastern music tinkled in the background and candles shimmered everywhere. Slim brown fingers rubbed his hard-set shoulders, his sore bruised back, his tense buttocks, calves and feet. He forced open his happily tired eyes to see the slim dark girl remove the towel from Elaine's hips and he was happy indeed. If he could just go back there for a little while. If he could just spend a few more months at the peak. Not long, but long enough to say goodbye and to choose which way to come down. That would be enough; let him go back there just for a little while. He turned to let the hot water play on his tense neck muscles. As he bowed his head he saw that he was standing in swirls of diluted blood.

He touched his finger tip to his right nostril, the one that had bled so profusely at the time of the fall, and looked at the result. There was no sign of bleeding. Then he did the same with his left nostril and this time he found that there was a thin, mucussy blood there, though the bleeding had now stopped. Perhaps he'd been massaging blood from his sinuses out through the nostril – was that possible? He resolved to monitor the situation and to go to hospital if necessary. He was too tired, hungry, thirsty and … happy. He was too happy to spend half the night in Casualty with the Christmas drunks, especially knowing that he looked like one.

He couldn't sit in the hotel restaurant frightening all the guests, so he found a kebab shop close to the hotel and took away a large doner and chips with extra chilli sauce and pickled jalapeños on the kebab and too much salt and vinegar on the chips – a feast for the taste buds. He hadn't had a kebab for years. The streets were now thick with brilliant white snow, two or three inches, and more was falling. The lights of the shops shone out yellow and warm and the dark silhouettes of evening shoppers conjured up a Dickensian romance. He started up Fore Street to try and find an off-licence to buy himself too much beer, but a sudden slip caused him to nearly fling his supper into the air and he lost interest in the idea. He had done enough slipping for today. He sat on his bed scoffing, plotting a future and enjoying English speaking television.

He was so tired that his eyes were closing even before he had finished eating. Rousing himself, he fished in his rucksack for his camera, but couldn't find it. He unzipped the many pockets one at a time, patting and probing them before putting on his glasses and double checking.

'The old bastard,' he said aloud, 'the smelly old git. The thieving bastard's stolen my camera.'

CHAPTER TWENTY-TWO

When the Englishman awoke there was blood on his pillow and in his mouth the cloying morning after taste of the kebab. Somewhere below him there was the slight whiff of bacon frying. Bacon! He sat up and fluids moved in his face and the smell was gone. But he had detected it, just a hint of it, he was sure he had, just a tiny hopeful waft. Would this be how it would happen – a slow, step by step, scent by scent recovery to a full sense of smell? Hints of taste, followed by set-backs, and then a flavour breakthrough? He would settle for that. As he showered he tried to smell the shampoo and as he ate his breakfast, he considered every bite, sniffing and ruminating, unsure as to whether he had picked up real flavour or not, confusing his sense of taste with his sense of smell, desperate for signs that he was making progress.

Outside the snow fell and the high tide dragged Seaton Bay's long shingle beach Eastwards in a clamour of stone and wash. The path climbed steep steps beside a sad looking café that hunched under the cliff for protection from the elements. At the top of the climb, despite what should have been the obvious nature of the route – just head West with the sea on your left – the Englishman instantly got lost. He was standing in a housing estate looking at his map when an elderly woman approached him. She wore no hat and her brushed back cotton white hair was almost invisible against the white background.

'Lost the coast path, my love?' she asked and, without waiting for an answer, said, 'follow me, darling. They've moved it.'

The Englishman couldn't keep up with her and neither, it transpired, could her dog, which pattered up to its scraggy knees in the snow behind them.

'Every day I bring the dog up here,' she was saying, as she battled her way in her wellington boots up an extremely steep and narrow lane. She was going so fast she was throwing up a fine white spray. The Englishman had to jog just to keep her in view. 'He says I shouldn't do it anymore, but the dog likes it.'

The Englishman looked back at the expressionless dog. He couldn't tell one way or another. 'There's nothing wrong with your lungs, is there?' he called, stopping to breath for a second and to unfasten his coat.

'Eh?' she called back, and then, 'come on!' and she sped on.

He ran up the hill to her. They moved from the steep lane onto a footpath with railings on the cliff edge. The dawdling dog was out of view, but the Englishman supposed he knew the routine. Then they were overlooking the pretty village of Beer and at last she stopped. Deep concrete steps led down to a narrow cutting that emerged onto the beach. Beyond it, a neat row of stone cottages leant into each other for support on a precipitous track parallel with the coastline. The rustic charm was self evident, but the climb looked long and dull.

'This is how far I come,' she said, and pointed to a bench.

The Englishman plonked himself on it. 'It's beautiful. Is this your bench?' But he said it to no-one; she had already turned and was hurtling back. She passed her dog on the way. It continued towards the Englishman, cocked a leg to the bench and, with a faraway look cast towards the sea, urinated on his espadrilles, warm and yellow. Then it turned and trundled after its ancient mistress.

The Englishman clambered sideways, down to the village, his hips and knees jarring. There was a bin into which dog owners could deposit dog mess and The Englishman posted the soiled espadrilles there. Then he was instantly climbing back up again. The old lady's pace had made him hot and, in spite of the heavy snow, he felt that he would have been better in shorts and tee-shirt. He was gasping and steaming by the time he settled into the exposed cliff-top section that would take him to Sidmouth. There would have been wonderful coastal views here on a clear day.

There was no shelter on the high cliff-top. The strong westerly wind blew the flakes against him as a blizzard. Only the fact that he was now walking in soft, deep, fresh snow enabled the Englishman to keep upright, but his feet were soaking and cold, his toes numb. He almost wished the old lady's dog would return and warm them. The path weaved between white dusted bushes as it descended towards Branscombe Mouth. The Englishman reached into the snow here and there, breaking off little snippets of shrubbery and holding them to his freezing nose. Nothing, but that might just be the cold - even rotting murder victims didn't give off much aroma inside the freezer drawers of a mortuary. Where the uneven hedgerow disappeared, so too did the path, for there was now no trace of it whatsoever through the snow. Keeping the sea to his left but steering a course well away from the edge, he trudged on. In places the slope was too steep to walk and he crouched down and slid on the soles of his string shoes and backside. In this manner it was not long until he was crunching awkwardly across Branscombe beach, the pebbles digging painfully through the thin string of the espadrilles like the knuckles of a Singaporean masseuse on a tender neck.

He felt well and he could have walked on and upwards, but he decided that he had ignored the Marine's advice too much over the last couple of days, so he stopped in the lee of an upturned boat for a ten minute break, a swig of warm tea and a change of socks and shoes.

He took his flask from the rucksack and started to sip. A couple of years earlier, a container ship had run aground here, its cargo infamously washing up on the beach. Infamous, because the tiny hamlet had been invaded by tens of thousands of treasure hunters desperate to get their hands on the booty. It had been a pretty lawless and indecently greedy affair. It had puzzled the Englishman how a modern ship could founder off the coast of England in the twenty first century, but looking out at the cruel sea today, he could easily understand how difficult navigation might be.

Turning his gaze back to the beach, he was surprised to see another lone walker sitting not far off, doing exactly the same as he was, sitting behind a boat for shelter, steaming cup to lips, rucksack and flask to one side. The Englishman hadn't seen any footprints at all today and so was certain the walker hadn't been in front of him. Only yesterday he would have seen him as a threat, as a pursuer, part of the Detective Chief Superintendent's plot. Now he saw only a young man enjoying the snowy wilderness, perhaps clearing his head after an office Christmas party. The walker acknowledged the Englishman with a silent nod through the snow and he returned the gesture.

The Detective Chief Superintendent must have had a motive for shoving the Englishman aside. Was it simply malice? The Ringleader had acted out of malice when he'd head-butted the young copper in the face. There hadn't been any need to do it. He and his gang could easily have run away with their loot, without smashing the young copper's face.

Soon, he was back on his feet and struggling upwards again, the sea to his back. The lone walker was in front of him. Halfway up the slope the path turned into a dense thicket and resumed its westward course. The trees were thin and spindly, but there were many of them and, leafless as they were, they shut out both light and snow. It was remarkably dark. The walker shuffled through the narrow and ill defined path ahead of him.

The Desk Officer might be malicious. Even at O'Raugherty's funeral there was something in the way the bastard had slid his empty beer glass to be filled that made the Englishman seethe. He was a bloody Detective Constable, for Christ's sake! The Englishman wouldn't have dared even to speak to a Detective Superintendent when he was a DC, let alone assume that the senior officer would buy him a drink. Thank Christ he was at the end of his career, it wasn't the same anymore. "The job's fucked," that's what policemen say. "It wasn't like this when I joined up, the job's fucked."

The little wood had darkened still further, but he still glimpsed the walker ahead of him. He had looked back at the Englishman once or twice.

The Englishman could hear the Desk Officer saying the job's fucked. He was exactly the type of person to use the expression. Someone who hadn't actually done much. The Englishman himself had been a desk officer once, and had enjoyed it, but to make a career of it? That was someone avoiding the sharp end. The Desk Officer had cultivated a deliberate air of experience and authority, he led you to believe that he'd been at the sharp end. He knew everyone and operational names rolled from his tongue. That's what irritated the Englishman about the desk officer: he'd not done his bit and he pretended he had. He'd sat at a desk and taken the glory for other people's work and connived to maintain his position there. The way he bandied about O'Raugherty's Operation Airtight was typical.

'There's been a bomb!'

The Englishman scrabbled around on the bedside cabinet for his reading glasses. Elaine murmured and turned her back. The air-conditioning was rattling and a large floor-fan whirled like a helicopter. He had been negotiating for the release of the children; Linda was desperately thirsty.

'Are you there? There's been a bomb.' The Desk Officer's voice was urgent.

The Englishman stumbled out of the noisy room and into the oppressive, damp heat of his office. He fell naked into his desk chair and switched on his computers: one official one on which he would receive the classified message about the bomb and the other his laptop, on which he could search Reuters and the other news agencies to see what they had discovered.

'What time is it? It's one o'clock in the morning!' Still pressing the phone to his ear, he got up from the office and pranced into the kitchen. The drinking water bottle stood empty on its dispenser; he had been too lazy to change the heavy 15 litre beast before going to bed. He picked up the kettle, gave it a little shake and switched it on. The skin across his shoulders was already coated in a smear of slimy sweat.

Back in his office, his laptop had booted into life, but the secure computer was sluggishly resisting waking up. He found the air-conditioning remote control on his desk and pointed it vaguely towards the ceiling. There was a bleep, then a long pause before the unit clattered into a semblance of life.

'Are you there? I need to know about a bomb.'

'Yes. You said. OK. I've got a pen. Tell me about it.'

'There's been a bomb in a church in Indonesia. A small home-made incendiary device In Klaten, Central Java.'

'Another one? In the middle of the night?'

'No, not in the middle of the night. It was earlier today.'

'Or yesterday, if you happen to be six hours ahead. How many people were injured? Anyone killed?'

'Not that we know of here in London. That's what we need you to find out. And we think it might be linked to a similar device in Mindanao. So we need a report on it before I finish late-turn reserve.'

'Mindanao? You mean in the Philippines?'

'That's right. You do know the area you cover, don't you?'

'Don't you start. Of course I know my patch. But Klaten to Mindanao…' he studied the map of the region above his desk, 'that's like Kiev to…Paris. It's got to be fifteen hundred miles. What makes you think they're linked?'

'The motive, they both seem to be Islamist terrorism, and the type of bomb – they're both home-made incendiary devices. So CTU needs a report, with photographs of the devices and your analysis, by 10 pm.'

'I can get photographs of the Indonesian device sent to me tomorrow, once Detachment 88 officers get to work, but I might not be able to get photos of the Filipino device for a couple of days. Maybe not at all.'

'No. The Detective Chief Superintendent wants the information this evening. He wants me to call him at home once I've received it. You'd better get hold of your contacts tonight. Do you know any of them well enough to get them out of bed?'

'I'm not getting anyone out of bed to discuss a near harmless incendiary device that was discovered at a remote church yesterday. It can wait until tomorrow.' The hiss of the secure computer's cooling fan suddenly stopped and the screen came to life.

'Is that what I should tell the boss?'

The Englishman tapped in his password. 'Wait. The secure line's up. Where does the information come from that links the two?'

'It comes from our analysis. There's no report on the secure system yet.'

'And the Mindanao bomb. When was that?'

'That was on the 4th.'

'Five days ago.'

'And analysis suggests that it's linked to the Klaten church bombs.'

'Whose analysis?'

'Analysis of all the available information to date. That's why a report from you is so important. To confirm that such a link exists. The Detective Chief Superintendent wants to brief the Commander on it first thing tomorrow.'

'If you remember, I did a report on the Mindanao bomb the day it happened. My sources are unable to provide a photo of the remains of the device. It's part of the ongoing campaign for a separate Muslim state in the Southern Philippines. It has nothing to do with churches in Indonesia.'

'Then you need better sources. My analysis suggests that there is footage of the Filipino device.'

'Your analysis. *Your* fucking analysis. You've been sitting, bored shitless, searching the internet, haven't you? You've found that video clip of a bomb in Mindanao…'

'There is some open-source video footage available. My initial assessment is that it's genuine footage of the Mindanao bomb. '

'Whilst my initial assessment is that the police officers seen in that clip are wearing Thai uniforms.'

'During Operation Airtight Detective Superintendent O'Raugherty said that it was my analysis that…'

'How long have you been doing that job?'

'Fourteen years. There's nothing I don't know about Southeast Asia.'

'Have you ever been here?'

'I made a field visit when I started in my role. But my analysis since…'

'…consists of the internet and pins in a map of the world.'

'I'm the longest serving desk officer.'

The Englishman's thoughts, the level ground and the shelter from the snow provided by the thicket had enabled him to walk at a good pace and he had all but caught up with the walker, who continued to glance back from time to time. Walkers liked solitude, they didn't like it when they fell in with another travelling at the same pace and in the same direction. If they'd wanted company they'd go and play golf. The Englishman could see that it was time to overtake and, with the walker just a few paces ahead of him, he accelerated.

He was at her shoulder when she turned – a woman of about his own age. Her mouth was agape. She raised her arm as if to strike him and a terrific screeching sound deafened him - a rape alarm.

'Get back! You ugly man!' she shrieked.

'Wait, please, please. I'm not a rapist…' He had to shout at the top of his voice just to be heard above the electronic squeal. He held his hands high.

'Get back!' she screamed. Holding the rape alarm aloft, she was waving a pepper spray in the other hand. Strands of grey hair blew out around her hood. Her face was angular, her features sharp and clear, lips and eyes without make up. Her knees were bent, her slim legs planted wide apart.

'Don't, please!' he shouted, 'I'm harmless.'

'Get back….,' she growled, her voice barely audible.

He felt like ducking below the line of fire, ripping the spray out of her hand with a satisfying snap, crackle and pop of her knuckles and punching her in the face, like a rubber terrorist. 'I'm injured,' he pleaded, 'that's why I'm ugly. I'm a policeman.'

'Get back….,' she snarled, and began to edge past

him, in the direction from which they'd come. He obliged by moving past her in the direction they'd been travelling a few moments ago. The path was narrow and, to keep a safe distance from each other they were obliged to squeeze through the undergrowth. As he stepped back onto the path, the Englishman saw that it had come to an abrupt end. He was standing on the edge of a ravine, barely visible from only a few paces away, its banks thick with the same spindly trees.

The alarm switched itself off. 'You've been following me. Why?' The pepper spray was ready to fire if his answer didn't satisfy.

Now he was the pursuer? 'I wasn't following you. I'm on the coast path.'

The spray jerked. The Englishman stood with his hands stretched above his head. 'You're not. The coast path doesn't come into these woods.'

'I'm sorry. Truly sorry. I didn't mean to frighten you. I wasn't paying attention. I followed you assuming you were on the coast path. I'm really sorry.'

She studied him for some moments.

'You don't look like a policeman,' she said.

'No. I know. I slipped on the snow yesterday. I've had a few very strange days.'

At last she dropped her arm. He kept his hands in the air. 'Do you want me to stay here while you walk away?' he offered, 'I know how frightening it must have been to feel hemmed in like that.'

'How do you know?' she barked.

He thought about trying to explain how he felt, at the peak, with nowhere to go. 'My wife and daughters. They were victims of a prowler.'

'The path's back there,' she said, and began to walk the way they'd come. He guessed he should follow.

'Can I put my hands down, now?'

'Do what you like.'

'So why were you on this path, if you know the way?' he ventured.

'I live in Branscombe. I wander all over these hills.'

'Then you knew all along that it was a dead end?'

'Of course.'

'Then you let me get too close.'

'What do you mean?'

'You waited too long to confront me. By the time you did, you had nowhere to go.'

'OK…'

'Then you were too close to me with the spray. You need to maintain a safe zone – a distance that gives you a chance to think and react. And to run away. I could easily have grabbed your wrists,'

'You didn't though.'

'That's because I'm not a rapist.'

'All men are rapists.'

The Englishman said no more. They emerged at the edge of the thicket onto the white hillside. There, at the junction of the two paths, was an acorn and an arrow pointing up the hill. It was clearly visible from the direction they had come from the beach. Without speaking, she pointed to the sign, then to the hill. The Englishman obeyed and did not look back to see which way she went.

It was an odd incident. How many women carried rape alarms and pepper sprays when walking on the hillsides of Devon? Why hadn't she said much earlier that he was walking the wrong way? It would have saved his tired legs and prevented the unpleasant confrontation. Why did she say all men were rapists? How must she have suffered to live her life like that –

constantly wary of men and carrying her weapons with her? She must have had them to hand. She must walk along, fingering them in her pockets. Forever a victim, men her pursuers. Somehow she misinterpreted the scent of a man to be the fear of the stalker about to attack. Why did she walk? Was it to sort her head out? Can you do so, carrying with you constant reminders of your nightmares?

He could see a parallel between the woman and himself. Pursued, trapped and angry – that was how he felt too. But whatever had happened to her, or whatever she perceived might happen to her, had taken over her life. She saw herself as a victim. And this galvanized the Englishman more than ever; he would not see himself as a victim. The Detective Chief Superintendent had broken him and was stalking him still, but the Englishman would look forward to a new life, not constantly behind him.

The coastal path soon turned inland and remained level for some two or three miles. There were now few places which weren't covered in white. The landscape had become Alpine and the Englishman felt the excitement of a child at being the first to make his footprints in the fresh snow. Only the beach and the sheer sections of cliff face seemed to evade the blanket. The Englishman felt closer to Scott in this environment and he wondered what the comparison was. What was it like to be so much colder than this? It was unimaginable; especially, perhaps, for a man now used to the Tropics. The Englishman wished that he'd written a journal. Something for the girls to read one day. We need to write down our stories, he thought. Without them no-one would know about Scott, and the Marine from Mandalay might as well never have existed.

He was now descending some steep, zigzagging steps, barely discernible through the whiteness. Going down was much harder than going up. His tired joints seemed to have lost all lubrication and his hips, knees and ankles ground drily together. When would this bloody holiday end? Complaining at each step, he eventually slid onto the pebbly beach of Weston Mouth. Sidmouth was just two or three miles away.

The Detective Chief Superintendent had been in Abbotsbury and in Chideock; he'd only not been in Seaton because he thought that the Englishman was heading to Sidmouth yesterday. Surely he would be in Sidmouth today? But why? And what would the Englishman say? What had changed since their last meeting? The Detective Chief Superintendent was kicking him out. The Englishman had been through a personal hell, but nothing had changed for his boss. Nothing. And when he thought about what he had to tell Elaine, Katherine and Linda, the Englishman saw that his experience of the last few days amounted to nothing.

Everything had happened inside his head. How could that be explained, even to a loving wife? So his sense of smell had returned. To Elaine and the girls this would mean he could taste his food, not a sense of the hope and opportunity of a future outside the police. What would he say to Elaine that was any different from what he was always going to have to tell her about his under-performance at work? "I've got really bad news Elaine. They say I'm no good at my job and we've got to come back to England. I've felt pretty bad about it, but now I feel a lot better. And my sense of smell came back for a few seconds." That's what it amounted to. Elaine hadn't had a week's walking holiday to get her mind around it. Neither had the girls. They would have to come home, find new schools, new jobs and start again. They would be devastated. It was all very well him coming to a unilateral decision that it was time to start afresh, time to leave the police, to look forward, but he had his family to think of. Even the Agent could see that.

There was only one sensible option: to ask the Detective Chief Superintendent for another chance. The Englishman would apologise and say that he'd had time to reflect and he could now see that he had been underperforming, of course he had. They could prepare an action plan and the Englishman would sign it and promise to improve. He would accept the evidence that the Detective Chief Superintendent had come up with and he'd knuckle down and he could have his job back. He would be stolid in his relationship with the desk officer – he would get on with him at all costs. Then he wouldn't even have to tell Elaine about any of this at all. The girls could stay at school. He and Elaine could enjoy the rest of their posting. He might not even have to retire. It was the pragmatic thing to do.

But what if the Detective Chief Superintendent had already found the evidence he needed? What if it was serious? He might consider that the Englishman was in breach of the discipline code, that he'd committed a disciplinary offence, that it was more than under-performance. That made a lot of sense. The Englishman was in more trouble than he thought. They had uncovered evidence of a disciplinary offence – neglect of duty, or bringing the service into disrepute. Yes, it made sense. The Detective Chief Superintendent was required to serve the notices in person. That was it. That enquiry he had refused to do in the middle of the night? It was possible - disobedience of a lawful order. Perhaps they were going to suspend him?

The more the Englishman trudged, the more sense it made. His brain was running at the same speed as his legs and his thought processes were clear. Walking helped like that, even the Agent had said it. The Englishman had finally sorted his head out, he had solved it at last. Like most puzzles, it was obvious now that the last piece had fallen into place. Of course, he had committed a disciplinary offence and the Detective Chief Superintendent was here to serve notices on him. They might dismiss him, never mind retirement. They were allowed to prevent him from retiring whilst they investigated a disciplinary offence, weren't they?

Before the Englishman knew it, he was descending Salcombe Hill into Sidmouth. It was the final night of his holiday and there was some small comfort for him in the thought that tomorrow he would sleep at home in Exmouth for the first time in a year.

CHAPTER TWENTY-THREE

It was three days before Christmas and Dukes Hotel in Sidmouth was busy with festive drinkers. Two or three groups of workers from offices or local factories were celebrating. Buxom ladies were resplendent in sparkling black evening dresses, sheer black tights and patent black high heels, gleaming. They flirted with the men and gossiped with their friends and pulled crackers and wore paper hats and were happy.

'So what are you doing for Christmas?' they asked each other.

The question forced the Englishman to consider his own Christmas. He was a guilty man, guilty of some wrong-doing at work which he had yet to fully understand. But worse, he was guilty of weakness; he had enjoyed a thirty-three year career in which he had been successful and popular, yet the very first time that this view of himself had been challenged, he had crumpled. He had sunk rapidly into depression, terror even and, worst of all, this terror had pushed him towards suicide. He had been unable to cope, weak. He wanted to see his family, of course, but he wanted to embrace them and cry with relief and self-pity. This was how his Christmas reunion would be.

The Englishman did not resent these happy people their Christmas, indeed, he enjoyed watching their uncomplicated fun. He sat alone at an inconspicuous small table and watched and listened. He ate a beef and ale pie with mash potato and vegetables. Pies – they were a thing to be admired. How he had loved pies. This one looked fine, though he preferred pies that had pastry walls and a bottom and weren't just a lid. The saltiness of the pastry and the even saltier taste of the chunky pie filling were satisfying and the smooth mashed potato was pleasingly heavy and dense. But he didn't eat many of the vegetables, they seemed to lack any taste at all and would have gone just as well with custard as they did with the gravy. He couldn't sit still. He sipped smooth draught bitter and it went straight through him so that he had to carefully arrange his reading glasses, beer and coat to save his table from being taken each of the several times that he went to the toilet. He constantly blew at his incompetent nose and prodded the swellings below his eyes with his finger tips.

The bread and butter pudding was wonderfully sweet with a firm gelatinous texture and he enjoyed it, but the beer tasted wrong afterwards and the Englishman went outside. It had stopped snowing. Sidmouth's narrow streets were busy with pedestrians. He walked up and down, thinking that he might buy some small trinkets for the girls, things he could carry in his rucksack, but he didn't see anything he liked. He bought some ibuprofen and a Mars bar in a small Co-op and went back to the hotel. He stood waiting for a few minutes whilst the busy bar staff served Christmas groups ordering huge trays of drinks, but then he went up to his room instead.

Just before midnight he telephoned reception to be

told that no one had left any messages for him. He went to bed, but his nose and eyes hurt him and he couldn't sleep. He sat up and rubbed his face, working his fingers up over his cheeks to the base of the swollen eye sockets. He was able to push quite hard, even into the pain. It helped to remove the dull ache by causing other sharp pains with his fingertips. His eye lids were dry and heavy and he pushed them into his eyes and it felt good. Running his fingers down the side of his nose, he pressed into the nasal cavity. In his right nostril there was a hard lump.

He took a wad of tissue from the toilet and blew gently down his right nostril. A terrific and dangerous pain, like a stab of light, pierced his right ear. He placed his finger tips on either side of his nose, high up, close to the corners of his eyes and dragged them downwards. The right finger definitely passed over a lump. He did it again. This time the lump moved slightly downwards. He was now able to feel a beginning of it when he ran his finger down the outside. Again coming in from the corner of his eye, he pushed at it and it moved downwards again. He blew gently, the lump moved and there was only a slight pain in his ear. Blowing and massaging, he eventually eased a dense, heavy slug of dried blood and mucus from his right nostril. It was an inch long. He stared at it on the piece of tissue with revolted fascination. It was as if a pathologist had just removed a bullet from his body. He wanted to bag it up and exhibit it but, instead, he flushed it down the toilet.

It was the first thing he thought of when he awoke the next morning. What difference had it made? It must have made a difference. It was the shower gel he smelt first. Then his deodorant. Things that were manufactured to be smelt. He had no idea why, but there was no repeat of the all encompassing aromatic experience on top of Golden Cap. He didn't pick up subtleties transmitted from great distances, he detected strong smells that were close to him. In the corridor there was a waft of some strong cleaning fluid and the breakfast room, a large conservatory where last night's Christmas parties had been sitting, smelt of cooking oil.

The Englishman approached his breakfast like a gourmet, tasting things carefully and slowly, taking his time to chew, looking at the glass panels of the conservatory roof as he came to a decision, trying everything there was to try. Porridge – no taste, just the sweetness of the sugar. Wholemeal toast – yes, he could detect a sumptuous wheatiness which he'd forgotten long ago, reminding him of All Bran - he used to like that but it just became little sharp tasteless sticks after his nose had been broken. Bacon and egg he couldn't taste at all, just the normal saltiness of the bacon. He could clearly taste the herbs in the sausages. Marmalade was simply delectable. He had continued to enjoy marmalade all these years, and, if it were a good one, he could detect both sweet and bitter tangs. But he had completely forgotten that it had a third taste, a subtle fruity roundness, the taste of oranges.

The tea was sublime. It was a new aroma, or at least one he had no recollection of: fragrant, leafy, floral, like fresh cut grass with added citrus. He had visited tea plantations in Puncak, just south of Jakarta, and he could see the slim women in their wide brimmed conical hats, baskets on their backs, as he sipped. It was the most refreshing thing he'd ever tasted. He asked the waitress what the tea was, anticipating that she would say Assam or Ceylon, English Breakfast, even. He needed to know so that he could buy it again. She told him it was PG Tips.

As he was pouring his second cup, the Detective Chief Superintendent bustled through the doorway. He looked briefly around the bar and sat down at the Englishman's table. He was casually dressed – a dark woollen overcoat over an open neck shirt and jeans. He hadn't shaved. He looked much older than he did in his chalk stripe suit. The Englishman put down his tea and stood up.

'Good morning, Sir. This is a surprise.' He smiled and held out his hand.

'Good morning to you too, Superintendent,' he shook the Englishman's hand heartily. 'Don't be silly, sit down. Now can I buy you breakfast?'

'No thanks, Sir. I've just finished.'

'Another tea, then?'

'Good idea, Sir. The tea's delicious.' The Englishman started towards the bar.

'Stay there, stay there. I'll order.'

The Detective Chief Superintendent walked away to order and the Englishman sat down. As he lifted his tea his hand shook.

The senior officer came back grinning. 'If you only knew the trouble I've had trying to track you down, you old sod!' He pulled an envelope from his overcoat and handed it to the Englishman. 'Here you go. You must be expecting this.'

The Englishman's cup rattled on its saucer as he lowered it to the table to take the notice. He put on his reading glasses and picked at the sealed envelope with inefficient fingers.

'Let me be the first to congratulate you.' The Detective Chief Superintendent held out his hand and again gave the Englishman's a strong, collegiate shake.

'Congratulate me?'

'You don't know? I thought you knew. QPM. The New Year's Honours list will be published next week. If I'd have known I'd have caught you at the conference. You're getting the Queen's Police Medal! Congratulations, eh?! Well done indeed, Superintendent.' As he spoke, a hint of some unidentified dank malodour pulled at the Englishman's novice nostrils.

The envelope finally came open. The Englishman took in a deep breath as he unfolded the single sheet, which fluttered in his hands as if in a breeze. The letter bore the crest of the Metropolitan Police Service and was signed by the Commissioner. It was addressed to the Englishman at his office in the British Embassy. The Commissioner asserted that his name would be on the New Year's list for those receiving the Queen's Police Medal for Distinguished Service.

'And this is why you've been trying to track me down?' His thin voice cracked as he spoke.

'Yes, of course. Why else?'

The Englishman's voice came loud and sharp. 'I thought it might have had something to do with our little chat on Friday. About me under-performing.'

'Ah yes, well. In a way it does. That's why I was so keen to meet you myself.' He shuffled closer, putting his arm across the back of the Englishman's chair. The conspiratorial huddle that he'd been in with the Desk Officer. As he spoke, the suspicion of a reek that the Englishman's new nose had picked up earlier came to him with revolting clarity - halitosis. The Detective Chief Superintendent had appallingly bad breath. 'You see. I didn't have all the information,' he confessed.

'You bloody well didn't, did you?'

'Don't be like that. I'm trying to explain. If I'd have known that the Ambassador had nominated you for the QPM, I'd have approached things a little differently.'

'The Ambassador? He nominated me for the QPM?'

'Well, it turns out you've had a bit of a career. I thought you'd come off uniform, you see.'

'The Ambassador?'

'Yes. This isn't easy for me, you know. He apparently felt that you were doing rather well, you see. A breath of fresh air. And he made a call and someone looked into your past, and well… - Congratulations!' He smiled widely. His breath smelt like oily estuary mud.

'Have you any idea what you've put me through?' The Englishman's words were clipped and tense.

'What I've put you through? You've been on holiday, don't forget. This has been awful for me, realising I'd made a bit of a faux pas, then trying to track you down all week to put it right. I even called Elaine out there and told her you'd got it.'

'A bit of a fucking faux pas?' The Englishman placed his hands on the table, either side of his tea cup. 'So you've been following me around just so that you can set things straight?'

'I need to put right what I said on Friday. I need you to go back to the Far East.'

'Why? Because the job can't do without me?' the Englishman asked.

'I can't sack a bloke who's just got the QPM, can I?'

'Why not? If there's evidence that I've under-performed, you should do the right thing.'

'But there's not any. You know that. Why should you and I fall out over someone else's mistake?' The Detective Chief Superintendent actually cuddled the

Englishman's shoulders. 'Eh?'

The Englishman pulled away, sliding his chair backwards a full three feet. 'Whose mistake? What are you talking about?' he asked.

'It was that bloody Desk Officer who told me you weren't up to it. You'll be pleased to know I've sacked him. Starts at Stoke Newington tomorrow. Late turn Christmas Day,' he sniggered.

'Was there any evidence?

'Against you? No, I've just said so. That's why the incompetent fool had to go. No place for him in CT.'

'No, against him.'

'Well of course there was. It was him. He told me that you weren't up to the job. He had to go. Him or me. It became quite clear on Friday afternoon that not only was there no evidence that you'd done a bad job, but that they're giving you a bloody medal for doing a good one!'

'And you just took the Desk Officer's word for it that I wasn't up to the job? He's a bloody DC!'

'I know. Sounds ridiculous in hindsight, doesn't it?' The Detective Chief Superintendent rolled his eyes playfully, 'but he's so experienced. And I'm new to CT, so he was really helpful.'

'Except he's a liar.'

'Well, so it turns out. That's why he had to go. He was undermining you and I have to be seen to have dealt with it.'

'You have to be seen to have dealt with it, do you? You don't feel that you should have dealt with it because it was the right thing to do?'

'Well. We all cover our arses don't we?' He looked surprised and confused. 'That's how we get to our rank, after all.'

'This is about saving your arse, isn't it?' he asked. 'It's got nothing to do with me at all.'

'Well. It's also about you. It just so happens that saving your arse saves mine too.'

The Englishman stood, blowing out a long puff of air. His eyes closed momentarily and he raked his fingers through his hair. For a few moments he stared out through the window at the snowy street. Then, sitting down again, he asked, 'how long have you been on Special Branch?'

'Nearly two years. I was on Community Policing. I came across on the Prevent ticket. Preventing Terrorism in Our Communities, you know. Everyone's doing it. You need counter-terrorism on your CV. When I heard you were from uniform, I thought you were the same as me. I didn't know you'd been a detective all your career.'

'That's why you don't know Blake.'

'Blake. Who's he?'

'Commander Blake. Retired SB. He's the owner of the bed and breakfast I was staying at two nights ago. You called there.'

'Blake Cottage. That silly old fool told me you were at Sidmouth last night.' The Detective Chief Superintendent lifted his own chair and once again shifted himself closer to the Englishman.

'That silly old fool is Commander Blake,' the Englishman said. 'He gave you a bum steer to give me a break - from you.' Then he added abruptly: 'What about the relationship problems you were so sure that I had?'

'There *were* relationship problems in your post. I should know. Partnership working is what I'm good at. It's what Preventing Terrorism in Our Communities is all about.'

'But I overcame them, didn't I?'

'Yes, according to the Ambassador, you did, yes.' He looked uncomfortably around the conservatory before continuing in his familiar, conniving manner. Again, the reek of his unwholesome insides wafted and hung in the space between their faces. 'Look. I know you won't think much of me for what I did. But I really need you to forget our little conversation on Friday and go back to Southeast Asia. This is my career. I won't go any higher than this. I can't afford to leave with a bad reputation. I'm looking for a job with the Foreign Office. I need counter terrorism experience on my CV.'

'And how will my going back help you?'

'It'd be like our little conversation never happened. Like I hadn't made that little faux...,' he hesitated, 'little fuck-up. You'd just go back to work and no-one would ever know any different. End of conference, your little walking break, Christmas and New Year with your sons, QPM, back to work in the embassy. No harm done, my career's back on track. What would the Commander say if you're suddenly not at work? He'll want to know why. He might even ask you. You might tell him the truth. Oh shit – don't do that, please.'

The Englishman did not speak and the Detective Chief Superintendent did not wait for him to.

'And what would the Foreign Office say if the man they recommended for the QPM is sacked by me? We can't upset the Foreign Office, for Heaven's sake, that's my next posting we're talking about. That'd be my career plan down the drain. This way, you get the medal, your job and the reflected credit comes my way. I'm your boss. If one of my officers gets the QPM, it makes me look good.'

'You're fucking unbelievable.'

'Look. You can't tell anyone about our conversation, alright? People will say I'm dishonest. People will say I was wrong to do what I did. I'll be finished.'

'You were dishonest. You told me there was evidence that I was under-performing.'

'Yes, but I was relying on that Desk Officer.'

'And what was his motive?'

'It was budgetary.'

'Budgetary?! Since when does a DC care about the budget? They can't spend it quickly enough usually!'

'The cutbacks are hitting hard. He came up with the idea. It was going to be much cheaper to put a constable into Southeast Asia than a superintendent. I thought it would look good to the Commander. Show him a bit of strategic planning and fiscal...'

'You were going to put that fucking malicious little shit bag into my post? You really have no fucking idea at all, do you?'

The Detective Chief Superintendent looked hurt. 'Well, it might not have been him. Anyway, that's all over now. He's gone and you've got the QPM. Will you take your old job back?'

'What about the budget?'

'Please?'

'You have no idea what you've put me through, have you? This has been the lowest week of my life. I have never felt as bad as this. I nearly...' The Englishman stopped.

'There won't be any evaluation.'

'You little bastard. You're a little, self serving shit bag. You know you haven't even said sorry?'

'Well, I do apologise.'

'You can't say it, can you?'

'Look I came all this way. I've had a terrible week trying to sort this out, worrying that I'd miss you or that you'd speak to someone about what I'd said. Thank God you didn't take your phone with you.'

'You make me sick.'

'Think of your family. Your boys - they've only just started to settle. You don't want to drag them back now. You'd be letting them down.'

'You bastard.'

'Will you go back to your post?'

The Englishman threw his hands up, clasped the back of his head, tipped back his chair and looked up at the ceiling, rocking precariously. Tipping forward, he looked at the letter again then sat contemplating, tapping the corner of the paper against his teeth.

'Yes, of course I'll go back,' he said at last.

'Great. That's marvellous then. Congratulations.' The Detective Chief Superintendent held out his hand and the Englishman shook it. 'I'll call you in the New Year then. Have a nice Christmas. Say hello to your wife and boys for me.' He was up and walking towards the door.

'They're girls.'

'What? Whatever. See you in the New Year.'

The Englishman watched him as he walked towards the door. 'I nearly died, for Christ's sake,' he said quietly, the words tumbling out broken, lacking clarity.

The Detective Chief Superintendent was just reaching out to pull the door open, when it swung abruptly into his face and the Agent barged in with his giant rucksack. He caught sight of the Englishman and strode untidily past the Detective Chief Superintendent as if he hadn't seen him.

'Bet you never thought you'd see me again, did you

boy?' A broad smile spread across his plucked cheeks.

'I smelt you a mile off.' The Englishman stood and moved towards his friend.

'Did your smell come back, boy? Well done! You couldn't have had a better Christmas present than that, could you boy?' There was a distinct Welsh lilt to his voice.

'No, I couldn't. Thank you.'

'Excepting maybe this, eh boy?' He held out the Englishman's camera. 'I seen the photos of your wife and that. I couldn't sell it after that. Knowing they was waiting on you to get back.' He looked into the Englishman's face with questioning, watery eyes.

The Englishman stared at the Nikon in the Agent's grubby palm and didn't know what to say.

'I'm trying to change, boy,' the Agent said, 'I'm sorry I took it.'

The Englishman took the camera and reached out for the Agent who shyly lifted his own arms. The two men hugged whilst the Detective Chief Superintendent stood speechless beside the door, his arms by his side, his mouth open. The Agent's greasy pong was almost pleasant in its honesty.

'Merry Christmas….Agent,' said the Englishman.

'Merry Christmas, boy,' the old tramp responded, as he eased himself out of the Englishman's grip.

'How did you find me?'

'The Commander here told me, boy,' he said, jerking his thumb towards the Detective Chief Superintendent at the door.

'Commander?' The Englishman looked towards the Detective Chief Superintendent.

'You ripped me off for twenty four pounds last night,' he whimpered.

The Agent turned towards the door. 'Never seen you in my life,' he said, contemptuously. His filthy lips parted in a smile as he looked back at the Englishman and said, 'Don't get too close to this one, boy. His breath stinks like a dog's arsehole!' And he was out into the snow, the heavy pub door slamming behind him.

'Call you after Christmas?' the Detective Chief Superintendent asked, rattling his finger and thumb like a telephone close to his ear.

There was a long silent pause as the Englishman looked first out at the disappearing old tramp and then into the enquiring face of the senior officer. 'No,' he said.

'What?' The Detective Chief Superintendent cocked his head to one side.

'No,' the Englishman reiterated, 'you can stick your fucking job right up your arse.'

The Detective Chief Superintendent's shoulders dropped and he shuffled a few paces nearer to the Englishman. 'What?! We just agreed. Your family – remember?'

'My family will stick by me. They always have. But you won't, will you? There is absolutely nothing I want from you.'

'Please?' He stepped forward as he spoke, gripping the Englishman's arm, his face once again close to the Englishman's. The stench was revolting, corrupt, the smell of a future that had nothing in it for the Englishman.

CHAPTER TWENTY-FOUR

The path followed the Esplanade to the West, hugged the beach for a while and then climbed steeply between the cliff top and the road to Budleigh Salterton. There was no snow falling, but the sky was cold and grey as if there were more yet to come. The broad expanse of grassland was thick with snow, potted with the footprints of walkers and dogs. Two boys were throwing snow balls at passing cars, easy targets as they tried to get traction on the narrow road, wheels spinning. At the top of the open section the path turned onto the road itself for a few slippery metres and then disappeared into woodland. As he stepped onto the road, a snowball hit the Englishman on the back of the head. He scooped up his own and hurled it back towards them.

'Fuck off!' one of them shouted. This is what he was coming back to.

Emerging from the woodland onto the very cliff edge, the Englishman stopped and admired the view east across the high brown cliffs towards Sidmouth, Golden Cap and beyond. Then he turned away from his past and headed west towards Exmouth and home.

It was Sunday lunchtime by the time that the process was completed and the Ringleader had been charged, fingerprinted and photographed. The Detective Sergeant was washing the fingerprint ink from his hands when the custody sergeant told him that the Ringleader's mother was waiting at the front counter for him.

She was carrying a foil covered plate. 'Can I give him his Sunday lunch?'

'How did you cook it without a kitchen?' the Detective Sergeant teased.

'I had to use my bleeding sister's. He's not a bad boy you know, and he'll probably be remanded in custody tomorrow, so the least I can do is cook his dinner for him. He sort of meant well when he gave me the nicked one, you know?'

'Do you want to take his dinner down to him? I'm sure the custody sergeant won't mind.'

'You're alright you are,' she said as he unlocked the door for her to enter the custody area.

They stopped in the charge room, where the custody sergeant had a quick look at the meal, scooped it unceremoniously onto a flimsy cardboard plate and put a plastic knife and fork on top. Whilst he was doing so, the Ringleader's mother spoke again.

'He's not a bad boy, you know, really. He's got a heart, but he's too aggressive. Maybe it's what he takes for his body-building. But he don't always like what he's done afterwards. I'll give you a for instance. He got nicked once for head-butting a young copper who was off duty. Broke his nose.'

The Detective Sergeant's breathing was suddenly shallow. 'I know about that,' he said.

'Well he's always regretted that. He said he didn't

need to do it.'

'That was me,' the Detective Sergeant blurted out.

The Ringleader's mother studied his face, as if looking for the marks, but she did not speak.

It was the custody sergeant who spoke next. 'You can take his dinner down to him love, if you like. Follow me - you can have a quick visit.'

The Detective Sergeant left them to it and, scraping up his papers from the charge desk, he wandered back towards the CID office. When he arrived, his phone was ringing.

It was the custody sergeant. 'Your prisoner wants to talk to you.'

The Detective Sergeant turned wearily. It had been a long weekend and he wanted to get home and see his baby daughter. Five minutes later, he was turning the heavy iron key in the old cell door.

'You wanted to speak to me?'

'Yes, mate.' The Ringleader sat on the edge of his blue rubber coated mattress. His empty dinner plate lay on the concrete floor beside the stainless steel toilet. The plastic knife and fork were neatly placed side by side. Despite his huge frame he looked like a child sitting on his bed at home.

'I want to tell you something big.' The words came out awkwardly, slowly.

'I can't offer you any deals'

'No, I'm not after nothing Sarge. I just need to get something off me chest.' He said, and yawned.

'Do you mind if I sit down?' the Detective Sergeant asked.

The Ringleader shuffled along towards the toilet and pulled his grey blanket out of the way, allowing the Detective Sergeant to sit beside him on his bed. They sat at an angle, with their knees towards each other.

'Do you want a solicitor?' the Detective Sergeant asked.

'No. It ain't like that. My Mum says it was you.'

'It was me who what?'

'It was you what I head-butted. That time a few years ago. In the shopping centre. With the jeans.' He was talking to his lap, his head hanging. Patches of damp spread out from his arm pits across the tight tee-shirt.

The young copper was covered in blood, mucus and vomit, kneeling on a pile of jeans in the middle of a shopping centre on a Saturday afternoon, looking like a scrote.

'Yes, it was me,' he said.

'Well, I never had to do it,' the Ringleader said quickly and quietly, now looking down at the floor between his huge thighs, rubbing his bare toe across the polished concrete floor. His speech stalled for a moment as he sought the right words. 'We, I, er, I mean, I could've run'.

The Detective Sergeant did not reply. Yes, you could have run, he thought. You could have got away without breaking my nose. Without ruining every meal I've ever eaten since. You could have taken the jeans. But you wanted to hurt me. That's what you wanted. It was pure malice.

Slowly the powerful neck lifted and the Ringleader looked the Detective Sergeant in the eye. Their faces were close just as they had been before the Ringleader had delivered his hammer blow.

'Geezers like me don't say sorry.' The Ringleader snarled this out and the Detective Sergeant flinched. 'But you're alright. I shouldn't have done it. I didn't need to. You was outnumbered. I don't want nothing off of you, mate. You don't have to shake me hand. You don't have to accept it, but I'm apologising, mate. I'll say it right clear.' He hesitated.

The Detective Sergeant went to speak but stopped. The Ringleader's fist suddenly came towards the Detective Sergeant's belly and he flinched again.

'You needn't be frightened of me, Sarge.' The Ringleader's knuckles unwound into a big open palm and he offered his hand to the police officer. 'I'm sorry,' he said, 'No strings. Just plain sorry.' His barrel chest heaved and he sucked in a quick lungful of air that stuttered over his bottom lip. The thick vein on his neck pumped. 'I'm sorry,' he said again. The Detective Sergeant looked down at the big hand and shook it.

The sea front at Exmouth was bitterly cold. The tide was out and a strong metallic smell of seaweed and shellfish was carried in on a brisk wind. The sand and snow were whipped inland and deep drifts of the cold abrasive mixture had formed against the sea wall. It was nearly dark, but there were plenty of people about. Family groups kicked along, the kids chattering excitedly. Across the estuary, a train, a thin strip of light, trundled in front of the sparkling houses of Star Cross. The same stretch of railway would have taken the Marine from Mandalay to his headquarters at Plymouth, his long journey coming to an end, his orders followed, duty done.

Tomorrow, Christmas Eve, Elaine, Katherine and Linda would be on the same train from Paddington. He passed the half-built bowling alley, its tarpaulins flapping noisily, and turning inland with his back to the wind, he walked away from the coast towards home. The smell of the houses was on him now, chimney smoke reminiscent of home in Shoreditch. It was a night just like this when he and his brother had collected the paraffin. At last his journey from the East was over. He stood at the top of his road, a battered, ugly man in heavy walking clothes and beach shoes.

He looked down the white road, the pavements indistinct under the thick white carpet, and across the white pitched rooftops of the bungalows to the estuary and the white hills beyond. The sky was a luminescent dark blue. The old iron lampposts were emitting white balls of light and the windows of the houses twinkled with fairy lamps.

He reached his house and it was not as it should have been - it was full of life. A plume of smoke rose from the chimney; the windows blazed with colour – the living glow from within and a confused array of multi coloured fairy lights that had been strung across the panes. Inside he could see Elaine, Katherine and Linda in a group on the rug in front of the blazing fire, playing a game or wrapping presents. A decorated Christmas tree stood proudly behind them. A bottle of red wine and two glasses stood beside the hearth.

A heavy green and red wreath hung on the front door, the pungent fragrance of the pine cutting through the crisp night air. The snow of the front garden had been mightily disturbed by a maelstrom of footprints and, here and there, patches of grass showed where snow had been scraped up. A lopsided tubular snowman stood happily, a policeman's helmet on his head. What looked like a medal made out of gold foil was pinned to its narrow chest.

A huge banner hung from the gutter, stretching from one side of the house to the other:

CONGRATULATIONS
MICHAEL TANNER QPM

Yawning, Michael Tanner slid carefully up to his front door and knocked.

ABOUT THE AUTHOR

Philip Tucker studied creative writing at the Open University in the United Kingdom. He was a police officer for more than 31 years, finishing his career as a counter terrorism officer working in British Embassies overseas. Having studied terrorism and security with Australia's Charles Sturt University, he now teaches investigation and counter terrorism strategy in Asia and Europe.

Printed in Great Britain
by Amazon